BOBBY'S SOCKS

Nathaniel Sewell

Martin Sisters Publishing

Published by

Ivy House Books, a division of Martin Sisters Publishing, LLC

www.martinsisterspublishing.com

Copyright © 2012 by Nathaniel Sewell

ISBN: 978-1-937273-18-7

Literary Fiction

Printed in the United States of America
Martin Sisters Publishing, LLC

DEDICATION

For Rebecca Dawn, my RD.

"All things truly wicked start from innocence."

~ Ernest Hemingway

Literary Fiction

An imprint of Martin Sisters Publishing, LLC

PROLOGUE

Surrounded by a dense green thicket of towering oak and pine trees, an apple-pie-shaped clearing within Appalachia was baked by the steamy August. As hopeful daylight began to fade behind grey shadows, childhood death crept toward the church camp. "Want to make out? Are you a good kisser?" Kimmi asked. Illuminated by the late afternoon sunshine sparkle stars, her hypnotic green eyes were bathed with mischief.

"I don't know," Robert said. He stuffed his hands in his khaki shorts pockets. For a nine-year-old girl with sandy blond hair, he thought she had kissable, full lips to the extreme. He reconsidered his words. "Well, yeah... I guess. Yeah, I think so."

"I'd sure kiss her," Breck said. A tall, athletic, blond-haired boy, he goofily shoved Robert toward Kimmi.

"I just want to kiss, Robert," Kimmi said, playing with the frayed ends of her cotton shorts. She pointed her forefinger at Breck. "I like Robert right now."

Kimmi sprang off the front stoop of the girl's cabin and hopscotched over to in front of Robert. She lured him toward her puckered lips, on her tip toes, she smashed up against Robert's plump mouth.

"Dude, she kissed you," Breck shrieked. He shook his head as if a housefly had invaded his brain.

Kimmi giggled. She smirked as she gazed up into Robert's hazel-colored eyes. For some odd reason, he thought she proudly studied his face—as if she had conquered her quarry. Kimmi poked her tongue between her lips and tapped the tip with her forefinger.

"Have you ever touched tongues? They call it French or whatnot." She grabbed Robert's warm hand. "My brother told me it's kinda cool."

"I don't know," Robert said. As Kimmi towed Robert along behind her, he glanced at the other wood plank cabins and back at

5

·Breck. He touched his lips, which were spackled with strawberry lip gloss. Kimmi's 'smash kiss' had vibrated his lip nerves. His skin tingled, stirring his soulful cauldron for intimate discovery.

"Oh, man! Dude," Breck said. He scooted to the corner of the camp cabin and hid behind the barnacled trunk of an ancient oak tree. "I'm freakin'. Are you goin' to touch her tongue?"

"Shut up. Go away." Robert grimaced at Breck and whispered. "You'll get us in trouble."

Kimmi lugged Robert by the hand along behind her to the middle of the cabin.

"Stick your tongue out," she said. She pointed at Robert's mouth, her fingernail chipped with remnants of a lovely purple polish.

"Okay," Robert whispered. His fuzzy cheeks blushed with a blameless red.

Kimmi stuck the tip end of her tongue out of her mouth. Robert did the same with his. He dipped down, and they touched the tips. Robert thought it had a slimy, sandpaper sensation, as if he had licked a soggy sponge, but he decided he might like it. In fact, he thought he might like to try it again someday, because his body felt…weird. A happy this-might-be-fun weird.

"Can you roll your tongue? I can roll my tongue," Kimmi said. Her tightly enveloped lips and tongue glistened like moist petals of a yet-to-bloom rose. "See, I can roll my tongue."

Robert tried to roll his, but his pug nose blocked out the sight.

"Did I do it?" Robert asked. He wanted to pluck his eyeballs out to examine his attempt.

"No, that's not right," Kimmi said. She patted Robert on his maturing chest. "Watch me."

Breck slinked past the tree trunk and pounced close to Robert. His tennis shoes skittered into the dirt, causing a minor dust cloud.

"Did you do it?" Breck asked.

"Go away." Kimmi coughed and waved away the dust invasion. She huffed and picked up jagged rock within wilted grass near the cabin's foundation and slung it at Breck. The rock smacked Breck square in the mouth, chipping his front permanent teeth.

"Oh!" Breck said. He Goliath backed away; his hands cupped his mouth, specked with tiny blood droplets. The Breck crying alarm sounded, and the—fun with Kimmi kissing—seminar ended. Campers and the camp counselors scampered toward the crime scene.

"What happened?" Mr. Gibson, the head church counselor, asked. He was a happy-faced, balding middle-aged man. He was followed by Mr. Diabolus and Mrs. Dumbwoody.

"I got hit whiff a wok," Breck said.

Robert nudged Kimmi behind him.

"I'm sorry," Robert said as he scrunched his face. "I didn't mean to hit you."

From behind Robert, Kimmi's guilty eyes peeked at Mr. Gibson's scowl.

"That's uncalled for, little boy," Mr. Diabolus said. Shaped like a sweet potato, he had a fat, round head, and a ruddy nose. "For such a good-looking little boy, why so mean? I know your father, he's not mean. He's a godly man."

"Yes indeed and your mother would teach you better," Mrs. Dumbwoody said. She had the facial features that resembled a hawk.

"Why'd you do this?" Mr. Gibson asked. He furrowed his bushy eyebrows, glancing over at Mr. Diabolus, and pressed Breck's mouth open to study the chipped teeth tips.

"It huts when I reeve," Breck said. He spat out white specks of his formerly permanent teeth.

"We'll get you help right away, dear," Mrs. Dumbwoody said.

"We were just kidding around," Robert said.

Mr. Gibson sighed as he stared over at Robert.

"Kimmi, I can see you hiding," Mr. Gibson said.

Kimmi revealed herself from behind Robert. She stepped sideways, concealed within the shadow of the cabin's roofline.

"You've anything to say?" Mr. Diabolus asked.

"She was just standing here," Robert said. He shrugged and scooted between Kimmi and Mr. Diabolus. "She wasn't even playing with us."

Mr. Gibson gently patted Breck on the back. He huffed. "Well, it's getting late. I guess we need to take you into town to find you a dentist," Mr. Gibson said, biting his lower lip.

Mr. Diabolus maneuvered toward Robert.

"I'll take care of Robby," Mr. Diabolus said.

"I don't know," Mr. Gibson said. He stared at Mr. Diabolus. He gazed up at the silvery moon emerging high in the darkening, cloudless sky.

"I'm an assistant principal. I've trained," Mr. Diabolus said. He fidgeted with his silver belt buckle. "I'll call the parents and have a stern talk with Robby. I'll update you when you return. Always a good idea to write up a report—document things, you know."

"My name's Robert," the boy said. He shuffled his feet, backtracked, and stumbled into Kimmi. She gripped Robert's waist for balance.

"Yes, we all know Mr. Diabolus, you've trained, just go easy on the boy," Mrs. Dumbwoody said. She shook her head and glanced over at Mr. Gibson. "He'll have to do for now, besides, I'll have a talkin' to his mother."

Mr. Gibson pensively studied Robert and Kimmi, and then looked over at Mr. Diabolus. The other campers curiously stared at him. He glanced back at them and clenched his jaw.

"Very well," Mr. Gibson said. "Let's get moving. Mr. Diabolus, I'm depending on you to get all the campers together for dinner. You're in charge until I get back. Just keep everyone together. Maybe have an after-dinner talent contest. But it's important to keep the children together. Don't want someone wandering off."

"I like contests," Kimmi said. She giggled, smiling up at Robert. "My Daddy said I'm a toughie."

Mr. Diabolus patted Robert on the head. "Yes, I'll do that straight away."

Mr. Gibson hesitantly glanced back at Robert as he escorted Breck, with Mrs. Dumbwoody, toward a white camp van parked in front of the meetinghouse. The camp kitchen billowed out fogs of dense steam; chicken spices scented the humid air. Standing at the corner of the cabin front, Mr. Diabolus menacingly pointed at Robert to follow him.

"Go to your cabin little one," Mr. Diabolus said. He waved Kimmi away as if she were a losing game show contestant. "Stay inside until you're asked by your counselor to come out for supper."

Kimmi patted Robert on the forearm and whispered, "Sorry."

"I'll be all right," Robert said.

She gulped and sheepishly strolled away, her hands stuffed in her pockets as she disappeared behind the cabin.

With Mr. Diabolus close behind him, Robert trudged up the stairs, past the squeaking screen door, and into the camp cabin.

"Boys, I'm in charge; go to the dinner hall—now," Mr. Diabolus said.

The campers averted eye contact with dead-camper-walking Robert. Mr. Diabolus sauntered into the back closet and unscrewed the fluorescent light bulb.

"Get inside. You'll get no supper tonight," Mr. Diabolus said. His intense, deep-set eyes stared through Robert. "You've a sister, right, Robby?"

"Yeah, why? And my name's Robert," he said, his hands in his khaki shorts pockets.

"I'll explain later." Mr. Diabolus snickered and grabbed Robert hard by the forearm to hustle him inside the closet. "I need to go call your father first. Get supper organized, and then I'll be back for you. Sit down on the floor and keep quiet. You need severe punishment for this. No supper for you."

"But Mr. Gibson…" Robert said.

"Hush; I'm in charge," Mr. Diabolus said. He locked Robert inside the closet.

The wooden floorboards were hard and full of splinters poking into Robert's legs. The square closet was dark as a cave formed from Kentucky limestone, except for the gap between the bottom of the door and the floorboards. Robert's arms grappled around his knees. He heard other campers whisper about him as they came and left for the meetinghouse. Then, it was deathly quiet, still, except for an oscillating fan blowing humid, hot air. A fox squirrel clawed across the shingled roof. A bird fluttered its wings. A barn owl hooted a harbinger, "Hoo, hoo, too-hoo." Then, Mr. Diabolus's shadow slid underneath the gap. It fidgeted back and forth; each careful step he took creaked at the intersection of the floor joists and rusty, floorboard nails.

"Anybody in here?" Mr. Diabolus said. "Dinner time." His murky shadow stood still, and then roused.

The screen door creaked closed, the front door knob clicked shut, the slide lock wedged into place, and then there was the snap of the dead bolt lock.

The closet lock clicked open, and the door swung back. Robert's eyesight blurred after sitting in darkness for over an hour, and he blinked rapidly. His right hand rose to block the piercing yellow light.

"Come with me, Robby," Mr. Diabolus said. His fingers dug into Robert's baby soft neck.

"Let me go." Robert tried to push Mr. Diabolus off him, but the man was well past six feet tall and, even though he was three hundred pounds of fat, he was quite strong.

"You do as you're told; I'm in charge," Mr. Diabolus said. He shoved Robert's chest square with the last bunk bed's corner post. Mr. Diabolus's thick forefinger knifed into the base of Robert's neck. "Pull your pants down—right now."

Robert pulled down his shorts. He knew the drill; his father had whipped him with a leather belt before. He usually snapped the loop, and then… *whack.*

"Pull down your undershorts, too," Mr. Diabolus said. He gripped Robert's neck, his fingers digging into unblemished skin. "Now, do it."

"That hurts," Robert said. He coughed. The cabin dust floated and swirled near him, as if he slid into home plate but was blocked by Mr. Diabolus.

"Shut up," Mr. Diabolus said. He fidgeted behind Robert and tugged the boy's underpants down to his ankles. "Or I'll go find your sister."

"Why? She's not done anything to you," Robert said. He tried to twist away from Mr. Diabolus. "Let go of me."

"Shut up. I told your father what you did." Mr. Diabolus chuckled and huffed. He unbuckled his belt and his pants fell to the floor. "You've been a very bad little boy. You've embarrassed him. It will cost him a lot of money to pay for Breck's dentist. You should be ashamed."

"Leave my sister alone," Robert said. His exposed skin felt cold, and the side of his face was pinned against the hard wooden surface. His stomach fluttered; his lungs pumped for oxygen. He stood like a good soldier, half-naked, as his stomach muscles flexed underneath his dark blue t-shirt. He clenched his jaw, bracing for the slaps from the leather belt. He figured he had two, maybe three coming. He wondered what Mr. Diabolus thought by asking him about his sister. She was not even at camp this year.

"Teach you," Mr. Diabolus said. After he looped the belt and snapped it, he bull-whipped Robert until his butt was a scolded cherry red.

Robert squeezed his eyelids shut and sucked in his breath as if he were diving to hide at the bottom of a deep swimming pool. He grappled his arms around the bunk bed's wooden post like the mast of a great ship battling a tempest storm, but there had been no siren

11

song of madness. He tried not to cry, but it was as if a thousand bees had stung him. Then, he figured he had gotten through the worst of it. He reemerged, exhaled, and loosened his death grip.

But Mr. Diabolus grunted like a rutting bull and mashed his groin up against Robert.

Robert's lungs emptied. His teeth chattered. Sandwiched against the wooden post, he intently stared at the locked cabin door. He felt Mr. Diabolus slither against him. He wanted to scream, but he could not breathe; he could not breathe.

"Let … go," Robert said. He moaned.

Mr. Diabolus caressed the shaking, shivering Robert with his clammy fingertips. Then he reached around and fondled Robert's penis like a dairy cow's udder.

"You breathe one word, I'll kill your sister. I'll kill you," Mr. Diabolus said. His hot, alcohol-tinged breath torched Robert's neck. "Remember, I'm always watching you, Robby."

Robert shook. He could not breathe; he could not breathe. Mr. Diabolus crushed his groin hard into Robert's backside. His grinding force lifted Robert up off his tennis shoes, and he bicycle air-pedaled toward oblivion.

"You like that," Mr. Diabolus whispered. He panted with hard breaths as he played with Robert like a lifeless, straw-stuffed scarecrow within a Nebraska cornfield. "You can feel it's fun. I can tell."

Robert thought he was dreaming, as if a part of him had just floated away, with ghostly specters watching his childhood die. His legs, feet, and hands dangled like a marionette above the wooden floor. The intermittent gust from the fan blew moist hair from his face. The fluorescent cabin lights were a milky haze with a solemn, constant buzz.

"Please … let … me go," Robert whimpered, as his body reacted and did what it naturally wanted to do, but Robert was not in control of his body. Mr. Diabolus was in control of Robert's body.

"I like begging." Mr. Diabolus ground his groin harder into Robert. His breathing was erratic, putrid, as he squeezed the lifelight out from behind Robert's eyes. "I own you; you'll be my plaything, Robby. Or do you want the same for your sister? You breathe one word, and I'll humiliate your father."

In the speed of sexual assault time, Robert went from being a child to an adult. The taste of Kimmi's sweet strawberry lip-gloss faded from his memory. The giddy feeling he had from the freshness of her first kiss drained into a sewer of lost souls.

But what Robert could not know was that his brain instantly, tragically scarred, as if the cataclysmic flash of a nuclear weapon had ignited inside his head. The mushroom cloud of shame and degradation shocked his stress gene.

"You'll always be my pretty one. There now, how did that feel? See? You liked it; don't lie," Mr. Diabolus said. He grasped Robert's neck with his pudgy fingers. "My little Robby, see, you made me happy, too. But you'll keep quiet, or you know what will happen to your sister. Now, pull your pants up, and remember what I said, Robby. I own you."

Mr. Diabolus kept his thick hand grappling Robert's neck as he nudged him toward the bathroom. Robert stumbled forward, his eyes glanced at life as if riding on a high-speed train whizzing past reality. He wanted to scream, to cry, but he couldn't. He felt as if a layer of manure had been wiped all over his body. His mind was lost within a wispy, milky cloud.

"You liked that," Mr. Diabolus said. He squeezed Robert's neck. "That felt good. It was a first for you? You liked it, didn't you?"

As Mr. Diabolus watched, the hot evening shower stung as if Robert stood under an acid waterfall.

The remainder of summer camp Robert kept quiet. The other kids assumed he had gotten in trouble and was told to be silent. He ignored Kimmi. *Protect her from Mr. Diabolus*, he thought. He ignored Breck's questions. He did not feel like playing. He was on high alert.

"You okay?" Mr. Gibson asked. He sat next to Robert at breakfast the next morning near a long buffet table. The half-open windows sparkled with the summer sun. An audience of hungry fox squirrels dangled from the mesh screens as campers laughed and teased. The open-air room was loud with normal childhood activity. But Robert had not slept through the night. He had instead staked out his cabin territory, closely watching Mr. Diabolus snore on a squeaky cot near the front door.

"I'm okay," Robert whispered. He stared down at the bowl of oatmeal swimming in milk.

Robert thought himself dirty, flawed. He had grown up in a Bible-thumping family. Sex was dirty, and sex with another man, unforgivable. Sex before marriage was a betrayal to God. It was a simple calculation; he was going to burn in hell. But he had a duty to his sister. He had to protect her.

"Yeah. Need to talk or tell me anything?" Mr. Gibson whispered, leaning down near Robert.

"Robert, got … in trouble," Breck said in a sing-song voice. He shot a wet paper wad through a plastic straw. The wad stuck to the side of Robert's forehead.

"Breck, stop," Mr. Gibson said, as he snagged the plastic cannon away from Breck.

"I'm okay," Robert whispered. He wiped off the goo.

"I understand Mr. Diabolus had a talkin' to ya?" Mr. Gibson asked with a cough.

"Yeah, I'm okay," Robert said. He glanced up without moving his head. Mr. Diabolus intently stared at him, and then looked away before Mr. Gibson caught his intimidating glare.

He had to protect his sister, he thought. He had to protect Kimmi. If he said anything, he would embarrass his father. He would get into big trouble.

Mr. Gibson sighed. He scowled over at Mr. Diabolus, who ignored him, and pushed his breakfast plate forward.

"Lord, have mercy," Mr. Gibson whispered. He covered his face with his hands and mumbled a brief prayer.

"Robert, got ... in trouble," Breck whispered.

"I'll leave you be," Mr. Gibson said. He scratched his forehead. "But Robert, if you need to talk, I'll listen."

Robert ignored everyone but Mr. Diabolus. He kept a vigilant watch of the older man. If Kimmi came near him, he walked away. He had to protect her; he liked her and did not want her to go to hell with him.

Some might say, "At least Mr. Diabolus didn't kill him. He'll get over it. It's just sex, right?" But never underestimate Lucifer's delight torturing the soul of the half-living. The creatures of the night were left behind in Robert's terrified memory to constantly pick and feed at his charred essence. Behind Robert's eyes lived shame, humiliation, and a sense of isolation in a crowded room.

Robert's fourth grade IQ test had showed potential, but his nine year old brain was instantly scarred from the near murderous sexual assault. Mr. Diabolus's crime triggered a gene negatively coated with protein instructions over Robert's DNA. A lost leviathan deep within Robert's mind, an evil shame based command, the constant nighttime whisper...

"Before anyone finds out – *kill yourself*."

NATHANIEL SEWELL

Chapter One

Nestled within a lush, forested locale, Briar Hill School was built within Central Kentucky, it overlooked picket-fenced pastures, centered by red-roofed, white clapboard horse barns. To the east of the two-story antebellum mansion, fields and fields of perfectly aligned, broad-leaf tobacco was planted in the fertile reddish-brown soil.

The drafty structure had been doubled in size with a puke-yellow tumorous growth from the back of the main house. Behind was a green metal gymnasium, and beyond, a modest football field encircled by a quarter-mile running track. The elementary school was housed in the main house, while the junior high was within the offending new space.

A bright yellow school bus made a wide turn onto the long, narrow, driveway leading up toward the school's front double doors. The old man driving, careful—for fear of death by hanging by the local historical society—not to damage the precious limestone rock fences fronting the property. The walls were crafted using an Irish dry-stone method, pre-Civil War, by terrified

17

African slaves, who were devoted to perfection, lest they be sold off one Sunday afternoon downtown at the old Cheapside Market.

Robert sat toward the back of the bouncing, diesel-fueled bus, directly behind Ardee. Neither could know from their seventh-grade year this bus ride was the beginning of their lifetime journey together, and that perhaps the mythical Moirae had spun their lives threads to be eternally interwoven.

Ardee kept her thick, auburn hair long, flowing just above her delicate shoulders. Her posture was upright as if she expected to be recognized, and she wore a simple, collared, navy blue blouse and pressed blue jeans. Sitting on a burnt orange bench seat, she made every attempt to work the bus, make eye contact, and learn each child's first name so that perhaps the other children might remember to vote for her in early November for school mayor. She had gotten on the bus after Robert.

Robert hoped to blend in with the circus clowns, trainers, and other high-wire acts bouncing about the bus seats, but she caught his attention. She noticed Robert's curious glance at her from the reflection of the bus window and, without any hesitation, twisted around to face him. Her delicate fingers, with fingernails cut short, curled over the seat back.

"Hi, I'm Ardee," she said without the slightest hint of filter from brain to mouth. "I just moved here; we move a lot. My Daddy's real important."

Robert stared back at her pleasant, happy, eager smile. His heart rapidly thumped inside his chest. He blushed.

"Robert," he mumbled.

"Do you go by Robby, or Bobby?" Ardee asked.

"I prefer, Robert." *What else could possibly go wrong in my life?* Robert thought. *And don't even think of calling me, Robby.*

"Nice to meet you Robert, but I prefer Bobby," Ardee said. "Bobby's a happy name, right?" She giggled, turned back around, and started to glide her fingers up and down the tips of her hair.

"As well, I guess," Robert said semi-sarcastically.

18

She acted as though she did not hear his response, pretending to ignore him. She assumed he was like other boys, but she had made a miscalculation.

Robert would hardly speak to her again for the rest of the fall term. Actually, he took great care to avoid her. If he saw her in the hallway, he would find an escape route. If she said hello, he mumbled and acted as though he had important business to attend too. He was bewildered by her; her beautiful face stirred him. But his heart was beaten to the point he could not feel his feet, as if he continually walked naked in below zero-degree weather. He thought she was the prettiest girl he had ever seen but was afraid he would hurt her. He knew she would ask questions, questions he did not want to answer. With one exception, just after Thanksgiving, when he was standing next to her in the lunch line, trying to decide between vitamin D milk and vitamin D milk.

"How was Thanksgiving?" Robert mumbled.

Ardee glanced up at him with a happy grin, as she sidestepped along the counter toward the cashier woman.

"I thought you were mad at me." Ardee said. She reached for a cup of applesauce. "Do you like horses?"

"Not me," Robert said. "I'd never hurt you." He purposefully brushed her arm as he pretended to investigate some of the pre-made rectangular pizzas steaming under heat lamps, which were guarded by two manatee-shaped kitchen workers in white polyester uniforms. He could smell just the hints of Ardee's perfume—perfume he suspected she had snuck from her mother's collection. Her full lips had a red cherry, lip-gloss luster.

"We had great fun. We had a bunch of people over," Ardee said. She stared down at her tray. "My Daddy cut the turkey, and we had stuffing and mashed potatoes, and whatnot. I think I ate till my belly was going to explode. Can I pat your belly? You can pat mine. I'm strong."

"Stop that." Robert blushed. He chuckled.

"Really, go ahead, you can pat my belly. My Daddy taught me how to do sit-ups. Uncle Charles showed up and brought Daddy some sort of present in a dark brown bottle. They talked and laughed past my bedtime. Although, I did sneak downstairs to watch them, but they didn't know," Ardee said. She twisted her head down. She whispered. "I like to stay up late. How 'bout you? You like to stay up late?"

Robert stared down at his empty tray with a solitary milk carton soldier. The black and white picture of a smiling missing child was on one side, the nutritional facts on another.

"Yeah, I wake up at night." Robert smirked. "Always think there's a boogie man in my room."

"You're so funny," Ardee said. She giggled and patted Robert along his forearm. "That's what all the other girls say about you."

"What if I said I didn't mean to be?" Robert asked.

"Ha, now I know you, Bobby," Ardee said.

"I guess so," Robert said.

He shrugged. He gulped. His heart was squeezed in a vise so tight his blood had stopped circulating. He wanted to run. He wanted to remain hidden. But he liked her. He just wanted to talk to her and tell her she was pretty. He wanted to innocently hug her. She seemed trustworthy. Maybe she would be his friend.

"When it gets warm again, you'll have to come over, and we'll go bike riding," Ardee said. She inspected her fork. "You like to run fast? I'm fast. Bet you can't beat me."

"Sure." Robert smirked at her. "I'll race you."

"Want to sit next to me?" Ardee asked.

"Okay," Robert said. He followed Ardee into the crowded bedlam of the lunchroom. There were four rows lined with three buffet-style tables stuck end-to-end, surrounded with plastic multi-colored chairs. Children of all races and creeds buzzed in and out and around the tables like busy social honeybees with middle-aged teachers observing and attempting to maintain order. Ardee appeared to be inspecting the lunchroom for just the right place to sit, but there was only one option—two plastic chairs in front of Willis. Willis sat alone.

"Hey Willis," Robert said in sallow tone.

"Hey," Willis said. He was an obese African-American boy, his voice like the sound from a slow tire leak. He was wearing a frayed crew neck t-shirt, large blue jeans, and a shiny military-gray winter coat. The hood was rimmed with fake fur.

"Willis, this is Ardee," Robert said. He nodded over toward her.

"I didn't think you could talk." Ardee pointed her brassy forefinger at Willis. "You're in my social studies class and, I think, Mrs. Kotchen's math class, I think she's pretty."

"Yeah, me too," Willis said. He tried to grin, which caused his cheeks to puff out like half-inflated balloons.

"We have PE," Robert said nervously to Ardee.

Before he could stop himself, he gulped, exhaled, and mumbled, "You're pretty."

Ardee turned her head and poked her face up at Robert.

"What?" Ardee asked, with a smirk and a giggle.

"Nothing," Robert said. He grinned. "Want me to draw you a happy heart?"

"English and PE," Willis said. As he breathed in, his chest seemed to hoist itself up to allow as much oxygen inside his lungs as possible. "I don't like PE, but Robert's real fast."

"No, I'm not," Robert said. He drank some of his milk from the carton and sadly glanced over at Willis.

"Where do you live Willis?" Ardee asked.

"I live with my mother on a farm." Willis bit off a piece of pizza. He talked and chewed at the same time. "She works there … in an office, in a barn."

"Which one?" Ardee asked. She quizzically studied the side of Robert's unblemished face as he drank milk.

"Keene farm," Willis said.

"I've ridden there," Ardee said. She twisted to look at Robert. "Do you ride Bobby? Do you like horses? Do you have your own bike?"

"I've seen you," Willis said. He adjusted in the seat. "You're good."

Robert felt a momentary sigh of relief. He did not have to admit he had grown up in the horse capital of the world, but had rarely been near a horse, not to mention thoroughbreds.

"I'm just learning," Ardee said to Willis. She twisted to stare at Robert in his eyes, as if to study his face for truth.

"Bobby, do you like horses? Have you ever had a pimple? I hate pimples. My mom has this weird stuff she puts on her face at night."

"I wish I could ride," Willis said, grinning. "I can't get on the horses. My mom's afraid I'll fall off."

"Oh, I think I will this season, but I'm already nervous," Ardee said. She closely examined the applesauce and felt her chin with her fingertip. "Bobby, look at this. I think it's a pimple on my chin."

"Why?" Robert asked. His heartbeat had returned to a normal rhythm. He hated personal questions.

"I hate to lose," Ardee said. She drank milk and pushed her food clumps across the plate with her fork. "I've got to learn all this stuff, like the rider cannot be obvious to the judges and whatnot."

"You do good," Willis said with a yawn. "You're a good shot, too."

"Thank you, Willis. It's fun. I have these cool boots. My Mommy got me these cool leather boots, but I can't wear them to school." Ardee bent her right leg and put her tennis shoe up onto the end of plastic chair. "They come up to my knee."

"I don't think it's a pimple," Robert said, finally gathering his thoughts enough to answer her question from earlier. He liked to have an excuse to look at her face, so he stared at her for as long as he thought he could get away with it.

"Saw her taking target practice," Willis said.

Ardee glanced at Willis and sort of grinned over at Robert. Her brown, doe eyes lit up as if backlit by a soulful searchlight.

"My Daddy wants me to be able to defend myself, not depend on a man, he says," Ardee said. She tapped Robert on his forearm. "And I do think I'm a good shot — not as good as Daddy, but I'm not scared. You have thick hair, Bobby. I wish I had thick hair."

"Hello," Mr. Diabolus said. He glided his fingers along the tabletop. "Robby ..."

Willis looked to his right-hand side out the lunchroom's row of rectangular windows, refusing to look at the older man.

"My hair's like a mop sometimes," Robert said in an almost inaudible whisper. Willis was silent, his eyes a dead stare.

"Bobby, remember, don't make me get my Daddy's gun," Ardee said. She nudged at Robert.

She touched the back of his left hand with her soft fingertips.

"I'll have to set you straight, as my Daddy says."

Willis averted his stare from Mr. Diabolus and started to snicker.

"Bobby?"

Ardee winked at Willis. She sat up straight, twisted her shoulders, and stared into Robert's eyes.

"You'll let me call you Bobby? Won't you?" Ardee asked Robert. She squeezed Robert's forearm. "And I'm the only one, right?"

Robert's cheeks flushed crimson, and his ears burned dark red. He mustered a brief glance into Ardee's brown eyes.

"Yeah, you can call me Bobby." Robert shrugged as he glanced behind her in search of Mr. Diabolus. *I have to protect Ardee*, he thought.

Willis chuckled, and his sunken eyes sparkled with amusement.

"Bobby, why do you have sad eyes?" Ardee asked. Her fingers spider-crawled across the tabletop onto his forearm. He did not move his forearm. He liked her warm hand. It made him feel safe.

"What?" Robert asked.

The school bell rang at ten minutes before fourth period, ending the conversation before she could ask again. Robert was oddly okay that she changed his name to Bobby. *She's the only one*, he thought.

And he did not realize he had sad eyes. He couldn't just look at his reflection in a bathroom mirror and see how he really appeared. Sure, he could inspect himself, comb his hair, wipe off the grime, but he had to stand in another person's socks to understand how he really appeared. Robert figured it was his life, his destiny to die young—to burn in hell.

Oddly enough, he felt safe near Ardee. Just talking to her, he could see she was happy and friendly. She was everything he was not—all he ever wanted to be. She was normal. All he wanted to do was hug her and tell her she was pretty. He would dream of hugging her, and then he would cry. He did not want her to know he was dirty, and he didn't want her to go to hell. He had to protect her.

"Nice to meet you, Mister Willis," Ardee said. She playfully patted Robert's forearm. "See you later, my Bobby."

Ardee glided her fingers off his shoulder, picked up her tray, and waltzed toward the trashcan. Before she left the lunchroom, she smiled back over at Robert, and he felt the first glimmer of happiness.

Chapter Two

The school bell rang, and the yellow oak classroom doors flung open. Waves of children, converged to flood over the shiny terrazzo floor. But Robert knew exactly where to look through the panoply, as Ardee emerged from her social studies class. After a brief pause, a happy glimpse at the side of her happy face, he grinned, stared down at his tennis shoes, and turned to go to his physical education class, where the students wore unisex uniforms—royal blue shorts and a stark white t-shirt, stamped with 'Property of Board of Education'.

"What can I do for you Mr. Diabolus?" Coach Burton asked. He was a thick, barrel-chested, tree stump of a man, with a distinct, crisp voice that could range from quiet to carnival barker levels. He had prematurely grey hair, but extraordinarily kind eyes hidden within his power-lifter's body.

"Oh … nothing," Mr. Diabolus said.

"You appear lost," Coach Burton said. He fiddled with his plastic wristwatch. "Diabolus? Now that's an interesting name."

"Oh, sorry, but I remember a few of the students from the elementary school and thought I'd check on them, I pastor their parents," Mr. Diabolus said. He cryptically smirked. He glided his puffy fingers down the side of a locker. "It's Greek; my last name is Greek. Never been there. My first name's Danny. Friends call me Dandy when the little boys aren't around."

Coach Burton stepped back slightly.

"Okay, Dan, I've got class in three minutes. Let me know if you need something," Coach Burton said. He furrowed his eyebrows as he marched out of the boy's locker room and out into the busy, loud gymnasium.

"Sure, sure," Mr. Diabolus said, though Coach Burton had left the locker room.

Coach Burton blew his whistle, and the sound vibrated off the empty metal walls and the yellow oak bleachers that were pushed back into tall, imposing storage units. The students, including Robert and Willis, were dressed out in their 'Property of' uniforms and had formed five single file lines, each five students deep. Robert and Willis sat Indian-style in the second and third rows.

"Damn, Willis, you sweatin' already," Taylor said. He was skinny, with buzz-cut blond hair—a kid with an agitator's personality. Taylor was one of those people in life that did not mean to start trouble, but just did not possess the filter inside his brain to shut his mouth. A few of his friends laughed, because they lacked the self-confidence to think independently.

"Yeah, you're sweaty fat," Bo said. Already north of six feet tall, he was thick as a concrete retaining wall, inside and out. "You need to shower again? You smell like sweat."

"Willis, what's wrong with you?" Breck asked.

Robert glanced over at Willis. He was sweating across his forehead and had moisture blotches emerging through his white t-shirt.

"Man, leave ol' Willis alone," Robert said. His skin tingled with goose pimples from the blasting air conditioning. The gym was at a subarctic temperature.

"Can't help it; he's right in front of me," Taylor said.

"Yeah, Mister Perfect, at least you don't have to look at him," Bo said.

"My teeth still hurt, Mister Perfect," Breck said, reminding Robert of the summer camp incident.

Robert just shook his head and shrugged his shoulders. "Sorry, Willis." He glanced behind him to grudgingly include Breck in his apology. "Breck."

Breck shrugged and sat with his lanky legs forward.

"It's okay," Willis said. "I'm just nervous I guess."

"What?" Robert asked Willis. He glanced over at him.

"Not now," Willis whispered.

Coach Burton blew his whistle.

"Taylor, pipe down. You'll be sweating soon enough," Coach Burton said.

"Coach, man, I can't see around old sweaty hog Willis," Taylor said.

"Yeah, sweaty hog," Bo said.

Coach Burton strolled over to Bo.

"Are you a parrot?" Coach Burton asked.

"Yes, he's a parrot," Breck said.

Bo appeared confused. He looked over at Taylor.

"What did you say?" Bo asked.

"Are you a parrot?" Coach Burton asked. He twirled his whistle rope. "And this time don't look over at Taylor for the answer. Quiet down, Breck."

"I ain't a parrot," Bo said.

"Then why do you repeat everything Taylor says?" Coach Burton asked. The rest of the class laughed.

From behind Coach Burton, Mr. Diabolus emerged from the boy's locker room. Robert spotted him, as if a specter from another dimension. He almost threw up his breakfast over the shiny basketball court. His face turned ashen, the approximate hue of a corpse. Coach Burton casually acknowledged Mr. Diabolus, but he noticed Robert's dead-faced, terrified expression. He glanced at Mr. Diabolus and then back down at Robert. He backed up and nudged the boy.

"You okay?" Coach Burton asked.

"What?" Robert asked. He appeared bewildered and lost in another parallel world. Only Willis knew why.

"You all right?" Coach Burton asked. He watched Mister Diabolus leave through the metal double doors. "It's cold enough in here to be a meat locker."

"Even *Mr. Perfect* sweats," Taylor said. He pointed at Robert. "Can't be. Look at him, Bo. Bet he smells better than sweaty hog Willis."

"Yeah, sweats like a hog dog," Bo said.

Coach Burton snapped his pudgy face over to stare down at Bo. "You are truly a strange boy. Sweats like a hog dog? Are you serious?" Coach Burton said. He shrugged. He shook his head.

"Why don't you think about your similes and metaphors while you give me laps around the gym. I'll tell you when to stop. Taylor, another word, and you'll be with him."

"Ah, man," Bo said. He rolled up and on to his high-top tennis shoes and jogged toward the back of the gym.

Robert wiped the sweat from his eyebrows with his t-shirt. He tried to stop breathing hard. His cheeks were a cherry red and his stomach a dense rubber ball without air—a boy with an instant spiked fever.

"You okay?" Coach Burton asked.

"I'm all right," Robert said. "Something I ate I guess. My stomach sort of hurts."

Willis closely watched Robert try to compose himself.

"Willis," Coach Burton said. "Go walk off whatever you two need to walk off and take Robert with you. I don't need anybody passing out today. Do you all have the flu? Feel sick?"

"I'm all right," Robert said. He huffed. "Just let me walk it off."

"What's up with you?" Breck said.

"Calm down, eat some mashed potatoes, and just take a walk," Coach Burton said. He bit his lower lip. His hands were on his hips. "If you're feeling bad and need to go home-"

Robert snapped his gaze up at Coach Burton.

"No, no," Robert said. "I'm all right."

"Good, good," Coach Burton said. He studied Willis and Robert for a brief moment. "Anything you all need to tell me?"

"Okay, I'll go," Willis abruptly said before Robert could answer.

Robert hopped up. His hands were on his bare thighs. It felt good to be on his feet, to get away from the crowded gym.

"Come on, Willis." Robert leaned down and helped Willis up.

Coach Burton followed behind them toward the back double doors.

"Sure you all don't have anything you want to tell me?" Coach Burton asked. He studied their faces.

"No, we'll be all right," Robert said.

"Yeah," Willis whispered.

"If you change your mind, let me know," Coach Burton said. He backed away and clapped his hands together. "Okay class, let's do some jumping jacks to loosen up."

Robert pushed open the doors and nudged Willis in front of him.

"Sorry, I'm slow," Willis said.

"No worries, I'm not going anyplace special," Robert said. They ambled behind the school, past the empty football stadiums metal bleachers, and onto the blacktopped track. It was late fall, the oak trees beginning to shed leaves and prepare to hide within the winter frosts. Eight running lanes segmented by white lines circled back to infinity. Robert and Willis stayed in the two outside lanes, out of the way of the other gym classes sporadically lapping the quarter mile.

"It smells like fall," Willis said.

"I guess," Robert said.

"The fields are being turned. I can smell the soil," Willis said. He sniffed. "That's what my mother tells me."

Robert also smelled the air and sensed the coming cool snap in the air—of early frosts, of a reminder that winter kills, of the loss of the humid, bright yellow sunshine of a summer day. The days would change to the dullish bouquet of soft peach, jack-o-lantern orange, and mustard yellow before fading into gray, winter mornings.

"You're not okay," Willis said.

"What?" Robert said. He stared at Willis with a puzzled expression—an expression most might perceive as anger, as opposed to him simply hiding from his truth.

"You're not okay," Willis said. "I may be fat, but I'm good at noticing things."

"I'm not all right. I thought junior high would be better, thought he'd finally disappear," Robert blurted out. "I can't think. It's like he follows me. If he gets near her—I'll...I'll try to kill him." He marched straight ahead.

A few classmates strolled past them in irregular groups of athletic types, gossipy types, geeky types and the lonely runner. After they turned along the backstretch, Robert stopped to clear his throat.

"I feel stupid," Willis said.

"You're not stupid," Robert said.

"That girl really likes you," Willis said.

Robert stared down at his tennis shoes and put his hands on top of his head.

"I know," Robert said. He puckered his lips. "I don't know. She'll think I'm a freak. I can't protect her. He's bigger than me."

"She's pretty," Willis said.

"She's very pretty...and smart," Robert said. "I don't know why she likes me." His face was as blank as a block of raw chiseled granite. "I don't know what to do. I don't want her near my family. If she finds out, she'll never talk to me again. She will think I'm weird, and then she'll tell all her friends. I can't do anything right. I'm bad anyway I go. I'm a freak."

"I know," Willis said. He huffed out.

Robert stopped walking and stared over at Willis.

"I'm scared," Robert said. "I'm really scared, and you're the only person I can talk to. Now I have to protect her, too. I thought he'd leave me alone."

"I'm fat, so they think I start sweating because I'm supposed to," Willis said. He shrugged. "I get real anxious, too. At night, I wake up, can't sleep. Do you sleep all night?"

"Not really. I feel cramped in my room, I turn on my light," Robert said. He stared across the football field and thought about the fun of football games. He could hide within the team; he could hide on the field. He was just one of the many, just a face in the crowd. He whispered past Willis. "Me too, I wake up all the time. Then I oversleep. Mom yells at me to get up. It's embarrassing."

"I watched you after health class, the day of that VD film. You started sweating. You left class like you needed to go to the bathroom and looked sick … but I know you weren't sick before class."

Robert scratched behind his head, squeezed his eyelids shut, and clenched his jaw. He felt a cool chill from the afternoon breeze against his embarrassment, his lifetime humiliation.

"Please don't tell anybody," Robert said.

"You know I won't. I just wanted to tell you, I don't think we got VD," Willis said. "But I don't have any pretty girls that like me. I'm not cursed."

Robert turned to start walking again, and Willis lumbered along beside him.

"Cursed?" Robert said. He gulped.

Willis patted his pudgy catcher's mitt of a hand against Robert's right forearm.

"I can disappear," Willis said. He wiped sweat from his puffy forehead. "You can't. People notice you, and you're good at stuff, even if you don't want them to notice you."

Robert glanced back over at Willis.

"Never thought I was cursed," Robert said. He furrowed his eyebrows. "Maybe I am?"

"I know you're my friend." Willis grinned. "You're the one person who is always nice to me. You tried to protect me."

"I don't feel anything sometimes," Robert said. "Do you? I think I should feel something, but I don't. I really like her. I think I will always like her for some reason. But I'm afraid I might hurt her, and I would rather die than have that happen."

"You wouldn't hurt her," Willis said. He shrugged. "But I think I'll die young. I just know it."

"Man, she has the zap on me," Robert said. He crinkled his face. "I've never liked a girl...you know, like that."

"I know. I'd sure like to sure kiss her," Willis said. He chuckled and rubbed his belly.

"I haven't done anything," Robert said. "I'd just like to hold her hand... You know, just hang out."

As Willis and Robert completed the quarter mile track in a slow record time and headed back toward the gymnasium, Willis coughed and stopped. Robert blankly stared at Willis, who knew where his charred, smoldering childhood embers had been left behind to die.

"Hey, you two turkeys, time's up," Coach Burton yelled, holding open one of the gyms double doors.

"Don't worry about me," Robert said. He patted Willis on the shoulder. "Come on; I'm good at bouncing back."

"I'm not," Willis said.

"We can walk it off. It was last year. We'll get past him," Robert said. He tried to grin at Willis and smacked him on the back.

"It can be real bad. He scares me," Willis said. He wiped a tear from his eyes. "Thanks for being nice to me... Thanks for trying to protect me that time."

Robert shook his head. "I'm your friend. I'll never tell on you," he said. "I won't squeal."

"I won't tell on you either," Willis whispered.

"Thanks. I don't want to get into trouble," Robert said.

NATHANIEL SEWELL

Chapter Three

The year before, when Robert was in sixth grade, on a resplendent spring day, the summertime break beckoned. Robert had started to notice girls, and girls had started to notice him. His body was changing. Ardee's pretty face had not yet infected his mind.

"What are you young boys doing?" Mr. Diabolus asked. He stood with his hands clasped behind his pear shape. He stared through Robert.

"Nothin'," Taylor said. Twitching his shoulders, he flicked the tubular cigarette away. It belched smoky, curvy rings of evidence from within the blades of grass.

"He was doin' nothin'," Bo said.

"Talyor was smokin', that's all." Breck shrugged.

"Shut up," Taylor said.

"I'm not takin' your crap, punk," Breck said.

Robert and Willis backed away. Taylor and Bo did not sense what they sensed. Breck ignored them. He shrugged and walked back toward the gym.

"Smoking is bad for your maturing lungs, little boys,' Mr. Diabolus said. He crinkled his nose like a sniffing pig and smirked over at Robert.

"We were just standing here," Robert said. He gulped, his throat packed thick with mucous.

"I don't care," Mr. Diabolus said. He fidgeted with his belt buckle. "All four of you, come. Breck go back to class. Now come; time to pay the piper."

The elementary school principal's office was busy with activity. From the two older assistants' dense perfume, it smelled like a bouquet of fresh cut flowers at a funeral parlor. The pine wood floorboards moaned under Mr. Diabolus's black leather shoes. He wore a powder blue polyester jacket and poorly-fitting black slacks. His rubber soled shoes squished as he pushed Willis and Robert out of the office. He had paddled Taylor, barked at Bo, and shooed them back to class.

"Mrs. White, taking these two to clean downstairs toilets. They're a mess," Mr. Diabolus said. He fidgeted with his silver belt buckle.

The ancient Mrs. White's hair matched her name. It was thinning, and her conservative dress was of a purple paisley print. She wore black horn-rimmed cat lady glasses. She had a sharp nose and a dull brain.

"Well, you two are lucky. Robert, of all the kids in school, you're the last one I'd think would take up smoking," Mrs. White said. Her thin lips judgmentally puckered.

"Not sure paddling will get our point across," Mr. Diabolus said, breathing through his mouth. "I know this one from church. He was bad at summer camp last year. Too bad for Robby. So I'll be back in an hour or so."

An hour was forever, Robert thought. He and Willis were in their gym clothes, with white t-shirts and navy blue short with 'Property of...' stamped on the left leg.

"Move. You two have toilets to clean," Mr. Diabolus said. He waved at Mrs. White, and she proudly acknowledged him back. "Good for you, Mr. Diabolus, good for you; that'll teach 'em," Mrs. White said. She shook her forefinger at Robert. "Robert, you and Willis should get on your hands and knees and pray to God for forgiveness; that's what the good book commands. Smoking is bad."

Mr. Diabolus fidgeted with his silver belt buckle. "Oh, in due time Mrs. White." He sneered at her. He poked Willis in his doughy back and directed Robert and Willis down the school's back stairs to the boys' basement bathroom.

"You two have been very bad," Mr. Diabolus said. He scratched and tugged his groin. "This must be my lucky day; I've my fatty and my pretty Robby—such a pretty boy."

"Let Willis go," Robert said. He whimpered. "Just leave my sister alone."

"No, let Robert go," Willis wheezed.

"Oh, how sweet," Mr. Diabolus said. He hooked his moist hands around both of their necks. "Sorry. You're both out of luck today, and if either of you breathe a word, it'll be the end of both of you. Robby, I might have to search out your sister—really give her a good beating. Get inside the bathroom. I'm going to enjoy this for a while."

Robert knew he could run away and warn his sister. Maybe his parents might finally listen, but there was Willis. He was too slow and too obese to get away. Robert was his only friend. Nobody liked to hang out with the smelly kid. The bathroom was desolately empty. A row of three porcelain urinals, two stalls and, near the door, two sinks with silver faucets. The left hand faucet dripped clear, clean water.

"Please, don't," Robert whispered. "Leave me alone ... I didn't do anything. I just want to be left alone."

"Oh, I love begging, but you know that," Mr. Diabolus said. He sighed. He chuckled. "You two stand next to the side of the stall.

It's a good dark color. Think it'll make my pictures perfect in this light."

Willis shivered. His eyes wide open, glazed over, he appeared as if in a milky daze. Robert fought back his instinct to scream and run. He had to figure out a way to protect Willis, to protect his sister. He had to keep Ardee away from him. He had to protect her. Mr. Diabolus likely knew she liked him. He could try to fight him off, but Mr. Diabolus was much bigger. He could not fight him off, and he would not leave Willis behind. He and Willis were trapped.

"Can't you see we're just boys?" Robert asked. He huffed, his lungs begging for oxygen, his heart pounding against his chest.

"Please, no – it hurts, it hurts."

"Shut up," Mr. Diabolus said. He wiggled his body toward the trashcan. "I own you," he said, as he opened the top of the trashcan to find a crumpled paper lunch bag inside. Within the bag was an old-style instamatic camera. "Been planning this day for a long time. I'm almost about to pass out."

"Please don't," Robert moaned. He gripped his hands over his knees. His mouth filled with mucous.

"Shh. If you cooperate, Robby, I'll go easy on you and leave your sister alone," Mr. Diabolus said. He adjusted his groin with his palm. "I've never cornered her, but I can easily. I see her at church all the time. Oh, by the way, I've already called your father at work. He knows you've been bad. Tell him what you want; it's too late. Might not be much fun at home tonight. I wonder how your sister is doing. I wonder if she would like me to take some photos. Maybe she's old enough to accept a man for her training?"

"You're a monster," Robert whimpered. His legs wobbled, and his teeth chattered. Tears involuntarily streamed down his puffy, crimson cheeks.

"I don't care. I have to do this; it's my life's calling for God, to train you," Mr. Diabolus said. He fidgeted with his silver belt buckle and tore off the camera packaging. "Now, stand next to each other."

Robert trembled next to Willis. He heard the camera click, then the battery-powered ejection motor buzzed. Each new triggered photo rolled the negative over the positive sheet to spread the developing reagent. Robert involuntarily shook and blinked when the camera auto-flashed, as if shot in the face with a handgun. After the fifth self-developing photo, the bathroom had the distinct scent of fear, hopelessness, and chemicals. Mr. Diabolus carefully peeled off the filmy positive layer to expose the captured negative image to the air. He neatly lined up each white-framed picture along the edge of the right hand sink. Eventually, Robert and Willis were naked and barefooted. The bathroom tile floor was starkly cold. Both were shivering, teeth chattering, humiliated.

"Oh, I'm so proud of you two," Mr. Diabolus said. He unbuckled his pants. "No more tears? No more complaining? I think you are enjoying this, my little plaything, Robby. As I please myself, I please God."

"Can we go please?" Robert asked. His voice was flat, monotone. His skin tingled as if acid had been poured over him. His skin burned, as if set on fire, and he knew his father was going to set him on fire again later that night. He would not get the opportunity to tell anyone; no one took time to listen. Robert glanced over at Willis. He was in a trance. Robert whispered. "Willis?"

Willis blankly stared down at the pale green and white checkerboard floor.

"Am I dead?" Willis whispered.

"Oh, now, my play things, almost done," Mr. Diabolus said. He checked his digital watch. "I am so efficient with time. I love being so meticulous. God called me to do this. You'll thank me someday."

"Please no more pictures," Robert whispered. He stood naked, his eyes dead. "Let Willis go; he can't run. Please don't touch my sister." He blankly gazed over at the bathroom door's silver lock.

"Oh, picture time is over my pretty, Robby. You've a pretty face. I never had pretty girls like me the way they like you," Mr. Diabolus said. His belly bounced up and down as he chuckled. "Hmm, don't you understand Robby. I own you."

"Please, no," Willis moaned.

Robert closed his eyes as Mr. Diabolus strolled toward him and Willis. He put his arms up as if to hide and tried to shield Willis, but Mr. Diabolus shoved Robert onto the dirty bathroom floor in front of the first urinal. For the next half hour, an unspeakable crime was committed. Robert knew no one would listen; no one would defend him. He realized no one cared. He was alone – isolated. He and Willis were completely humiliated—degradation they could never wash off, an invisible layer of shame they would always feel, a sensation they couldn't explain unless someone else had experienced the torture of being powerless. He shook his head to wake up from the living nightmare as he heard the door lock of the bathroom cage click open.

Then, it was as if it never happened—like it was a dream. Robert and Willis sleepwalked back toward the gym.

"Where have you two been?" Coach Burton said.

"We got sent the principal's office," Robert mumbled.

"For what?" Coach Burton asked.

"Taylor was out back smoking," Robert said, walking toward the locker room. "We were with him."

"Whatever. Get showered up. You both look rumpled," Coach Burton said. He crossed his muscled arms. "Teach you to stay away from cigarettes, and Taylor, for that fact." He shrugged. He squinted. Then he twirled the rope of his whistle around his fingers. "Need to tell me anything?"

Willis and Robert stared down at their tennis shoes.

"No, we're all right," Robert mumbled.

"Sure?" Coach Burton asked.

"Yeah," Willis said.

Neither Willis nor Robert said another word. What would the other kids think? Robert thought he had to protect Ardee. If she found out that he was a freak, she would never talk to him again. Willis and Robert had a tragic bond, a lifetime bond, and neither would betray the other, as if they were two foxhole brothers who had fought a valiant struggle and had scenes from a bloody battle as a continuous loop within their dreams. They would live forever as shadows of themselves—behind their eyes, half-living souls of who they should have been. Both reminded with a gentle whisper, *kill yourself, before everyone finds out.*

Chapter Four

"How was school today?" Mrs. Scott asked, without looking at Robert. She had thick dark brown hair, a round youthful face with kind, naïve eyes. Robert's face favored hers in appearance.

"It was all right, I guess," Robert said. He thought about how Mr. Diabolus seemed to follow him at school. He whispered, "Better than last year…"

"What's that?" Mrs. Scott asked.

"Nothing," Robert said. He stared down at his tennis shoes.

The kitchen smelled of boiling chicken and spices from the stock his mother was making. She busied herself with domestic work—a bit of cleaning, folding clothes from a dryer, and preparing the evening dinner. His sister, Laina, sat on the other side of the kitchen table, studying her pre-calculus. *She likes to study*, Robert thought.

"That's good, dear," Mrs. Scott said.

Robert turned his shoulders and looked across the round kitchen table to find his sister ignoring them as she read. She had brown hair like Robert, but her facial features were sharper, her

43

nose a little longer, her mouth a little wider, and her eyes full of life. And if anyone ticked her off, her green eyes became death rays and everyone prayed their maker would help them survive. It did not matter what book or class she absorbed. She always seemed enthralled by learning, but mostly ignoring the nearby reality of the family holding pattern she had to get through for the next four years, until she could escape to college.

"Do you think God loves me?" Robert asked. He watched his mother freeze in place, stopped her busybody, mind-blocking, domestic duties. She shook her head as if a bumblebee had flown inside her ear and bounced around her brain.

"What?" Laina asked, as she put down her book. "Are you serious?"

"Yeah, do you all think some people are cursed?" Robert asked. His cheeks blushed crimson.

Robert's mother strolled over and sat on the dining chair between him and his sister. It creaked in the joints from overuse. She leaned forward to pat Robert on the head as if he were an obeying golden retriever.

"Why do you think such things?" Mrs. Scott asked.

"I don't know," Robert said. He sat back in the chair and crossed his arms. The kitchen started to seem cramped and warm, and the descending darkness through the floor-to-ceiling windows behind Laina made him think Satan had decided to join in their conversation.

"Is something bothering you?" Mrs. Scott asked. She clasped her fingers together. "You've been, well..."

"Strange," Laina piped in. "But you're my brother so, I guess that goes without saying."

Mrs. Scott snapped her gaze over at her daughter.

"Laina, not nice," Mrs. Scott said. She looked back over at Robert. "You have been distant recently. What's wrong?"

"Well, I'm just saying," Laina said. She gave Mrs. Scott a weird look and circled her forefingers around her head. "Say it with me, 'Mister Cuckoo Clock' over there."

"See, Laina thinks I'm cursed," Robert said. He stared at his sister through a bouquet of red and white foxgloves dying inside an oriental vase.

"You're not cursed," Mrs. Scott said. "And God loves everyone, bless the little children. Just pray about it; I'm sure that will make it all better."

Laina pursed her thin lips. She tapped them with her forefinger.

"Robert have you been eating mom's flowers?" Laina smirked. "You know these flowers are poisonous, and the first sign before death is hallucinations."

Robert scowled at his older sister. "No!"

"Enough," Mrs. Scott said. She put her against her chin and appeared to be thinking. "I didn't consider that."

She quickly got up, took the vase into the kitchen, and threw out the flowers into the garbage can, and she was careful to wash her hands, at least three times. She appeared to be examining them closely to determine if the naked eye could see poisonous microbial particulates.

"I'm cursed," Robert said. He slumped back in the wooden chair.

Laina rolled her eyes and stared up at the ceiling.

"Come on," Laina said. She sighed. "You're not cursed, unless for some reason God decided to curse you by being cute, popular, a good athlete, smart, and having all sorts of girlfriends. And don't think I haven't noticed the one you've been flirting with lately...I notice all. Yeah, you're cursed, you moron."

"Flirting?" Mrs. Scott asked. She perked up and released her paranoid potentially-poisonous-flower thoughts. "Do tell..."

"Yeah, I just think he's smitten with puppy love," Laina said. She smirked and crossed her willowy legs to bask in the complete destruction of her little brother.

"I'm not doing anything," Robert said.

"Well, let's hope so," Mrs. Scott said. She turned her head and wagged her forefinger down at Robert. "Lustful hearts are the devil's playground."

"I'm not doing anything," Robert said. "I've not even tried to kiss her."

Laina instantly lost the ability to hold in her delight.

"Idiot! You are such an easy mark," Laina said. She leaned her head back. "Why are you so stupid?"

"Young man, you treat all women with respect." Mrs. Scott angrily shook her head. "I'll need to talk to your father about this. We don't treat girls like sexual objects."

"I'm not doing anything," Robert moaned. He wanted to run out the front door, down the residential street, and find a nearby tobacco field to hide. Maybe he could hide out there, as a troll hides under a bridge, and scare away any other kids who wanted to hide with him. It would be great to be left all alone.

Mrs. Scott appeared as though she had actually swallowed the foxglove flowers and her insides now rotted from the thought her precious little boy might be a sexual predator.

"If you two will excuse me," Mrs. Scott said.

Robert felt sick to his stomach, and his ears started to blaze a deep, dark red hue. He was close to tears of total frustration and desolation. And his mother wondered why he told her nothing.

"Sorry, I took it too far," Laina said.

"It doesn't matter," Robert said. He collapsed back into the chair. "I'm not doing anything."

"I know," Laina said.

"Then why'd you set me up?" Robert huffed. "You know what a sap I am."

"Sport, I guess," Laina said. She shrugged. "Sorry, I was just messing with you, and then Mom has to go all Bible thumper on you. Didn't see that coming."

"It doesn't matter," Robert said. He crossed his arms. "I'm sure I'll get a lecture on premarital sex and lust tonight."

"Good point." Laina smirked over at Robert. "Besides, I'll never get asked out by a normal boy. I can't stand those happy hee-haw morons at church."

"I think they're all living in snow globes," Robert said. He stared at his sister. "I just fake it now. I'm tired of fighting."

"I know, little brother," Laina said. "I know; me, too."

Robert glanced at her resigned face and down at his tennis shoes. He could feel his heart pulse through his burning ears. After talking to Willis, he had started to get a queasy sensation of the memories he had buried at the bottom on his turbulent adolescent sea. The thoughts had lost their papier-mâché filters and were starting to bubble up like the big chunks from the bottom of a cesspool.

"Laina, remember summer camp, when I was in fifth grade?" Robert asked.

"No, because I wasn't there," Laina said. She continued reading and did not look over at Robert.

Robert thought there were times when he would like to have someone in his life he could trust—someone who he could look into their eyes and they would understand him. He would not need to say anything; they would just know him. Someone who did not hide behind the idea of God, but instead would ask him head on, what was eating him from the inside out. What caused him to wake up in the middle of the night. What caused him to think he would be dead before dawn or was destined to die in some tragic way. Sexually transmitted disease, airplane crash, crushed in a car accident, or any number of headline-getting 'accidents' that God had chosen from his list of extermination techniques. But Mrs. Scott swiftly returned to the kitchen reenergized from a prayer for Robert and Laina's lustful souls.

"Okay, all will be just fine," Mrs. Scott said. She adjusted her hair. "How 'bout, let's act like nothing happened."

*

After dinner that night, Robert knew his evening would become complicated.

"What's this I hear about you lusting after a little girl?" Mr. Scott said. He had dark, deathly blue eyes and a prominent nose.

"Tell your father everything." Mrs. Scott said. She nodded her head at Robert.

"Sorry, I've got a test in the morning," Laina said. She shrugged over at Robert and disappeared to her room. Robert heard her lock her door.

"I didn't do anything," Robert said.

"You look guilty to me," Mr. Scott said. He sipped his coffee.

"What are you hiding?" Mrs. Scott pointed over at Robert. "Thou shalt not lie."

Robert's mouth gaped open, and he huffed. "I'm not hiding anything."

"Tell me about this girl." Mrs. Scott gave Robert a *Mother Superior* stare.

"You are not allowed to flirt with a girl. That's for adults," Mr. Scott said. He adjusted his powder blue button-down shirt collar. "You are not approved for that activity."

"Whatever," Robert said. He stared forward. "You all don't listen to me."

Mr. Scott snapped over and grabbed Robert by his ear.

"Don't you ever give me that attitude." Mr. Scott tugged at Robert as if he was a disobedient animal.

"Mr. Diabolus has been doing things to me." Robert started to cry. He cried for someone to listen; he cried for his parents to defend him.

Mr. Scott instantly released Robert from his grip.

"What did you say?" Mrs. Scott said.

"Mr. Diabolus, he touched me," Robert whispered. "He took pictures of me – and Willis."

"Come now, Dan touched you?" Mr. Scott slinked back into the dining table chair. He comically looked over at Mrs. Scott and smirked at her.

"Robert, you should be ashamed," Mrs. Scott said. Her jaw dropped so far, it seemed unhinged. "That's a horrible thing to say."

"My son has a vivid imagination. Hey, dummy, Dan is an ordained minister in the church." Mr. Scott chuckled. "I should know; I was there. I helped with the service."

Robert stared at the purity-white lace tablecloth with his heart thumping and his cheeks blushing with a rosy red. He knew he had crossed a magical, unseen line. He would get a beating—a whipping that he would never forget.

"Robert, honey, you can't be serious." Mrs. Scott said. She narrowed her eye lids. She puckered her lips.

"I'm not making it up," Robert said. He wanted to keep crying, but he stopped. There would be plenty of crying during the night, when he wanted to sleep but couldn't. He would wake up and pace. His thirteen-year-old body was sexually on fire, and he hated the constant nagging of his body. *My dirty body*, he thought.

"Well, I do know one thing, I'm going to beat that imagination right out of you," Mr. Scott said. He sprang up and wiped off his black leather belt. "Get up boy."

Mrs. Scott looked away as she cleared the kitchen table of dishes. She disappeared from Robert's view as his father whipped him the way a jockey would a losing racehorse near the finish line.

Robert took the whipping without crying. Instead, his eyes were dead. He would never make the mistake twice; he would keep his mouth shut.

"There, that'll teach you," Mr. Scott said. He combed his hair with his fingers. "I do know one thing. I'll need to talk to Dan. I've known him for years. He's always at my prayer breakfasts. The man has taken an oath—has sacrificed to look after children. You'll need to tell him you're sorry. I'm sure he'll be shocked.

Boy, you will not embarrass me before God. Perhaps through prayer, you'll learn not to have such an evil imagination."

"I don't know what has gotten into you," Mrs. Scott said. She straightened the lace tablecloth.

"Yes, you'll apologize," Mr. Scott said. "Have you said this to anyone else? You will not embarrass the family."

"We would have to leave the church," Mrs. Scott said.

"I've worked too hard to allow that." Mr. Scott straightened his collar and buckled his belt. "Boy, go to your room and pray I don't feel moved to revisit this. You will not embarrass me."

Chapter Five

Early the next morning, the ghostly mist began to evaporate above the harvested stalks of sweet corn and tilled over tobacco fields. Sunlight began to reveal the lush, forest green, canary yellow, and carrot orange rolling Central Kentucky terrain. Robert stood at the school bus stop with his sister, Laina, and three neighborhood children. They ignored the odor of hay, manure, and winterized soil. He was lost in his own thoughts—thoughts he was unable to define. In the pit of his stomach, something he could not see was pulling at his subconscious strings. His sister thought it odd her chatterbox of a brother had disappeared into a quiet, reflective boy.

"What's up, chicken butt?" Laina nudged him.

"What?" Robert asked. He looked past her at three thoroughbreds foraging for breakfast on the other side of a line of white four-plank fences. He could hear them snort and scratch their hooves against the dense soil.

"Attention K-Mart shoppers; earth to Robert," Laina said. She waved her hand in front of his blank face.

"I'm all right," Robert said, glancing over at Laina.

"Sorry. I didn't mean to get you in trouble." She adjusted her book bag strap. "Didn't think Dad would come down on you like that, Mom kind of went off the deep end."

"It's not the first time." Robert shrugged and pursed his lips. "I'll be all right."

"Get your homework done?" Laina asked.

"Naw, I'll do it at school," Robert said. "Couldn't concentrate last night."

"Bad idea," Laina said. She checked the clasp of her book bag.

"I can't concentrate. Get distracted," Robert said. He crinkled his face. "I try, I really try, to study like you."

"Well, you better get with the plan," Laina said. "It only will get harder and harder, and you don't want to get stuck here."

The school bus brakes squeaked a quarter of a mile away from within the dense fog curtaining the country road. The children's paddy wagon approached, as the diesel engine belched.

"Well, maybe your pretty friend will sit next to you," Laina said. She elbowed him and smirked as they climbed up the bus stairs and walked down the center aisle. Robert just sat in the seat and glanced over at his sister.

"Like, what will I do?" Robert asked.

"I'm sorry, I'm just trying to make you feel better," Laina said. "Don't worry about them. They're wacky."

"I guess so." Robert leaned against the bus window. "I didn't do anything, and they make me feel like I'm going to burn in hell. I hate church. All they talk about is death and not doing anything. I think they're all hiding."

Laina fiddled with her book bag zipper. "Let it go little brother." She stared forward to the half-full school bus. "You need to learn to tune them out."

"It's kind of hard. They're our parents," Robert said.

He smelled the bus exhaust fumes and heard the low, dull hum of the rest of the students as they waddled like bobble-heads down the long, narrow road toward Briar Hill. He sighed and tried to perk up, aware that at least his sister cared about him. He glanced over and half smiled at her. She tapped him on the leg. It was not her fault she had a wicked sense of humor.

The school bus tooled along for another twenty minutes, stopping at a few modest homes for the nearby farm laborers families, a housing development like Laina and Robert's and then in front of Ardee's house. She hopped up to the top of the bus stairs and looked around the bus until she saw her man. She said hello to a few friends, skipping her way to sit next to Robert. And yes, his heart thumped hard enough to make his ears burn and his face turned shades of pale pink and red. Robert figured it was t-minus ten seconds before nuclear warhead Laina's launch sequence.

"Can I sit next to you Bobby?" Ardee bounced in next to Robert, playfully leaned her shoulder against his, and giggled.

"Sure," Robert said. He felt like he had no actual oxygen left in his lungs. He knew within a Nano second what would happen next. Ten, nine, eight, seven…

"Bobby?" Laina laughed. "Who might that be?"

"My Bobby." Ardee giggled, showing a row of perfect white teeth. She leaned back against the bus seat and pointed at Robert.

Robert wondered if it was possible to teleport through time, and if there really was a wormhole that he dropped through. Even if he dropped into a world run by barnyard chickens, at least he would die trying to minimize the sister-fed grains of his humiliation.

"Hi, I'm 'Bobby's' sister." Laina smirked at Ardee, and then leaned forward to find Robert inspecting the cold bus windowpane for microscopic germs.

Laina simply grinned like any great hunter about to bag her lifetime prey. It was a moment all sisters dreamt of, a choice moment of sibling torment, savored, and not wasted, for this was a moment that, decades later, Laina would have in her bag of top ten Robert Scott embarrassment moments.

"Oh, I know. I'm Ardee."

"Nice to meet you." Laina patted Ardee on the leg and leaned across the dirty center aisle. "He is cute I guess."

Robert closed his eyes and accepted his fate—the fate of having his sister remove each morsel of his dignity. When he got home later that night, any lustful thoughts, any thought of kissing Ardee, would forever be burnt in the ash heap of his parents paranoid view of the evils of premarital sex. As if an innocent kiss even counted. All Robert was hoping for was to hold her soft, warm hand and maybe, just maybe, kiss her on the cheek. For one of the first moments in his life, he decided to risk his heart.

"I think he's cute." Ardee smiled at Laina. "But he's so shy."

"Oh, he's not shy," Laina said.

"Then he should ask me to go to a movie on Saturday." Ardee smiled and winked at Laina.

"Now that's a great idea," Laina said. It was as if she had gotten a perfect inside-out facial suntan from her bright pride. She felt that she now controlled all of Robert's sunshine. And for the cherry on top of her morning bus ride to academic purgatory, she had a new name for her little brother—*Bobby.*

Robert reemerged from his soul searching and attempt to hide in plain sight from his sister.

"What? How am I going to do that? I don't drive," Robert said. He could feel the grinding of his Adams apple against his throat as he glanced over at Ardee. "I mean I want to, but…"

"Shut up, Bobby. I'll help you," Laina said. She frowned. She decided that at least someone in the family should have innocent fun.

"I'm excited." Ardee nudged Robert. "Let's go see something funny. I like funny."

She reached over and grabbed Robert's hand. He did not move his hand away. Her hand made him feel safe, as safe as a newborn puppy hugged by a little girl. Robert lost the ability to speak, paralyzed by the thought of his sister nearby and being asked out

on his first "sort of" date. And he was holding Ardee's hand. His
brain squished inside his head, and he felt pulled along as he
walked off the bus and inside the school, still holding Ardee's
hand.

"See you later Bobby," Ardee said.

"Sure." That was all he could think to say.

Of course, Robert, aka "Bobby", spent the rest of the day
stewing in his own angst-ridden juices. He wondered how he had
somehow asked Ardee to a movie. It was not a date, Robert
thought. Only old people had dates. And how had this all come
about? Was there some sort of female conspiracy to drive him to
an adolescent heart attack?

The thought of talking with his parents caused his brain to
solidify as hard as the prehistoric rocks he was learning about in
science class. But little brothers do not always appreciate the
wisdom of older sisters, in particular, understanding a girl's soft-
tipped Cupids arrow. A fresh wound into an unblemished heart
began to pour out a lifetime of vulnerable feelings—an eternal scar
of friendship and purity that, if he were brutally honest with
himself, would always be there.

That night at the dinner table, Laina, the chief negotiator on
behalf of Robert, aka "My Bobby", coughed to clear her throat
after she managed to swallow down her mother's newest version
of meatloaf.

"Yes, dear?" Mrs. Scott asked Laina.

"Meatloaf was great mom," Laina said. She coughed. "Right,
Robert? Moms love compliments."

Robert grimaced at his sister. Whatever this was on the dinner
plate was certainly not "great". It was, more accurately, caked
together dried-out cat food with baked-on ketchup. *However, the
mandarin oranges from a can are quite tasty*, he thought. But she
gave him one of her looks, as if to say, "Fall in line, stupid."

"Yeah, it's great mom," Robert said with a cough.

Mr. Scott sat at the head of the table. He moved his tongue around the inside of his mouth, searching for charred meatloaf remnants to clear out, and studied his children with a "what are you two up to" glance.

"Tastes just great, dear," Mr. Scott said slowly.

Mrs. Scott gasped in pleasure, and then threatened her family with some sort of chocolate pudding concoction she had read about in Southern Living.

"Thank you all. It's nice to be appreciated," Mrs. Scott said.

Robert glanced over at Laina and realized he was learning the first tenets from a master salesperson—warm up your pigeons before you pluck all their feathers.

"I have no doubt it'll be unique," Laina said.

"You're being quite calm tonight," Mr. Scott said.

Robert pursed his lips. It seemed his father was suspicious of Laina's praise. She typically sat quietly, hocked down dinner, and then found a window of opportunity to disappear to her room to study. Her snake rattle only came out when either of her parents became overly inquisitive about her life.

"Oh? Sorry, I'm just in a good mood," Laina said. The bait had been thrown on the table, now it was a matter of being patient, let them peck a bit; let them peck.

"Wonderful. Did you get a blessing today at school?" Mrs. Scott asked.

"Me? Not today, although I feel blessed every day," Laina said. She grinned over at her mother.

Robert did not move his head. He just shifted his eyes at his sister, then at his mother, and finally over at his father. Perhaps if he chose not to move a muscle, they might have a conversation as if he was not actually in the room.

"Okay, I'll bite." Mr. Scott leaned back. "What's up?"

"I happened to meet Robert's little friend," Laina said.

Robert's cheeks flushed. His heart thumped against his chest, and he had the distinct feeling he was having an out-of-body experience.

"Yes?" Mr. Scott said. He and his wife stared over at Robert, who decided he would listen to his sister and keep quiet.

"She's very sweet," Laina said, elongating the word sweet.

"Not worried about her. Has Robert been behaving?" Mr. Scott asked.

"Are you kidding? I think her name's Ardee?" Laina said. She paused for just the right amount of time; after all, it was how a patient angler is rewarded, cast the line, and dangle the lure as if a real horse fly flopping in a stream. She glanced over at Robert.

"Yeah, that's her," Robert said. He immediately went back into hiding mode.

"Oh? I'll be the judge of that," Mrs. Scott said.

"She's a total tomboy. She could beat Robert up." Laina laughed. "Oh, another thing. I'm ninety-nine percent she comes from a Christian home."

"Well, nice to hear that," Mr. and Mrs. Scott said in stereo. They gave Robert an approving glance from within their fundamentalist snow globes.

"You didn't tell me that," Mrs. Scott said to Robert.

"Sorry," Robert said. She did not seem to care last night as dad gave him a beating for no apparent reason and made him certain he would burn in hell from impure thoughts, even though he did not have them. He just liked holding Ardee's hand. He just liked talking to her.

Laina tried to chew more "meat loaf", or whatever it was. Robert realized she was stalling. Let the parents think Robert had been innocently burned at the stake.

"Almost forgot. I was talking with her on the bus and suggested she and Robert should go to a movie," Laina said. She tried to swallow. "Maybe Saturday afternoon…"

"Laina, I'm not sure," Mrs. Scott said.

"I thought you all wanted Robert to learn to be a gentleman, a nice Christian boy?" Laina asked. "It was my idea. I was thinking... you know."

"Well, yes," Mrs. Scott said.

"I was just thinking," Laina said. She immediately yanked back on her invisible fishing line and set her hook. "She's so shy, a perfect girl for Robert to practice what you two preach—be a good, Christian boy."

"Well, that's true dear," Mr. Scott said.

"Then you'll drive them? That way you can supervise," Laina said.

"I suppose that would be the right thing to do," Mrs. Scott said.

Robert sat at the kitchen table in stunned silence, amazed at his sister's parental sales skills.

"All right, if you all think it's okay," Mr. Scott said. He shrugged. "I have a prayer breakfast at seven. I'll take you after that, okay, Robert?"

"Okay," Robert said. He did not know what else to say. Laina had turned them so fast, as if they were her willing sheep. He looked over at his sister. She just sat there, beaming within the saintly hallow of her older sister glory. And Robert knew he would have the sword of Laina hanging over his head for the rest of his life.

Chapter Six

Three-thirty in the morning. It did not matter to Robert what time it was; he just could not drift off to sleep. And almost every morning, the sun's golden, angelic beams bore through his window before he had the chance to fly into the Peter Pan night. The ghostly shadows of the furniture were his constant nighttime security detail, his silent friends. In the new morning, light glistened with the refreshed vibrancy of a kaleidoscope of color. A framed print of a prayerful little blond-haired boy hung above his bed. It was a reminder to Robert that God and Satan constantly watched over him.

Almost every night, just after he had disappeared into the ether of rest, he became his own sporadic alarm clock. His heavy breathing an instant on, every few hours he would awake with drops of sweat painting his forehead and behind his ears, his brown hair moist and matted. Someone else, it seemed, was using his body during the middle of the night, and he was not a friend of Robert's. On the other hand, was he just dreaming? Robert could not remember his dreams; he vaguely remembered tiny fragments of scenes that seemed terrifyingly real. He leaned up on the double bed, the white cotton sheets dotted with his personal smell and moisture.

It was desolately dark outside except for a faint haunting street lamp that hung low, like a distant baby moon. Through the night, he was either chilled to the bone and snaked the cotton blanket between his knees and around his neck, or he pushed back all the covers, lying there panting with his hands above his head as if he had run a fast quarter mile. Most of the time, he slipped off his pajama bottoms, dangled his naked right leg outside the covers, like a human thermometer, to balance his body's internal temperature. He gulped the thickness within his throat. *Water, a glass of water, or maybe a glass of cold milk might calm my stomach*, he thought.

"Robert," a strange, yet familiar, voice whispered from within his dream.

Robert heard the voice but could not quite place it with a face.

"Wake up, Robert," the voice asked. He heard a *tap tap tap*, like knuckles on a wooden surface.

Robert blinked his eyes rapidly and realized he was looking at his forearm, which was curled under his head, resting atop his school desk. The voice grew a bit louder, and the laughter from his classmates became a certain dagger to his conscious mind. Mrs. Lange rhythmically tapped her long fingers on his desk. Her voice sounded between bemusement and concern.

"Robert, are you all right?" Mrs. Lange asked.

Robert abruptly sat up straight in his desk chair. He expelled air suddenly, as if he had been holding his breath at the bottom of a pool, and looked up at his social studies teacher. She had auburn hair, like his friend Ardee, but cut just at the mid-point of her neck, a button of a nose, and piercing, dark blue eyes. She appeared perplexed, her thin spindly arms crossed.

"I'm all right," Robert said.

A wave of giggles washed over Robert. He did not look around the classroom; he didn't need to. He knew what had happened, and there was no going back.

"We were timing you, dude," Taylor said.

"Yeah, over ten minutes," Bo said. "Dude…"

The rest of the class laughed.

"Sleepy time for Robert," Taylor said.

"Yeah, sleepy dog." Bo flicked the back of Robert's head.

Robert shoved the front of Bo's desk. It tottered for a second, but Bo shoved Robert's right shoulder as he righted himself. Robert wheeled around to retaliate.

"Let's go," Robert said. "Come on, you stinkin' loser dick."

Willis got up from his desk and bull rushed Bo, encasing the boy in a mountain of blobby brown flesh. He then sat on Bo and growled over at Taylor.

"Leave him alone," Willis said.

"Hey, man, no problem here." Taylor put his hands up.

"Willis, stop," Mrs. Lange said. "Sit down Robert."

"Hey, what'd I do?" Bo shook his head and gazed around the classroom. "Get off me, Willis."

"Willis, what's gotten into you?" Mrs. Lange grabbed Willis by his left arm and escorted him back to his desk.

"Sorry. They should shut up," Willis said. His face sallow, stone like.

"Boys, enough already." Mrs. Lange appeared perplexed. Her hands were on her narrow hips as she trudged to the front of the classroom.

"Willis started it," Taylor said.

"Taylor, be quiet," Mrs. Lange said. "Another word and you can stand in the corner until the end of class."

"But I…" Taylor simply lacked a brain filter—a filter he would desperately need in life.

"Taylor, you know the drill," Mrs. Lange said. She did not even turn around before pointing her arm like a traffic cop, advising him to pull over into the front corner next to her desk.

"Dude, she did warn you." Bo rubbed his pimple-infested forehead. "Willis, you must weigh ten thousand pounds."

Willis ignored Bo and re-stuffed himself in his desk chair like a massive marshmallow man. He studied the back of Robert's head, thinking he knew why Robert was dead tired. He was afraid to fall asleep at night, too.

"Enough foolishness," Mrs. Lange said. "Okay, I assume everyone has completed the reading assignment. Let's talk about the Bill of Rights?"

Robert reached into his book bag to pull out his social studies textbook. As he was gripping the top of the book, he noticed a folded piece of notebook paper. On the outside of the paper was a heart shape, drawn with a pink magic marker. He slowly glanced around the classroom and unfolded it under his desktop.

Bobby,

Hi! I like you.

Ardee

Robert quickly refolded the paper and stuffed it back into this book bag, grinning faintly. He felt like a happy glimmer of sunshine had just hugged him.

Chapter Seven

"Remember to behave," Mr. Scott said dryly to Robert.

Robert thought about the whipping with a leather belt he took after the day he and Willis were attacked at school by Mr. Diabolus. Mr. Diabolus owned his life.

"Yes, sir," Robert said as he and Ardee scampered from the car toward the Cineplex.

Robert knew he was not supposed to have lustful thoughts. He had been stuck in church with the 'adults' who he thought could not seem to leave each other alone. He understood the concept of lust; all he needed to do was pay attention in church. He knew he was likely going to burn in hell. He did not need reminding from his father.

"Thank you for driving, Mr. Scott," Ardee said.

"You're welcome, dear." Mr. Scott tapped his watch. "Two-thirty. I'll be waiting here."

Robert was careful not to even act as if he wanted to hold Ardee's hand. Although he had sat in the back seat next to Ardee as his father drove them toward the movie theatre and thought about holding her hand. He could tell something was on her mind. She was normally more giggly and gregarious. He just thought that perhaps she was unsure what to think of his *stiff shirt* of a father.

"You look pretty," Robert said.

"You're sweet," Ardee said. She was wearing a pink, long sleeved, collared blouse, blue jeans, and tennis shoes.

"I liked your note," Robert said. He glanced at Ardee. She was beautiful.

When you are thirteen you cannot help but be honest, if you like someone, you like them, it was just the nature of things. It did not matter your parents social status, if they had some money, or all the machinations adults calculated into relationships. When you are thirteen, you cannot help but be honest, true to your heart. And inside of Robert's heart, there was the picture of Ardee. He was thirteen. She was thirteen. He was a child, but he was not a child. She would always be an instamatic photo of perfection.

Ardee smiled and giggled, but Robert could tell there was something she was not telling him. He had learned at an early age how to sense what someone thought behind their eyes.

"We're moving, Bobby," Ardee finally said. She shrugged and tried to act as if it was just life—their ships were about to navigate into different ports of call.

"Oh," Robert said. His mind went snow-white blank, but in a sense, he felt relief that Ardee would be away from him. He would not have to protect her. She would be safe.

"My parents just told me," Ardee said. "Daddy got a better job, so we're going to move soon."

Robert stood almost frozen looking up at the movie register. He thought it was a cruel trick from God to allow him a tiny window of happiness, to innocently care about Ardee, and then, *poof*, she would disappear from his life. Robert should have expected the surprise; he would never make the mistake twice. Only a fool would love someone as he puppy-loved Ardee and then allow God to trick him. God might have His ways, but Robert had his ways too. His anxiety marinated his life as if he lived within the depths of hell. *So give me your best shot Mr. Higher Power*, he thought.

"I'll miss you," Robert said. He also felt like another hole was punched in his heart.

"What are we going to see?" Ardee asked. She shrugged and whispered, "I'll miss your sad eyes."

"I don't know. I like funny. You like funny?" Robert asked. "We need to pick something funny -"

"Yeah, I like funny," Ardee said. She reached over and grabbed Robert's hand. Her hand was baby soft and warm—warmth that could only be felt from the innocence of honesty.

They shared a sugary carbonated beverage with two bendy straws and a gallon of popcorn. A funny movie inside a dark theatre with an amazingly pretty girl with a happy laugh—what more could Robert want? It would be an awesome day for any male from thirteen years old to one hundred thirteen years old, but Robert thought Ardee was like a fragile baby bird. He did not want to hurt her or pluck off any of her delicate feathers. To him, she was perfect. If you constantly look at the world through dirty eyeballs, as if someone dipped you in acid bath, well, you might feel lost. So he held her hand tightly and prayed he could remember the moment. He wanted to kiss her again, but he did not. He wanted to cry. He wanted to scream. He just sat there silently. But he never let go of her hand.

"Are you all right?" Ardee asked. She kissed Robert on the cheek.

"Yeah, why?" Robert whispered.

"Because you're squeezing awfully tight." Ardee giggled. "But I like holding your hand." She sighed and leaned her head against his shoulder.

"I like it, too," Robert said. He loosened his grip. "Better?" He leaned in near her, close enough to feel her breath along his nose and against his cheek.

"Yeah," Ardee whispered and kissed Robert on the cheek again. "You'll always be my Bobby?"

For one of the few times in his life, Robert felt safe—safe near Ardee—and did not feel dirty. He knew she would never do anything intentionally to hurt him. She would always be his friend, and he trusted her.

"Yeah, I'll always be your Bobby," Robert whispered. And he wished the movie blipping across the screen would never end.

Chapter Eight

"Robert, I'm not sure quite what to say," Coach Burton said. He studied his manila file folder and flipped over several notebook pages affixed to the top.

Robert assumed it was his student file, since his name was typed in block letters along the tab.

"Just so you know I've already talked with your parents."

"What'd I do?" Robert squirmed in the plastic chair.

The guidance office seemed cramped, the air stale and the room abnormally warm. Enough sunlight bore through the misty sheers that curtained the window behind Coach Burton to almost blind Robert.

"Don't stress," Coach Burton said. "I *have* to talk with them before I talk to you. It's the rules."

"So?" Robert said.

"I like you. You're a good kid," Coach Burton said. "You're rarely in trouble, been one of my better football and basketball players…and you're okay at track, too." Coach Burton glanced up at Robert.

"Thanks," Robert said. He wondered what this was all leading toward. He did not like the thought that his parents were snooping into his life. He didn't want them knowing what he really thought. He didn't want *anyone* to know what he thought.

"But you're, well... You seem disinterested," Coach Burton said. "Your grades are good, but your teachers know you can do a lot better. For you, getting a B is just getting by in school. Any reason why?"

"I don't know." Robert shrugged.

"I don't mean to pry. I know you really liked that girl that moved away, but that's been two years. I know you have a harem of girls chasing you up and down the halls. So I know you can't still be down about that, and you're always a good teammate. You play hard for me," Coach Burton said. "What am I missing? You're too smart to just get by in your classes. You're not lazy or destined for mediocrity. I sense you're not engaged in things."

Robert knew Coach Burton had his best interests in mind. He'd just never had anyone ask him why he didn't study. Of course, that excluded Laina, but she was too busy hatching her own plan to escape to college to worry about Robert.

In reality, Robert never studied. He tried to mimic his sister's study habits, but he was too embarrassed to tell anyone he couldn't concentrate for more than fifteen minutes. He would start to read—he liked to read—or do math, which he also liked, but his mind would wander—wander into an intense daydream, as if he were looking at the world through foggy binoculars. His body nagged at him as if his groin were attached to a crazed human serpent. He was like any boy fighting through puberty, and he hated the feelings in his aroused body. It was not a pleasurable feeling. He related the feelings to severe pain, shame, filth, and being dirty. They were sensations he begged to go away and leave him alone.

Athletics allowed him to release some of his pent up angst. He loved to run off his puberty steam engine, but he was having girls flirt with him. He liked some of them and was afraid he would hurt

68

them, so he usually ignored them or said something mean. Either way was effective. He did not know what to do. He was not going to allow anyone close to him again the way Ardee had been.

So, he tried to memorize what he heard the teacher say or saw written on the chalkboard, and that usually worked—at least it worked well enough to get a B.

"I don't know. I get distracted," Robert said.

"Distracted?" Coach Burton asked.

"Yeah, when it's quiet, I get distracted." Robert decided it was okay to talk to Coach Burton.

"Funny, I'm just the opposite. I need it quiet as an empty church to read," Coach Burton said.

Robert stared down at his tennis shoes. "Have you ever loved someone?"

Coach Burton sat back in his office chair and swiveled in it, acting as if he needed to adjust the height.

"Now, I have to admit," Coach Burton chuckled. He piano tapped his fingers, "I didn't expect you to ask me that."

"I'm just curious. What's it feel like?" Robert's face was blank, unemotional, as if he were a robot full of circuit boards and software programs hoping to load data to improve efficiency.

"Well, I think you know… You just know," Coach Burton said. "You feel it—whatever 'it' is."

Robert glanced at the half-full metal bookshelf behind Coach Burton's husky right shoulder. "Does love make you feel safe?"

"Hmm, I guess so. I think if you love someone, or they love you, you should definitely should feel safe with them," Coach Burton said. He opened his eyes wide and talked out of the corner of his mouth. "Trust me. If you're going to spend a long time around them, being safe is the least of your worries."

Robert paused for several minutes, pursed his lips, and folded his arms. He remembered going to the movie with Ardee—how he felt safe next to her, holding her soft hand.

"So, why did you want to talk to me?" Robert asked.

Coach Burton rubbed his forehead and thought it was an odd question, but it seemed to him that Robert had opened up his internal world for a minute. He had a glimpse of what Robert was thinking behind his hazel irises and then, just as quickly, the boy disappeared and went back into hiding.

"Ah, I know you've got high school football practice in the late summer, but I was contacted by the university. They've got a three-week summer program I'm recommending you attend," Coach Burton said.

"Why?" Robert asked. He stared at Coach Burton as if he did not care.

"For students that we think can do better, a program is set up to try to spark your interest," Coach Burton said. He breathed out slowly and methodically.

"So, I'm a loser?" Robert said.

"No, it's not like that," Coach Burton said.

"Hmm, sounds like loser to me."

"Well, that's not what they're, rather, *who* they are searching for—just someone, like you, who has a lot of potential," Coach Burton said.

Robert sighed, sitting still and quiet. "What's wrong with me? What did I do wrong?"

"Nothing," Coach Burton said. "Nothing—"

Robert shrugged his shoulders and looked down at the tile floor. "Can't be just nothing. It doesn't matter either way, what's been done, is done. I'll always be a loser."

"I hardly think you're a loser," Coach Burton said. "Perhaps the class will spark an interest in you that you want to follow, maybe writing?"

"So, what do I have to do?"

And the years silently whispered past Robert. Ardee, Willis and Mr. Diabolus disappeared from his life. Memories hid, waiting to be reborn within Robert's fractured brain. Memories that emerged deep in the night.

"Maybe now, *kill yourself*—don't let anyone find out."

Chapter Nine

"Oobie, what're you doing down there, little buddy?" Steven asked. His nude body was a milky specter as he bounced his dangling body parts down the townhouse's stairs. He flopped down next to Robert, who was wearing boxer shorts and a white t-shirt and sitting on the bottom stair bare footed.

"Naked Nan!" Steven said in buzzed Tarzan mode.

"You just love messing with me?" Robert said.

"Oh, Oobie, it's three in the morning. It's when Naked Man comes out," Steven said. He draped his long, skinny arm around Robert. "I need a girlfriend to play with... so do you. They like to play, too."

"You know, if someone just happened to come to our front door over there and look through that window, they'd swear we're having a moment," Robert said.

"Naked Man has no boundaries," Steven said. He patted Robert on the back. "You need to loosen up little buddy. I'm just joshin' with ya."

"I know." Robert grinned. His thick brown hair was mangled, and his icy cold feet were digging into the carpeted floor. He wondered how he had stumbled into living with a man who walked around the apartment naked. Robert admired Steven's freedom; he wished he had the same courage. At first Naked Man disturbed him, now, he welcomed the distraction. Maybe he could snag some of Steven's courage and ask a girl out on a 'real' date and let his Naked Man come out.

"You know, I think you need find yourself a cute girl and let your little fella spit," Steven said. "Let's go to the kitchen. This carpet's chafing my nuts."

"Why not?" Robert loped behind Steven.

"Beer?" Steven asked.

The interior refrigerator light splashed along Steven's gangly arms and legs and lit up half of his rear moon. Robert was thankful that the dark side of the moon was left to his imagination.

"I think I've had enough for a while," Robert said. "Besides, I need to get back in shape. I'm turning into Porky Pig."

"You've gotten a bit of a belly lately," Steven said.

Robert patted his waist. "Yeah, don't want anybody thinking I'm pregnant,"

He slid open the sliding glass door and moved two of the wooden kitchen chairs out onto their side patio, the corner of which was blocked by a mature pin oak. It was a cool spring morning, the time of night when most are dreaming they are kings and queens of their make believe universes. "I know better...than to get fat. I've no excuses."

"Ah, we'll go joggin'. Get ya back to your fighting weight." Steven flicked off the exterior security light and leaned down on the wooden chair. "Don't want Naked Man to scare anybody."

"You ever sat out this time of night and listened to the stillness?" Robert asked.

"To be honest Oobie, nope. You can't listen to stillness." He swigged the beer and wiped a few escaping drops from his thin lips with his forearm. "I just take things as they come. You think too much. I do like this snap in the air, like tonight."

Robert leaned forward with his elbows on his knees and, with his forefinger, flicked the side of their barbecue grill, which was shaped like an upside-down black metal spaceship.

"You know that knucklehead Ernie almost shot me tonight?" Robert said.

"See? You need to relax." Steven laughed.

"Hard to relax when you almost get shot." Robert sighed.

Steven pursed his lips and shrugged his wide athletic shoulders.

"Was kind of stupid, droppin' a bullet into a charcoal fire," Steven said. He swigged the beer again. "I have to admit, when I heard it bounce off the inside of the grill, sort of got my attention."

"Ernie just doesn't sense danger," Robert said. "Known him for years, can't accuse him of being boring."

"He's just doing all his stupid stuff now, while he's still young," Steven said.

"Yeah, you've got that right, Naked Man," Robert said.

"See, you should have your own Naked Man. Sit out here naked to the world. Might help you to relax," Steve said. "Cleanse your spirit."

"Right now, I might get harpooned for my blubber," Robert said.

"Ah, you're not that bad, just chubby." Steven reached over and pinched the underside of Robert's arm.

"Dude, that flippin' hurts."

"Sorry, you have the softest skin of anybody I know," Steven said. "You're like a grown up cherub, with that baby soft skin and more hair on your head than I've got over my entire body. Maybe you should get yourself some wings to wear with your Naked Man."

"Wings? I know I'm not gay, but our neighbors have got to wonder about us." Robert rubbed the inside of his arm from where

Steven had pinched him. "I think you bruised me. At least I'll look good in my coffin."

"Man, you're such a fatalist," Steven said.

"Now, that's some fancy talk," Robert said. "I'm serious; I think I'll have a bruise."

"Sorry, it's that baby soft skin. I had to pinch you. Listen to Naked Man; Naked Man knows things." Steven pointed his left hand forefinger at Robert.

"Do tell, Naked Man," Robert said.

"I've lived with your crazy behind for almost two years," Steven said. "You're so stinkin' funny ninety percent of the time, but get you near a girl that likes you or right now…"

Robert crossed his arms and glanced over at Steven.

"Right now?" Robert said.

"You look like you're ready to blow your head off," Steven said. He leaned over and tapped Robert on the thigh. "Now don't go doin' that, we'd lose our security deposit."

"Geez, I'm not," Robert said. "I'm not a quitter."

"I just don't think you're aware of how you look, you look mad," Steven said. "And I know you're not mad…I can just tell…you have some bumble bee of a thought buzzin' around and around, inside your head."

Robert grinned over at Steven.

"Naked Man, I think you're not right," Robert said.

"I'm serious, you need to relax and stop thinking so much. Goin' to give yourself a heart attack," Steven said.

"I know, sometimes I just get…" Robert said. He huffed, staring across the townhome complex, as if the other rows of red brick townhouses were silent, stiff upright witnesses. "…wound up. I wake up in a cold sweat and think I'm about to die."

"Naked Man sleeps like baby," Steve said. "You have nightmares? See yourself spooning with Naked Man?"

Robert laughed and scratched behind his ear. "That's a visual. I don't ever remember my dreams or nightmares of Naked Man."

Cars brake lights lit up at the main intersection into the complex, like pale red beacons in the early morning.

"Besides, my little fellow's so small, you might not even notice I'm there," Steve said. "Oobie, we need to find you a girl to play with that big ol' *Mr. Happy* you keep hidden."

"I am officially at creeped-out stage." Robert smirked and covered his face with his hands.

"Oobie, I'm just half kidding with you—just joshin' ya." Steven drank down the remainder of the beer. "I do worry about you. You're a good guy. I've liked living with you, but you've got to let go of your dark side. It's just going to keep eating you up from the inside out."

"I think I must be nuts," Robert said.

"You're not nuts, you just need to let yourself go, have some fun. Life's short; play hard."

Robert paused for several minutes and stared over at Steven, his face blank and unemotional. "You ever had an almost constant sensation that something bad is going to happen to you?"

"Hmm, not really. I don't like to think that way," Steven said.

"I don't like to, either, but when it gets pitch black outside, something wakes me up. It won't leave me alone, like a ghost or something is inside me."

"You're serious?" Steven asked.

"Yeah. I can't run it out of me, and I can't get drunk enough for it to leave me alone."

Steven sat studying Robert. He felt chilled and not from the springtime temperature. "I don't know what to say."

"Nothing to say. I just feel cursed," Robert said. "I get frustrated. I say mean things, most of the time to girls I really like, or say something stupid...or..."

"Or? Don't leave Naked Man hanging," Steven said.

"Ah, well, Naked Man really is dangling," Robert said. He crossed his legs. "Or I clam up like I'm a mute... I guess I'm just scared I would hurt somebody."

"Hey, everybody gets their heart broken," Steven said. "Oobie, you do have a quick, wicked tongue. Hey, by the way, I don't think you're welcome in Japan. Those dudes likely called home and said you're not welcome."

"Funny, Naked Man. I feel kind of bad about that. Just don't like someone calling me Bobby," Robert said.

Steven uncrossed his legs and scratched himself. The wooden chair creaked as he leaned his head back against the brick side of the townhouse. "I don't think those boys will ever play darts with us again." He balanced the empty beer bottle on his forehead. "Little Japanese guy looked like he'd been shot in the head. He won't be callin' you Bobby again."

"Yeah, I'll leave that black death Jagermeister alone from now on," Robert said. "I'll never live this down. I almost died from alcohol poisoning."

"Mista Oobie, you can't be drinkin' with Ernie. He outweighs us both by about a hundred pounds. He hides his weight. The boy is thick," Steven said. "He's like a big circus bear. He's thick, man, and I don't think it's possible for him to get drunk... Big, happy circus bear."

"Can't believe he almost shot me," Robert said.

"Oobie, if it was meant that you'd get shot, it would have happened," Steven said. "Listen to Naked Man; Naked Man knows these things."

Chapter 10

Robert woke the next morning at just past nine-thirty and wiped sleep crusties from the corners of his puffy eyelids. He did not have to show up at his part-time job until the middle of the afternoon, and he had one class left before graduation into professional unemployment. It was 'Money and Capital Markets – 702', of which he had none, nor any real knowledge. He had slogged back to bed by four-fifteen, and had a fitful wrestling match with his overpowering subconscious. He shrugged off his thoughts, pushed them back into safe hiding, aware they would come back to haunt him next time he drifted off to sleep. He opened his dresser drawer to find a pair of blue running shorts. He already had a wrinkled t-shirt on that he thought would work. His musty running shoes left lonely for nearly six months were in the corner of his closet, just below the childhood picture he hid from view. His mother had hung it above his bed. To Robert it was a reminder of his innocence, when he expected to be happy.

Today will be a new day, start of some better habits, Robert thought. He twisted his shoulders and semi-stretched.

"Hey, Oobie, goin' for a run?" Steven asked. He sat at the kitchen table drinking orange juice and reading a textbook on marketing science—better known as common sense.

"Figured I'd give it a try," Robert said. "Likely drop dead of a heart attack…but Naked Man will come find me."

"Nope, only at night. Naked Man only comes out at night." Steven flipped a page. "Want me to go with you? Need a pacer?"

"Naw, I'm good." Robert pushed his baseball cap down on his head, strolled out the front door, down the front stoop, and walked along the parking lot's blacktopped surface.

It was warm day. A few cotton candy clouds licked by the mid-morning sun, and there was a modest southerly breeze and the city's rhythm and hum of normal, everyday life.

Robert figured he would jog his quasi-normal three-mile route—normal being once every six months. Head to the end of the complex, turn left along the concrete sidewalk, and venture into a middle-class housing development. He loped along the path and turned directly into the wind. He blinked his eyelids rapidly and slogged perhaps half a mile before he had to stop and catch his breath. With his hands on his knees, his heart thumped, his lungs burned, and he felt the pangs from thinking himself the village fool.

"Man, I'm out of shape," Robert wheezed.

He thought there was nothing like running to release his inner angst. It was free to anybody who wasn't crippled, feeble or wheelchair bound. Even a brisk walk would work—the point was to just get outside. Being outside was great medicine. It was the one thing he would do as a boy, the times he enjoyed the most, left alone. He just wanted to be left alone, even though he already felt isolated from the rest of the world. His inner terror, his anger, was not something he told anyone else about. He was certain nobody cared. Everybody else had their own problems. Running was the one solace he had that no one could steal from him, to run until he had burned off all his energy. It burned off his shame, his frustration, as if trapped inside an invisible box filled with acid.

Robert walked across the street, onto the sidewalk, past a happy couple planting fresh flowers around a young oak tree in front of their ranch style house. He grinned at the couple with an out-of-breath wave. They both smiled back and said hello. He seemed like a happy, sweating young man, they likely thought.

Robert walked past several more single story red brick houses, some recently built with white brick, some a few years older or with for sale signs out front.

For some odd reason, he thought about his childhood friend, Ardee. He prayed she was happy—that she was loved and respected. He remembered going to a movie with her. It was the exact moment he had realized something was wrong with him. He felt ashamed he couldn't have just kissed her. At the time, he was terrified he would hurt her. He would have rather burned in hell than hurt his childhood friend. She was funny and had a great laugh. He had just liked her for being her.

After he had gotten home after seeing her, he'd gone for a very long run down a narrow country road. He got as far from home as he dared run before screaming and crying in concert with the tobacco fields, grazing horses, and cows. Then, as always his routine, he had composed himself and jogged home, acting as if nothing bothered him. He had known she was someone who would never hurt him. He'd felt safe just holding her hand. But she was long gone now, living her own life, and she would forever be a happy memory, a memory he would hide away from his nightmares.

Now, there was no one with whom he could confide his feelings, with whom he felt safe, like he had felt safe with her. He trusted no one with his dark, childhood information. No one who he thought wouldn't judge him, tell him just to shake it off, or worse, ignore him by telling him to be a respectful young man and go pray. As if God would just snap celestial fingers and his shame would dissipate into the ether of dark matter.

And what if he did risk a relationship? He knew he would eventually have to tell his partner, but when? When do you tell someone you care about, "By the way, minor detail about me, I was molested as a child. I was humiliated. So, I panic when I want to kiss you. I don't know exactly why, so, will you be patient with me? I'm a bit confused by the whole sex thing, and I'm not really interested in kids. Not sure I'd be a very good parent." Not a topic of conversation for a first date, but, on which date? When exactly? *Better to remain alone*, he thought, *than to humiliate myself again.*

Robert crested the top of the residential street littered with modest cars or the occasional chrome-infested pickup truck. A few homes had basketball hoops backboards bolted above their garage doors. He turned and glanced at the couple behind him, still tending to their front yard. They appeared happy and content digging and planting in the black soil.

To be together, near each other, Robert thought.

He was certain he would never feel that way, to allow someone to love him. How *could* someone love him? He was quite aware he did not love himself, and how would he tell someone about his childhood? How could they possibly understand? He felt like a freak.

Robert clenched his jaw and kept walking along the sidewalk. He was tired of being alone. He was frustrated that he could not seem to say the right thing or just be himself around someone he liked. Nothing just came easy anymore; everything a struggle. His life was forced.

After another half-mile, Robert decided to turn left and head back toward the townhouse. About a third of the way down the connector street was a rectangular neighborhood park, with metal swings, a row of seesaws, a circular path, and a little league baseball field. Robert plopped down on one of the park benches.

Neither rain, nor sleet, nor snow would bother this dead concrete park bench.

A tiny boy emerged from a nearby ranch-style home. He was wearing khaki pants, a long sleeve shirt, and brown shoes, and his brown hair was wild and free. Not far behind, a young blonde, petite woman, maybe thirty years old, followed behind, with a light jacket draped over her arm. The boy raced to the swing and began to twist and move back and forth, his legs pumping underneath. He giggled and asked his mother to watch him climb higher and higher into the sky.

"Watch, Mommy, watch," the boy yelled.

His mother glanced over at Robert. He casually grinned at her and waved. She waved back and turned to watch her child.

Robert sighed and leaned forward to inspect a colony of red and black ants scurry for survival between his tennis shoes and along the cracks in the concrete sidewalk. Robert clenched his jaw and took in as deep a breath as he could manage, trying to clear his mind. After a scene from his childhood flashed in his mind, from when he had been a little boy at summer camp, he almost vomited on the concrete sidewalk.

"Go away," Robert whispered to his living nightmare.

Robert's stomach condensed into a tight rubber ball. His brain flashed with still-life pictures, screams, tears, shame, and his skin sizzled on fire. He wiped a tear from his right eyelash with his forefinger and acted as if it was just sweat from his brief workout.

Robert swallowed and his tongue felt thick, his throat stuffed with mucous. He got up and decided to retrace his steps, heading away from the mother and child. His skin flushed and his heart played an irregular rhythm without the joy of music.

"Breathe," Robert whispered.

Robert acted as if he was out of breath, as he strolled past the happy couple planting flowers.

"Nice work. Looks pretty," Robert said. He half grinned.

"Thank you," the couple said in stereo.

Robert pushed his hands and arms above his head and twisted his neck, slowly inhaling and exhaling. He stood at the intersection of life and death. Across the road and to his left was the entrance to his complex. All he had to do was walk in front of that hulking city bus—*whoosh.* The strong breeze smacked Robert's face as it blew past by him. Maybe that speeding car—no. Maybe that big truck—yeah, that would do the job. Yeah, maybe a distracted driver. He'd just have to walk forward; the newspaper story would say it was a freak accident. *Robert Nobody, crushed by chrome-infested pickup truck with his brains splattered down the street. The county coroner had to scoop up his flattened carcass with a shovel.*

"Breathe," Robert whispered. He glanced left, right, and left again. The breeze washed his face, blowing his tormented tears away. He wanted to scream—a scream to get his innocence back, for a normal childhood, for a home where no one argued, no one insulted, no one yelled, for a place he could have felt safe, as safe as holding a happy, innocent girl's hand.

Robert thought about the 9mm handgun under Ernie's seat. It would only take one bullet, *pow.* A flash in the face like an instamatic camera flash, and all the shame would turn to black—an endless sleep. Or, he could get high, simply overdose and drift off into death.

"Breathe deeply," Robert whispered. "Keep breathing." He fought to a grin through his contorted face, achieving a half-smile before he walked back to the townhouse.

"Proud of you, Oobie," Steven said. He crunched his cereal and swigged his orange juice.

"Thanks."

"You okay?" Steven asked.

"I'm good. I'm all right," Robert said. He strolled up stairs, took a warm shower, and napped for a blissful hour in the fetal position. Then the childhood slideshow started after he closed his eyes. He was back at summer camp, dangling in the air. He blinked his eyes. He was naked, standing next to Willis. The still life pictures were unrelenting as the whisper came from nowhere. "Kill yourself—don't let anyone find out."

And through the hot summer Robert tried to build on better habits, but then, it was his birthday. He hated his birthday. It was the annual remembrance he was growing old – alone.

Chapter 11

"Come on, Oobie, it's your birthday," Steven said. He snapped his rough, callused fingers in front of Robert's watery eyes. He was wearing tan shorts frayed at the seams, a white Jimmy Buffet concert tour t-shirt, and Mississippi barge-sized rubber flip-flops.

Inside the main bar, a local cover band's speakers were set at 'eardrum damage'. The wood decking thumped with a bass-drum heartbeat, causing a train of black ants to marimba dance in an insect conga line past Robert's tennis shoes.

"Leave me ... alone." Robert burped and slurred. His voice was raspy, and his thick hair was dispersed like a field of trampled hay. He pre-puked over his baggy, untucked baby blue button down with the sleeves rolled up to his elbows. He wobbled back against the wooden bench, as a nervous, sweating beer bottle precariously dangled in his right hand fingertips.

The summertime heat just south of the Mason-Dixon Line barely abated below a thousand degrees, with humidity dense enough to write your name in the air. The tiki hut-themed bar, a thousand miles north of the subtropics, was well stocked with college girls of all shapes, sizes and socioeconomic expectations. The breeding pool current frothed and eddied to lure enough inexperienced bait near until one realized, too late, the true hunter was about to set her hook and snag her prey—unless that prey lacked a pulse, or was Robert.

"Lean him back so he doesn't fall over," Ernie said. Under the clear, starry, citronella smoky night, he resembled a happy, hairy, brown bear in baggy blue jeans, waiting for the distracted trainer to underestimate his intentions.

"Good idea," Steven said.

"You okay little buddy?" Ernie patted Robert's puffy cheeks. "Should've cut you off earlier. I think the last birthday shot those girls bought 'em did old Oobie in." He looked back over his husky shoulder at Steven.

"Screw you," Robert said, a bobcat sneer without the threat of any sharp fangs. "They're just teasing me … just a bunch a tramps."

Steven and Ernie smacked each other on the shoulders, shook their heads, and grinned.

"Yep, that's our Bobby," Steven said.

Robert clenched his paunchy jaw line and scowled up at his friend — at least his friend when he was sober.

"Not … Bobby," Robert belched out, pointing unsteadily at them with his forefinger. "No one … calls me Bobby anymore."

"Calm down. We're just pullin' your chain," Steven said.

"Okay, little buddy, we won't call you Bobby." Ernie picked Robert up from underneath his sweat-stained armpits like moving a straw stuffed scarecrow in a cornfield and heaved him back against the bench seat. Robert moaned as if punched in the stomach with the butt end of a baseball bat.

"Yep, not Bobby. But you're our little Oobie?" Steven swigged his domestic beer and wiped his lips with the back of his hairy, freckled hand.

"No Bobby. Bobby's been dead for a long time," Robert mumbled. He aggressively shook his head to agree with himself. If you could have peeled off his unblemished face, the other side would have been pockmarked with the bloody lashes from a living nightmare. He twisted to balance his head and shoulder inside a vertical gap in the fence. Mucous strings glistened on his full lower lip, dive-bombing his khaki shorts.

"Either way, try to sit here and don't say anything," Steven said. He glanced over at Ernie.

"No kiddin'," Ernie said. He leaned down near Robert's face. "Hear me? I know you don't want to get lucky, but don't ruin it again for us, okay?"

"Screw off." Robert snorted in heavy breaths through his pug nose. His eyes were barely open, like alligator eye slits at the water's surface.

"Well, at least that's the idea," Steven said sarcastically.

Steven and Ernie shrugged, and glanced around the open-air bar, blazing with citronella torches and candles with the sharp, distinct smell of repellent ambiance. They wondered if they could leave the snorting, sleeping Robert in the corner for a few hours for safekeeping.

"Hey, guys," Amanda said. She was a spindly thin, brown-haired woman, and a 'friend' of Steven's. "Ernie, meet my friend Christy."

Christy was barely taller than five three, perhaps with heels on. She was blessed with the kind of thick, shoulder-length brown hair other women paid hairstylists to fake, a cute button nose, round eyes, and a perfect, curvy, gymnasts shape.

"Hey, girl," Steven said.

Amanda stared down at Robert and shook her head in bewilderment, as Ernie mentally took an inventory of Christy. Unfortunately for Ernie, there would be no ticket sales for the human bear versus gymnast feature wrestling match he imagined.

"He's so stinkin' cute," Amanda said.

"Don't wake Oobie up. You know how he gets," Ernie said. He pressed along his bushy eyebrows with the back of his thumb to wick away sweat from the humid night.

Amanda crossed her thin arms and sipped her draft beer, confident she had failed her cupid homework.

"Yeah, I know," Amanda said. "Why don't you boys take him home before he says somethin' stupid? He can be downright mean."

"He looks sick to me," Christy said.

Steven pursed his lips and stared up at the pock-marked moon, as though it were perhaps a harbinger before a death in the night.

"Sweet thing, we're not goin' anywhere," Amanda said. She glided her forefinger along Steven's forearm. She leaned in closer to him and whispered. "Tell Christy why ya'll call him Oobie?"

"Actually, he did it for us. That's slurred 'Bobby' at three in the mornin'." Steven chuckled, and his eyes twinkled in the patio's torch light. "We'd been throwin' darts with a bunch of Japanese guys over at the Brew Pub."

"It was stinkin' hilarious. One of them called him … Robby, or was it Bobby?" Ernie snickered, sucking in his gut like a hairy puffer fish hoping to breed. "He almost blew a gasket."

"Poor Japanese dude didn't mean anything by it," Steven said. "He was just tryin' to be friendly."

"What's wrong with Robby?" Christy asked. She gripped the end of the beer bottle and wiggled as if she was warming up to do the splits.

"He's real prickly about his name," Steven said.

Ernie grinned and held up his meaty left arm.

"So, Oobie was in a full Jagermeister mood—I think he was five shots in, plus I don't know how many pitchers of beer we had downed—tryin' to keep up with me. He's real competitive, you know," Ernie said. He winked over at Steven.

"Yeah, he can't stand to lose," Steven said. "He gets sort of wound up." He shrugged, glancing down at Christy.

"He told the guy his name was not 'Bobby' or, for that fact, 'Oobie', and I quote in slurred Oobie-Japanese accent, 'or as ya re-tawd ba-rain might trans-rate, 'Mista Oobie'," Ernie said. Steven and Ernie cackled. They glanced down at the slumped over, snoring Robert. Amanda and Christy did not appear to think the story was amusing.

"You can't throw your voice like him. He makes me piss my pants when he gets warmed up, but that's pretty much it, and our little *Oobie* was born," Steven said. They clinked the bottom of their beer bottles, clueless to their friend's crumpled train wreck into alcoholism.

"Yeah, the next day, while we stuffed him with bacon cheese burgers, he had no idea why we were calling him Oobie," Ernie said.

"You know, Oobie says 'bacon's the elixir of the gods' for hangovers," Steven said. He shrugged. He smirked.

"Okay, you got me on the bacon comment." Amanda giggled and put her hand over her plump lips.

"Bacon's full of fat," Christy said.

"Yeah, Oobie thinks that's the reason it's great for a hangover. The fat sucks up your crap," Steven said. He chuckled. "I don't know."

"Too funny. I do love me some 'Mista Oobie'," Amanda said. She pursed her lips looking over at Christy. "He's so easy to talk to when he's sober. He is actually quite charming, but he's one of those people who is hard to get to know—impossible to get close to. I retired from trying to set him up."

"He looks sick to me. I think he needs help," Christy said. Her doll-like face crinkled and contorted.

"He just shouldn't drink. It brings out his demons," Amanda said.

Steven stared down at Robert.

"Yeah, I think you're right," Steven whispered. He swigged his beer.

"How so?" Amanda asked.

"Man sakes," Steven whispered. He shook his head. "Oobie's got a nasty dark side. Some nights I catch him downstairs fumbling about the kitchen, lookin' like he'd taken a midnight shower and acting like a ghost bit him."

"What's he say?" Amanda asked quietly.

Steven shrugged, shook his head, and crossed his muscular arms.

"Same thing. 'I'm fine, just couldn't sleep,'" Steven said. "I think somethin' did bite him, just not sure what."

Ernie and Amanda decided to inspect the bar's dirty wooden plank floor while Christy stared down at Robert. She furrowed her thin eyebrows, and then she turned her back to him.

"Hey, Oobie?" Steven asked. He poked Robert's shoulder. "He's out. Happy birthday Oobie. Same as last year."

"I don't understand him," Ernie said. "Man, he's had some pretty girls that liked him, girls that don't even know I exist, and he just blows 'em off."

"Or, more likely, he says something nasty," Steven said. He stared at Robert. He frowned, and a deep wrinkled sliced across his forehead.

"Yeah, sorry to say, he's gifted," Amanda said. "Take him home … He's such a buzz kill."

Steven flicked his longneck beer bottle into a nearby garbage drum. It shattered when it hit the other bottles, not unlike what had already happened to Robert's invisible heart.

"Yep, just hope he doesn't yack in my car," Steven said. "Oobie, wake up. Time to go-" Steven leaned his friend up against the railing surrounding the bar.

Robert shook his head as if to shoo away evil spirits. His breathing was hard, his eyes prize-fighter swollen and rimmed with internal redness.

"Come this way, Oobie," Steven said. "You know the drill."

Ernie frowned and fell in behind to sort of nudge Robert out of the back of the bar.

"Little buddy, I think you are officially a turd," Ernie whispered in Robert's ear. He glanced back at Christy. "But I tell him that as a friend."

"See you, boys." Amanda stared up into the dark night. She turned away from the alcoholic's slow death march. "Come on, Christy. Let's go lure us some tipsy drink sponsors. I need to get you on scholarship."

Steven and Ernie dragged and prodded Robert out of a place his grandfather would have called a "den of iniquity." Once past the line of gawking partygoers, a wobbly-kneed Robert traversed the narrow single-lane back street like a beginning snow skier, without the benefit of balance poles or fluffy white powder. Instead, he caught the toe of his tennis shoes, tripped, and did a face plant, skidding his cheek against the paved street. His face was thinly scratched, as if an alley cat had clawed him, and droplets of his blood bubbled from underneath the smooth peach of his skin.

"Damn it, Oobie." Ernie bent down and leaned Robert up against a restaurant's garbage dumpster. The foul blend of odors welcomed Robert's addition.

"I'm—" Robert gagged.

"Heads up," Ernie said as he sprang back from Robert.

Robert vomited everything from inside, except the constant anxiety, which he kept under the mental locks and key that drove him toward suicide.

"There we go," Steven said. "At least he did it outside this time. Oobie, you're a mess."

"I know." Robert huffed.

"Dang it, let's get him up," Ernie said. "This is the last time … you hear me?"

Robert wiped his mouth with the bottom of his shirtsleeve. He pulled his knees toward his chest and dangled his arms over his knees. He smelled like damp clothes left in a tobacco barn for six

-months. He was a prizefighter down for the final count but had not even gotten inside the ring.

"I'm a mess," Robert said.

"No kiddin', Bobby. Get up!" Ernie's patience was at an end. He had bigger plans for his Friday evening than playing nursemaid to a drunk man.

"Just leave me here," Robert said. "Let me die."

"Is he all right?"

Steven and Ernie twisted as they sensed a young woman, maybe just north of five feet six, haltingly walk toward them. She was wearing a simple white collared blouse, fashionable blue jeans and flats. She had happy, doe-like eyes, but her angelic face was contorted.

"Is he all right?" she asked again. Her voice was clear, strong, with a slight southern accent.

Steven and Ernie liked the fact Robert had attracted a pretty girl toward them.

"I think we need to get him loaded more often," Ernie whispered into Steven's ear. "He's good bait."

Steven shoved Ernie and smirked at him.

"Yes," Steve said to the woman. "We share an apartment. It's not far... We can handle him; this isn't his first rodeo."

"Yeah, he'll be all right. He just had too much cotton candy at the fair tonight," Ernie said.

She ignored them, slinking down near Robert, and intently stared at him. Even in the eerie dusk of a hot summer night, she instantly knew his once kind, boyish face.

"Bobby?" She sat down on her knees near Robert and nudged him. "Bobby? Bobby Scott."

Steven and Ernie snapped a glance at each other as if they'd been hit over the head with a snow shovel.

"Ah, I'd be careful. He's not a big fan of being called Bobby," Ernie said. He glanced at Steven. "I said it just to get his goat."

She ignored them and kept nudging Robert with her forefinger again, and again, and again until he opened his eyes. He blinked rapidly, coughed, and burped. His eyes were covered in a milky coating as he tried to focus on her face. His head bobbed back and forth, but his eyes were fixed and certain. Even in his drunken haze, he knew the face. He thought perhaps he was dead, and this was God's messenger to keep him calm before he was sucked into a hazy white light.

"This is a bad dream," Robert whispered. "Ardee? Am I dead?"

"What happened to you? You look sad." Ardee's lower lip quivered. "What happened to my little friend, Bobby?"

Robert stared blankly at his childhood friend. He felt as if she had discovered him hiding underneath his life's rubble. It had been well over a decade, and he thought she was still as beautiful as the first day he saw her. He stared down in humiliation at the gravel between his scuffed up knees as a few stubborn tears trickled down his dirt and vomit caked face.

"Just let me die," Robert said. "You always said I had sad eyes." He closed his eyelids, huffed, and covered his head with his clammy hands.

Ardee crossed her arms and studied his face. A hint of irritation emerged in her eyes. Her hands on her hips, she paused for a moment, clenched her jaw, and twisted her shoulders like a Greek goddess about to fling a discus.

"Oh, no you don't!" She yanked her right arm back and smacked Robert across top of his head with an open hand. As he lowered his left hand, she smacked him hard, leaving a red handprint—a sign Ardee had marked her territory. Robert collapsed onto the road, and Ardee pounced on top of him, shoving him and hitting him in the arm.

"Come on, Ardee," Robert said feeling his cheek. "Stings … get off me."

"Bobby! Get up! You know better than to lay down in the street like a dog. I demand better of you." She wheeled around and sprang up, pulling her shoulders back to face Steven and Ernie. They both backed up a few steps from her intense brown eyes; her face held a solid kick-you-in-the-groin promise. She pointed at them with a perfectly manicured dagger-like forefinger.

"Where are you two knuckleheads takin' him?" Ardee asked.

"Home," Steven said. His hands were up in front of his chest in arrest mode. "Honest."

Steven and Ernie appeared stunned and perplexed, as if the assistant school principal had caught them smoking behind the gymnasium.

"Wrong answer," Ardee said. She stared down at the crumpled Robert and closed her eyes in exasperation. She leaned her head back and sucked in a deep breath, staring up into heaven as if asking God what the deal was. "I'm taking him, and you two are going to help me. I'll not let him just lay there and die. He was my friend. You do not turn your back on your friends, no matter what. That's not right."

Chapter 12

"You could've killed him," Ardee said.

"Naw. He's a big boy." Ernie had Robert's left arm dangling over his hairy neck.

"Hey, moron, you're big; he's not. Ever heard of alcohol poisoning?" Ardee said. She scooted a few feet in front as Ernie and Steve dragged Robert along the parking lot toward her black SUV.

"Oobie, you in there?" Steven asked. "Come on, little buddy."

"I'm all right. Better put me down," Robert said, and dropped to his knees. He vomited and then dry heaved for ten minutes. Sweat spots emerged along his back through his baby blue button down.

"Oh, man," Ernie said.

"Bobby, you're a mess," Ardee said. She leaned down and patted Robert on the back. "Need to get you some water—get you hydrated."

"This is a nightmare. You're not real," Robert said. He shook his head as if to chase away evil spirits. He huffed and dry heaved while on all fours, gulped for air, and then leaned back on his knees.

"She sure looks real to me," Ernie growled under his breath.

"Sorry, I guess we let him get out of hand," Steven said.

"How long's he being doing this?" Ardee had her hands on her hips, standing like a staff sergeant between Robert and her SUV. "Get him on the front seat."

Steven and Ernie shrugged. They picked up Robert and leaned him against the truck. Ernie held him in place.

"I don't know. We must've started about six tonight," Ernie said.

"No, how long's he been drinking like this?" Ardee asked.

"To pass-out stage. He looks awful."

Steven, like a human forklift, picked up Robert and set him in the front seat. He clicked the seat belt across Robert and stood back from the SUV with Ernie, shaking his head.

"Come to think of it, he's gotten worse the last six months," Steven said. He scratched the top of his balding head. "Stopped workin' out, been acting spooked, you know, not been himself."

"Yeah, he can be real distant—dark," Ernie said. With his fingertips, he played with facial stubble. "He's been like that most of his life. Say, I think I remember your name?"

Ardee crossed her arms and pursed her lips, staring at Ernie.

"I think I was his first sort-of date." Ardee half-grinned. "We went to a movie…long, long time ago. We were just kids, but he was always so sweet to me."

"Yeah, I remember now," Ernie said. He smirked. "Need us to follow you?"

"Nope, I've got him from here," Ardee said. "I'm taking him to the hospital. I'm not standing by and let him just die in the street. You two should know better." Ardee twisted open her purse and pulled out her car keys. She steadily drove out of the parking lot and on to the nearby access road.

"Well, only Robert," Ernie said.

"What?" Steven asked as they turned around and headed back toward the bar.

"Only Robert can get picked up by a pretty girl he hasn't seen in eons while he's passed out." Ernie chuckled. "He's gifted. By the way, you think I've got a chance with that cute Christy chick?" Steven shrugged, walking next to Ernie.

"Honestly?"

"Yeah,"

"Nope, I can tell she's not digging your hairy chili. Better luck next time," Steven said. "Sorry."

*

"Bobby. Bobby, try to stay awake," Ardee said.

Robert's breathing was shallow, his lips glistened with mucous, and he had a powerful personal odor. Ardee reached over to grab his left wrist, she checked his pulse with her middle and forefingers.

"Your heart's racing." She turned up the air conditioning and pointed the vents at Robert's face.

"Please, we're just boys," Robert mumbled and moaned. He slinked forward, and the safety belt caught him. He slumped down across the center console.

"I don't understand," Ardee said. "Bobby, try to stay awake. I'm taking you to the medical center, okay? If I don't get you taken care of, you could easily have a heart attack. You hear me?"

Robert turned his head, mumbling and moaning. He snapped his hands up as if to protect his face. His eyes fluttered, as if he were having a vivid nightmare.

"No," Robert mumbled. "Please don't..."

"Hey, I'm trying to help you," Ardee said. "Geez, thanks for nothing." She scowled and drove her SUV across Limestone Street, periodically glancing over at the shaking, shivering Robert, but she had to stop for a red light three blocks from the medical center.

"I'm sorry... I'm begging," Robert mumbled. His hands pawed at the windshield.

"Bobby, wake up." Ardee tried to shake Robert awake. "Bobby, come on, wake up."

Robert fiercely shook his head. His face crinkled, and his eyes squished shut. He moaned deeply, and tears began to emerge from underneath his long eyelashes.

"Let me go," Robert begged. "Let Willis go..."

Ardee pulled into the active hospital's parking garage and toward the emergency department. After taking a parking stub, she circled up two concrete decks until she finally found an open space near a stairwell. She reached over and held Roberts clammy hand.

"Bobby, we're here," Ardee said. "Try to breathe. Breathe. I can't carry you, and I can't leave you alone."

"Don't touch me," Robert screamed. He snapped his hands up in front of his face and curled into a fetal position.

In the dim, yellowish light cast across the parking structure from nearby streetlights, Ardee closely watched Robert's swollen, doughy face. She realized he was not dreaming, nor was he screaming at her. He was reliving a horrifying experience from the depth of his subconscious, something real from his life had reached out to bite him. The buckets of beer and shots of liquor were a poor man's truth serum.

"Don't make me," Robert moaned. He cried as if he were a child. The corners of his mouth turned down, and strings of saliva dripped off his chin. His nose oozed rivers of regret.

"Oh, God," Ardee whispered. She brushed back Robert's hair and felt his crimson cheek. "You're on fire."

"No, no," Robert said, "I won't. No picture." He crumbled and cried, his face hunched against the cold, hard plastic center column.

Ardee leaned back in the bucket seat. She crooked her head and nervously fiddled with the ends of her auburn colored hair. "Picture?"

A minute later, Robert's hurricane of emotions subsided, and he was dead-man-still, but breathing. Ardee checked his pulse, and it had subsided back to a normal rhythm.

She scampered down the two flights of concrete stairs and convinced a husky, male orderly to let her borrow him and the wheelchair he was pushing.

Chapter 13

Robert groggily opened his eyes, blinking rapidly as his pupils adjusted to the stark hospital light. He was lying reclined on a semi-comfortable gurney, covered by a winter-white bed sheet, surrounded by a flimsy, blue-gray curtain that concealed a modest space within the ER. His dingy clothes lay folded in a nearby plastic container. His head throbbed; he could feel his heartbeat pulsate through his temple. The emergency room hummed and smelled of disinfectants. The top of his right hand stung from a crisscrossed gauze-taped needle, from which a intravenous tube snaked over his pasty white arm, twisted at the elbow, and continued up into the bottom of a glucose bag hooked to a metal pole. His tongue felt thick, and his skin tingled from a cold sensation. He felt like dozing off, but he gulped and sniffed the air.

"How you feeling?" Ardee asked. She appeared tired, with dark gray puffiness under her eyes and her hair pulled back in a ponytail.

Robert coughed and shook his head before exhaling and staring up at her with his mouth partially open.

"How?" Robert appeared perplexed. He studied her face, her brown eyes, and she seemed years younger than her face belied.

"I have no idea." Ardee crossed her arms and appeared exasperated. "Bobby, you need help."

"I'm all right," Robert said. "I'm sorry... I should know better."

"Never thought my childhood friend would be a drunk," Ardee said. "At least, that's what I'm looking at."

She pursed her lips and tapped Robert on the shoulder before turning and sitting on a nearby cushioned chair. She sat back, crossing her arms and her slender, athletic legs.

"I don't know what to say," Robert said. He scrunched his face and clenched his jaw. His stomach tightened into a ball of humiliation.

"And I don't want to hear any excuses," Ardee said. "I've had enough worthless men in my life. You all always have excuses, and so I'll have none of that... Just so we get that straight."

"All right," Robert said. "Sorry you found me like that, but I can take care of myself."

"Really?" Ardee said. "You don't have any health insurance; you're barely getting' by—"

"Yeah," Robert said. "I'm doing all right. I'm getting things together."

Ardee took in a deep breath. She smirked and tapped her shoe against the off-white tiled floor. "I'm really, really angry with you right now," Ardee said.

Robert stared over at Ardee. "Why? I haven't seen you in a long time."

"I had higher expectations for you," Ardee said. "Even though we were kids, you respected me. I could tell in your eyes. You'd have done anything for me, but now, I don't know who you are, and you're a hot mess."

"So what?"

"I expected better of you," Ardee said. "What happened to you?"

Robert glanced at Ardee, and then he stared forward, watching nurses in pink uniforms scamper in and out of treatment spaces and physicians in hospital scrubs examining patient charts.

"I'm all right," Robert said.

"That's bull. Nobody drinks like you are drinkin', unless there's something eating at them... It's how we're made. You can't hide from yourself. Trying to kill yourself?"

Robert closed his eyes and stuffed his head back into the pillow.

"How'd you get so smart?" Robert asked. He huffed.

"Psychology degree comes in handy from time to time," Ardee said. "Oh, another minor detail, while I was carting your drunk behind over here, saving your life—no thanks to your friends, in your drunken haze you started acting like someone was beating you, taking a picture, or what not. What's that all about?"

Robert snapped his gaze over at Ardee and crossed his legs. He breathed in methodically and combed his hair with his fingers as his cheeks flushed crimson.

"Hmm, I must've been hallucinating," he mumbled. "I'm all right."

"Goofball." Ardee crossed her arms again. "No, you're not, but I've not seen you in a longtime, so I guess it's none of my business. Just wasn't going to let you die in the street."

"I wasn't going to die," Robert said.

"Hey, you're not invincible. What've you gone dumb on me?" Ardee said. "I cannot believe how you've turned into this—a chubby drunk. I'm disgusted with you; that's why I'm mad at you."

Robert snapped his head over, and stared into Ardee's eyes—a gaze of instant, intense rage, of time lost, of terror, and of shame. He breathed out a gust of air from his angst filled lungs. He

-clenched his jaw in a vain attempt at keeping a tear from escaping down his cheek.

"I think I know," Robert growled. "If you must know... Really want to know? Well, all right, let's go—"

"I'm sorry. I'll stop picking," Ardee said.

She put her hands up and averted Robert's gaze, but Robert would have none of her attitude. He was feeling like the end of a struck matchstick. His blood boiled a gasoline flame back into his broken heart.

"Remember when we went to a movie?" Robert whispered. He stared down at the bottom of the hospital bed.

"Yeah," Ardee whispered. She had known something was wrong with him then. She knew something was still wrong with her Bobby now.

"I didn't want to hurt you," Robert said.

"Are you kidding?" Ardee shrugged. "We were innocent kids. I just figured you were being overly respectful, which now, I do appreciate." She chuckled lightly.

"I wasn't," Robert said in a dead, dry manner.

Ardee shook her head and stared up at the textured ceiling. "Wasn't what? You're being cryptic."

"Innocent." He glanced over at Ardee. "First time I wanted to kiss a girl I really liked. I just liked holding your hand, but I was afraid I'd hurt you."

Ardee sat forward and closely studied Robert's suddenly blank, unemotional face. But it was his eyes; they hid an unmerciful pain, an unmerciful theft.

"Bobby, what're you trying to tell me?" Ardee slipped forward to touch his left forearm. "This isn't a time to be funny...or cynical."

"I'm not," Robert said. "And I don't know why this all just popped into my freakish head right now."

Ardee sprang up and glanced at the hospital equipment blipping Robert's vital signs.

"Be quiet, just be quiet, stop," Ardee whispered. Her hand slid down his arm and held his hand. "This isn't the time. I'm sorry. I—I didn't mean to pick at you."

"I just didn't want to hurt you," Robert said. He clenched his jaw and tried holding back his tears, but his bloodshot eyes were ringed with moisture.

"Shh, I know. Just be quiet; try to go to sleep," Ardee said. She tightly squeezed Robert's hand. "I'll be here when you wake up. I promise."

"But you want to know why I get so drunk, don't you?" Robert said. He exasperatedly huffed out. "Why I'm a freak? I've been a freak my whole life. I'd be better off dead."

"Shh, listen to me." Ardee bit her lower lip. She squeezed his hand tight but couldn't look him in the eye. "You're upset; I'm upset, but now is not the time. Get some rest, and then I'll take you home. We'll talk then. I know someone you need to talk to."

Robert shoved his head back, huffed, and closed his eyes. Ardee brushed his hair back and kissed his forehead. She slid the chair closer to the bed and reached up to hold Robert's hand, leaning her head against the side of the bed. She stared vacuously into the emergency department wondering about the hot mess she had stumbled into. *Was Bobby abused somehow?*

"Dear God," Ardee whispered. "It all makes sense now."

Chapter 14

"There's nothing to be afraid of," Ardee said. She drove her SUV through the apartment complex parking lot.

"Over there, to the left," Robert said.

"Bobby, you need to talk to someone, but I'm not trying to tell you what to do."

"I don't know," he said. "You know I'm broke."

Ardee parked in front of Robert's apartment. "Just call me, okay?"

Robert got out of her SUV and sauntered past the front toward the sidewalk leading toward the front door. Ardee switched off her truck and slowly stepped out. Robert turned around, surprised. She walked up to Robert and hugged him tightly for several seconds. He smelled her flowery perfume and felt the warmth of her arms.

"I'll be all right," Robert said. His face flushed and he cleared his throat. He couldn't look her in the eyes.

"Do you think I'd ever hurt you?" Ardee asked.

"Never," Robert said.

"Then I'll call you instead," Ardee said. "It's a date?"

Robert took a moment to just breathe as he examined his tennis shoes.

"I'll do it." Robert hesitantly hugged Ardee. "I trust you."

"I'd never do anything to hurt you." Ardee touched Robert's cheek with her hand. She backed away and got in her SUV. She smiled at Robert through the windshield.

He watched her drive away, down the parking lot until her truck disappeared into the busy city traffic. He wondered if he would really see her again. He wasn't sure how to feel. As always, he was just confused and bewildered.

"Oobie, did your little fella get to spit last night?" Steven said. He was bare-chested and bare-footed near the open front door. "She didn't take you to the hospital, did she? I think ol' Oobie got lucky last night."

Robert smirked and shook his head, walking past Steven into the townhouse.

"Nothing happened," Robert said. "She's a nice girl."

"So? Nice girls need lovin' too." Steven slapped Robert on the back and chuckled. "If nothin' happened, she sure gave you a serious hug. I'd let her hug me like that."

From the cupboard above the coffee maker, Robert snagged a coffee mug. "She took me to the hospital."

"Seriously?" Steven asked.

"Yep. Made sure I didn't suffocate in my own puke," Robert said. He grunted.

"You were pretty well toasted," Steven said. "That sucks. She's a pretty girl."

"Yeah, I knew her when I was a kid; that's all. She was just being a do-gooder." Robert placed the coffee mug back inside the cupboard.

"You all right?" Steven asked, twisting his neck to pop it.

Robert turned toward Steven and slinked back against the Formica countertop, staring outside through the glass of the sliding door.

"I—I don't," Robert mumbled, rubbing his forehead.

"Oobie? You in there?"

"No, I'm not all right." Robert shook his head. "Think I'll go take a nap. I'm exhausted."

"Cool." Steven smirked. "I'll keep Naked Man under wraps."

"I appreciate that," Robert said.

He slogged up the stairs, kicked off his tennis shoes into his bedroom closet, and slipped under the rumpled blanket. He tried to rest, to close his eyes, to allow his mind to slip into sleep, but there was a ghost within his subconscious, waiting for him—an evil film director with a brief, terrifying slide show.

Robert shook awake after thirty minutes with his body covered in sweat. He trembled as if caught outside naked on a cold day. He sprang back up and went into the bathroom where he hit his knees and hugged the toilet. He dry heaved for fifteen minutes, until each side of his face was covered in mucous strings. The porcelain goddess's surface was a stark wintertime chill.

Standing like a soldier under a warm shower, he could not wash off his angst. His tears dripped down his life's bathroom drain. He went downstairs and silently stared at the television as Steven quietly surfed through the endless channels, but there was nothing on.

NATHANIEL SEWELL

Chapter 15

Robert sat still, but his heartbeat raced faster than a thoroughbred pounding past the last turn at Keeneland. His face flushed crimson; his ears burned a blood red. Ardee sat next to him and unsatisfactorily flipped through an oversized glossy fashion magazine.

"You'll be just fine." She patted him on the leg. "It's okay to be nervous."

"I guess." Robert glanced at the wall of framed degrees—some gold leafed, some in simple black or brown lacquer. The reception area was empty and quiet. A round *In Session* sign hung on the office doorknob—a door that Robert assumed would lead inside a psychiatrist's office. They sat in one of the three groupings of chairs and cushioned couches. A simple glass-covered coffee table set in front of them, with a random sampling of sports, fashion, and celebrity magazines.

"Bobby, Dr. Richie was one of my professors," Ardee said. "She's rock solid, so no worries. She knows her stuff. She agreed to do me a favor for you."

"Do you think I'm crazy?" Robert asked.

"We're all crazy," Ardee said. "I just think you're in a rut and need to take care of yourself."

"All right."

"Sometimes there are things in our subconscious that get in our way," Ardee said. "Just that simple. And Dr. Richie might be able to get it out of you."

"Why are you doing this?" Robert asked.

Ardee continued to flip through the magazine pages, but then she stopped and stared forward, down at the fake oriental carpet before gazing up into Robert's eyes.

"You're my friend, and I don't think you share what you're really thinking. You have these beautiful hazel eyes, but they're sad." Ardee crossed her arms.

"Oh, I never realized I was that pathetic." Robert combed his fingers through his thick brown hair.

"I don't know. I feel like, if I was in trouble, and I called you in the middle of the night, I know you'd come help me. No questions asked, you'd do anything to help me, but you'd never say it." Ardee sighed. "But it's in your eyes. Even when we were kids, I could tell you really cared about me, but you were always distant. I could never figure you out."

Robert smirked and cleared his throat. "Yeah, you're right. I'd do anything for you."

Ardee crossed her legs and sat back. She turned the magazine pages, stopping carefully to study a picture of a fashion model. "I thought so." She reached over and patted Robert on the leg. "I always listen to my instinct. That's how God talks to me."

"It hurts to tell people how you feel." Robert stared down at his brown shoes.

"This is not real. These girls are unhealthy," Ardee said. She slinked in next to Robert and pointed at a few waifish models. "What are they sixteen? Maybe younger? They're not real. Look at their eyes. They have dead eyes."

"Yeah," Robert said.

He liked the scent of her perfume. *A lavender hint*, he thought, *or was it a lily fragrance?* It seemed to fit her better than how she smelled at Briar Hill. Then, she was a pretty girl; now, she was a beautiful woman.

"They're children, and young girls should be left alone," Ardee said. "They're innocent, or at least should be. I'm sure they get pawed at. That's what all my boyfriends seemed to want to do, and once they get what they want, the phone stops ringing."

"Yeah." Robert thought about the loss of his own innocence. The emerging slide show caused him to squirm in the leather office chair. The triggered memories had started a nightly reality television show, but the camera angle was shot through his terrified eyes.

"They shouldn't be dressed up like adults and paraded half-naked," Ardee said.

"Yeah, I know you're right," Robert said. His hands started involuntarily shaking, and he instantly sensed tears in his eyes—tears he could not control or stop from traversing down his cheeks. He felt like running—running outside the office building, running anywhere but nowhere—until he collapsed. Maybe if he were lucky, he would have a heart attack and die on the street.

"Taking pictures of a half-naked girl," Ardee said. "This stuff is disgusting. It's not real. No wonder young girls become anorexic, with these pictures plastered about—pictures taken of a half-naked child. Perverts."

"Stop," Robert said. He smashed his lips together and gushed air out of his lungs like an over-exerted swimmer.

Ardee snapped her gaze over at Robert's face. "What?" She appeared confused.

"I'm sorry," Robert said. "I'm a hot mess."

"God, you're fragile," Ardee said. "You have any idea how fragile you are?"

"I'm sorry," Robert said. His breathing was heavy. He wiped his face. "I'm not much of a man."

Then it struck Ardee like paparazzi flashbulbs fired all at once, and her stomach twisted into knots. She knew—she knew just enough about psychology to be dangerous. She sensed her temper rising like a tempest.

"Be quiet," Ardee said. "Just be quiet."

"What'd I say?" Robert said.

"Nothing." Ardee said. "You need to buck up Bobby, and fight through this. You're too good of a man to be fragile. I'll never find you a girlfriend if you're a wet noodle."

"I'm trying," Robert said.

"Girls don't like wimpy," Ardee said. "Girls want a man that will defend them, and make them feel safe—make them laugh. Hear me?"

"I know," Robert said.

"Then get whatever's eating at you, inside your mind, get it *out*." She smacked Robert's leg. "And whatever Dr. Richie asks you, don't filter, don't be afraid. Just be courageous and strong, and say it. Secrets are bad. Hear me?"

"All right," Robert said. "Will you come inside and sit with me?"

"Not sure I can do that," Ardee said.

"I don't care." He grabbed her warm hand. "I'd feel safe if you just sat in the room—just be in the room with me…"

Ardee grimaced and flipped the magazine on the coffee table. "I don't know. It's about trust in there, and I don't want to invade your private thoughts. I just want you to be happy."

Robert reached over and grabbed Ardee's hand again. His own hand was clammy and shaking.

"I feel lost," Robert said. "Like I'm going to die. That's not normal, is it?"

Ardee squeezed his hand. "No." She scowled at Robert. She knew her temper could get the best of her, and the thought of her

Bobby somehow abused caused her pilot light of justice to flicker into a blue-hot flame. "It's not normal Bobby. It's not normal."

"Sorry I'm a freak," Robert said.

"Shut up. Just shut up, and stop saying you're sorry."

*

The office was quiet—the quiet of an empty Catholic cathedral—but comfortable. A simple, walnut Shaker-style desk was in the far corner. Above a credenza covered with pictures, there was a colorful modern art painting within an ornate gold leafed frame. The office smelled of a calming French vanilla candle, and there were stacks of manila patient file folders. Robert figured they moved steadily from the in pile to the out pile. His name was neatly typed in block letters on the folder resting on Dr. Richie's lap.

"So, you go by Bobby?" Dr. Richie asked. She glanced over at Ardee and then at Robert. She was middle aged, with jet-black hair cut boyishly short. She wore artsy, wood-grain finished rectangular glasses, a frilly ecru blouse, navy blue dress pants, and flat, open-toed Birkenstocks.

"I guess so," Robert said. He was sitting upright in a cushioned sofa chair.

"No, it's *your* name," Dr. Richie said.

"Bobby will work." Robert glanced over at Ardee, who grinned at him.

"What's so funny?" Dr. Richie scooted back in her office chair. She crossed her legs and allowed her shoe to dangle off her foot.

"I sort of named him," Ardee said. "When we were kids. Most of the time he's rather picky about his name—just not with me."

"Most people call me Robert," he explained.

"Well, I guess I should feel honored." Dr. Richie chuckled. "Bobby, have you ever submitted to therapy before?"

"No." He coughed to clear his throat.

Therapy? If I didn't feel freakish before, well, the word "therapy" and sitting in an office with a Doctor-For-Crazy-

117

People, is a simple confirmation I'm nuts, crazy, over-the-side, looney, pick your intangible noun, Robert thought. He preferred freak. Because that was how he felt—freakish, as if he had a cycloptic eyeball in the center of his forehead.

"Okay, what are your notions about therapy?" Dr. Richie asked. She shifted her petite frame, and balanced on her left elbow on the office chair. Her fingers adjusted her glasses from the bottom of her nose, sliding them back up.

"I don't know. I guess you'll realize I'm a freak, or you'll put me on some drug, or I don't know…" Robert shrugged. "Hypnotize me?"

"Okay, that's why I asked," Dr. Richie said. "Those are stereotypes. But that's not how the hard effort of this sort of therapy works. Drugs do play a part sometimes. Medications do help people, but hypnosis can be rather controversial, so I prefer to talk—mostly listen. From listening, we sometimes find the sources for coping. Sounds simple, but it's hard effort—effort based solely on trust. Without trust, this relationship will not work, so I'm asking you to trust me. That's the hard part."

"What are you going to do to me then?" Robert asked.

"Do? I'll *do* nothing to you," Dr. Richie said. She smirked. Her eyes were calm—Zen like. "We'll just talk. I suspect you will learn your own answers. Bobby, you're not crazy, so the first thing you need to do is get that thought out of your head."

Robert crossed his arms and stared over at a quiet Ardee. She was hiding in a corner of the office next to an expansive window on the second floor of the office building.

"Will I have to come see you for the rest of my life?" Robert asked.

"Oh, it's not like that," Dr. Richie said, reflecting. She glanced up at the square tiled ceiling. "It's up to you. Sometimes clients visit me once, and they feel benefitted; others clients I've had for years and years. Everybody is different, every story unique. Each person has their own life finger print."

"All right." He tightened his arms and clenched his jaw. He thought he might cry for no apparent reason. *Why cry?* Robert thought. His stomach ached, and his feet felt cold.

"Okay, a few ground rules. Whatever you tell me is between us only. If I see you out in public, I'll not act like I know you, unless you come over to me," Dr. Richie said. "Goes for you too, Ardee?"

"I understand," Ardee whispered.

"You're a good friend," Dr. Richie said to Ardee.

She turned and faced Robert squarely, opening up her arms. "Bobby, I don't sit here and take notes. I think there are a couple of things you need to understand. I am not judging you. This is my work— my passion as a physician—to help you heal— but instead of healing a body part, I hope to help you find the tools to cope. I get depressed; it's part of human condition. Feeling alive is scary, so you should realize you are not a crazy. You are not like my hospital patients who have serious psychological problems. They are people unable to exist in society, through no fault of their own. In other words, I suspect you're not crazy. That's a whole different subset of the population, okay?"

"Okay," Robert said.

"It took courage to walk in here. Ardee might have made the appointment, but nobody made you visit me," Dr. Richie said.

"All right." He could hardly breathe.

"I'm just going to ask you some questions, and how you answer is up to you. What you want to tell me is up to you," Dr. Richie said. "Do you understand me?"

"Yeah, I think," Robert said. He thought there was a powerful tidal current circulating within his stomach, hidden within, like a tormented leviathan snaking its way up toward his pulverized heart.

"I think—I hope—you'll realize by just talking through your feelings," Dr. Richie said, "how just telling someone, someone who will listen, inside a quiet, safe place can be helpful. It's as if we are all inside a canoe gliding along a calm stream… If that makes sense to you?"

"Yeah, I get ya," Robert whispered.

"Very good. Now, we might hit some tough rapids, but we'll get through them. Very soon, I'm going to stop talking so much. I'm going to ask you questions." Dr. Richie clasped her fingers together. "I don't offer solutions. I might offer recommendations; I might not say anything. The solutions come from how you view things. I'm here to listen and help you build your own bag of tools to deal with problems. Does this make sense?"

"Yeah, in an odd way," Robert said.

He thought it mad that he was inside the office—as in circus clown mad—and even madder that he was about to cry. He could not seem to understand why… Why was he about to cry? He glanced over at Ardee. How did she stumble back into his life? Why was life so random?

The smoked glass concealed the outside with a sheer curtain. Ardee had her hands on her lap, and she was looking down at the floorboards glistening from reflected sunlight.

"So, tell me about Bobby?" Dr. Richie asked. Her eyes were kind, welcoming, and she was non-judgmental. She would not express an obvious emotion or say another word, save for a few basic questions, for the next twenty minutes. Bobby started talking and talking, randomly bringing up his family, his childhood, and the time he took Ardee to a movie. He talked about everything, save a few things he could barely remember. As he talked, he started to reveal himself, uncovering clues to nasty scars—scars he could not heal or see.

"Well, that was easy enough," Dr. Richie said. "Feel weird?"

"Yeah." Robert blew his nose and wiped away the torrent of tears. "This is how it works? I come in here and spill my guts, and then everybody holds hands, sings *kum ba ya, my Lord, kum ba ya*?"

"You're funny," Dr. Richie said. "I like that."

"Sometimes it's a curse."

"A curse?" Dr. Richie asked. "Why is it a curse? And I'm curious. You used a few words I found interesting when describing your parents and yourself. Let's see… Cold, naïve, betrayed, but mostly you said you felt alone, numb, isolated…afraid."

"I don't know," Robert said, but his memory was beginning to reveal sinister moments from his life—moments he had hoped to keep buried. He hoped to hide from them, and then wake up one day to find they had never happened. That was a fantasy, though. The reality of his childhood was much harsher to accept. Flashes in his mind's eye went off.

"Bobby, it's okay to cry here. It's also fine to be funny. I like to laugh, and don't you like to laugh?" Dr. Richie asked. She paused, staring at Robert. "Why do you feel cursed?"

Robert stopped crying and fidgeting. Dr. Richie sat back in her office chair and waited, never taking her gaze off of Robert's face. The office was whisper quiet. Ardee stared across the room at nothing.

"I was a little boy," Robert whispered. "First time I knew something was wrong with me."

"Tell me, where were you?" Dr. Richie asked. "Try to put yourself there. Be specific; who were you with?"

"I was with her." Robert pointed at Ardee. "I wanted to kiss her, but I didn't. I was afraid to hurt her. I thought I needed to protect her. I knew I shouldn't be thinking that. It didn't make sense."

"Well, she looks like she can take care of herself," Dr. Richie said. "I bet Ardee was a very pretty young girl."

"Yeah," Robert said wistfully. "She was very pretty. I mostly liked her laugh. I *loved* her laugh. I felt safe with her."

"Safe? There's no shame in not wanting to kiss a pretty girl. You were a boy. You were both just learning about life. Innocent," Dr. Richie said. "But why would you be afraid to hurt her?"

"I was not an innocent little boy," Robert said. His voice was a monotone. He stared at Dr. Richie, without even a minor glint of emotion on his face. "I saw him six months ago. First time I'd stepped in church in years, and it was like someone hit me in the stomach. I panicked, broke out in a sweat, ran out of there, collapsed next to my car, and threw up. I barely made it back to my apartment."

"Who?" Dr. Richie asked. "Slow down; slow down. Let's back up. You were a little boy. Why would you think you would hurt Ardee? And you weren't innocent?"

"What?" Ardee said. She snapped forward, her face crinkled into a mystified expression.

Robert stared down at Dr. Richie's sandals. He thought it was funny she was wearing Birkenstocks with thick, colorful winter socks. He breathed methodically out of his mouth, and then he told them about summer camp, when he was just past nine years old. They were quiet and reflective for several minutes. Robert thought it seemed like hours.

"It hurts," Robert said. His face a stonewall of nothing. "He got me good, didn't he?"

"Bobby, look at me," Dr. Richie said. Her tone was commanding. She talked slow. Each word precise. "You said the first time... Slow down, and let's back up. What else happened?"

"What?" Robert said. His eyes appeared as if they were bloodshot moons lost deep in outer space.

Dr. Richie leaned forward, her elbows on the edge of her knees. "Bobby, you were a boy. You're a victim of a crime. Do you hear me?"

"Yeah," Robert said.

"Breathe. Take in a deep breath," Dr. Richie said. "We can stop. It's up to you, and I'm here for you. This is not a sprint. Tell me what you want to do."

"No, just give me a moment." He wiped his face.

Ardee slowly got up and slipped over to the chair next to Robert. She reached over and held his hand.

"I'm sorry I said you were fragile," Ardee said.

"It's okay. It's not your fault," Robert said.

"Bobby, we have all the time in the world today. Say what you want. Just try to organize your thoughts." Dr. Richie whispered. "Take your time."

"I know you wouldn't hurt me," Ardee said, wiping away a tear from her eyelid. They sat quietly for several more minutes.

"I was at Briar Hill. We were in fifth grade. Willis and me were out behind the gym before PE, hanging out with Taylor and Bo," Robert said. "Breck was there, too. He caught Taylor smoking. We were just standing there watching Taylor, and we weren't doing anything."

"That was a long time ago," Ardee whispered.

"Bobby, take your time," Dr. Richie said. "Sometimes trauma causes us not to remember. It's a mechanism our brain triggers to protect us, so try to fight. I'm right here, and I'm not going anywhere. Say whatever you want."

"He..."

"Do you remember a name? The pronoun *he* is all you've said," Dr. Richie asked. "Try to be specific."

"Diabolus, Mr. Diabolus. He got me at summer camp, and he got me again at school. I had no place to hide." Robert moaned. He closed his drenched eyes and clenched his hands into fists. "I was a boy! He ruined my life!"

"I remember him," Ardee said. She stared over at Dr. Richie. "He was creepy... Like he slithered everywhere."

"So he caught someone smoking?" Dr. Richie asked.

Robert took in an exaggerated breath and wiped his face dry.

"Yeah. Took us up to principal's office." Robert glanced at Ardee. "Sorry I'm fatally flawed."

"Stop. That's nonsense," Ardee said.

"Do you want to stop?" Dr. Richie asked.

"No, no. I'm tired of being alone," Robert said. "He paddled Taylor and made him cry. He told Bo never to get caught again and then told them to go back to class. Then it was just me and Willis, and my heart almost exploded. I have never been scared like that since. I was terrified, but I couldn't run. I felt frozen, like it was summer camp all over again."

Then he told them everything—sort of like unclogging a septic tank. He shared every detail he could remember—kissing Kimmi, her throwing a rock at Breck, and then desolation.

Dr. Richie gazed at Robert's patient file, fumbling with the stiff edges with her fingertips. Her face flushed a pale pink and harvest peach. She then glided her palm along the smooth surface of the file folder.

"I need a drink of water." Dr. Richie coughed. "Bobby? Ardee?"

"I'm sorry," Robert said. He breathed hard breaths. "My body betrayed me. I don't like to be touched. I don't think girls will understand. I need time to get comfortable."

His eyes were backlit by an empty, dull, black space. He wiped perspiration from his hairline with the back of his shirtsleeve.

"Sorry?" Ardee said. She shook her head. "That was one unbelievable brain dump. I can't seem to think." She clenched her jaw and pushed Robert by the shoulder her hands balled into fists.

"My God, that monster, you have nothing to be sorry about, Bobby."

"Ardee, calm down," Dr. Richie said. "Bobby, she's right. Do not be sorry. You're a victim; you and your friend, Willis, were victims of a violent, sexual assault. It's one step short of murder."

"I just feel like a freak," Robert whispered. "I have nightmares. He got promoted to assistant principal at junior high school. He seemed to follow me, but he never touched me again. I guess he got what he wanted. He enjoyed terrorizing Willis and me. I have these images that pop up in my mind without any warning. They paralyze me."

"I'm going to kill the SOB," Ardee said.

"Ardee, remember our agreement," Dr. Richie said.

"But the maggot is still out there!"

"I'm duty bound," Dr. Richie said. Her hands shook as she picked up the glass of water. Sunrays peeked through the side window. As Dr. Richie sipped, reflected rainbows of bright, happy color emerged through the glass prism. "Besides, we are both here for Bobby, right?"

"This happens in horror movies," Ardee said. "This happens to other people, not my childhood friend. I can't think straight."

"I just feel robbed," Robert said. He stared at Ardee. "I'd never do anything to hurt you. I would rather be dead than to hurt you. You were my friend. You always seemed happy... I was happy for you."

Ardee sprang up, crossed her arms, and paced in a circle near the office door, staring down at her shoes.

"Now it all makes sense—why you were so distant, why you'd clam up sometimes. I never could figure out what you were thinking. I just thought you didn't like me, but then you'd say something sweet, and this other person would appear," Ardee said. She collapsed back on the cushion chair next to Robert. "I'm sick to my stomach."

Dr. Richie leaned forward. She slipped off her artsy glasses and waved her hand in front of Robert's face.

"Bobby, let's keep talking," Dr. Richie said. "How do you feel? We can stop if we need to process. This takes time to process."

Robert blinked his eyes rapidly. He breathed in through his nose and out of his mouth.

"Numb," he finally said. "I feel I'm having an out of body experience, like I'm dreaming."

"You never told anyone?" Ardee asked. A jagged wrinkle snaked across her forehead.

"Relax. This is my gig," Dr. Richie said.

Robert stared past her, staring into his childhood.

"No one cared after the first time. I tried to act as if nothing happened. I didn't want to get spanked again. My father had a nasty temper, and I didn't want to embarrass him by telling anyone. I knew they'd ask questions," Robert said. He scratched the top of his head. "Mostly, I was worried about my sister. I just took the beating kept my mouth shut." He shrugged. "They weren't listening anyway. I told them, but they didn't believe me."

"And your mother?" Dr. Richie asked.

"She loved me, I think, but she always just acted like nothing happened. I thought they would notice something was wrong with me." He sighed. "She didn't want to listen. Just told me to pray."

"First time you've used the word love. How do you define love?" Dr. Richie adjusted her glasses and intently studied Robert's placid, unblemished face.

"I don't know. I've never really thought about it," Robert said. He smirked and crossed his arms. "One time she accused me of being gay... I may not be a playboy, but I'm not gay."

"You lost me," Dr. Richie said.

"Sorry, it's all coming at me so fast—all these thoughts," Robert said. He pressed his both his hands against his ears to stop the flow of memories.

"I know. That's why I think we'll need to carry this conversation forward later in the week," Dr. Richie said. "Give you some time to process. I will help you sort through your feelings. I think you'll be surprised how you'll find your own answers. It takes trust, honesty, and patience. And, by the way, sexual assault and accepting someone is gay are two different issues. One has nothing to do with the other."

"I had a couple of older friends I'd play basketball with or get pizza. They took me under their wing, as it were. I used to like to talk to my friends' fathers. They seemed interested in what I had to say...but my mother weirded me out by wondering why I hung out with some older friends. I was just trying to find a positive mentor,

I guess. That was all. I couldn't talk to kids my age. I was afraid. I couldn't make mistakes, and I didn't want them asking questions."

"And tell me about these friends your age?" Dr. Richie pointed at Ardee. "You liked Ardee, even after you were assaulted. You still must have felt something."

Robert glanced over at Ardee and thought about the innocent movie experiment and all his years of hiding.

"I felt dirty," Robert said. "It's hard to explain. I loved Ardee; how could I not? I liked several girls, but I would panic, so I just kept quiet or acted goofy. I mimicked other people and thought it best not to take any chances. I didn't want them to get hurt. I couldn't make mistakes."

"I can tell you for certain, you're not dirty," Dr. Richie said, "but I can't get your childhood back. For that, I'm sorry.

"I'm sorry, Bobby," Ardee said.

"But I can help you if you trust me. This takes time. Each person has their own time line, all right?" Dr. Richie.

Robert wiped his face with his cold, clammy fingers. "Church made it worse, warning us of the evil of premarital sex." His voice oozed sarcasm, and he shook his head as if to release his frustrations. "I thought God was about love, but all I heard was that I was damned; I was going to hell… Those people just talk and parrot. They don't listen. There are evil people even there, too."

Ardee had her hands tucked under her thighs. She was shaking her head and tapping her shoe against the carpet. "No one defended you?"

"All right, I think we're finished for now," Dr. Richie said. "Bobby, listen to me. First and foremost, this was not your fault. You are a helpless victim. Unfortunately, I deal with this regularly. Predators are everywhere—at school, at church, at home—and it's all a matter of the age of the victim, and the power and control someone has over them."

"Never thought of myself as a victim," Robert said, crinkling the corners of his eyelids.

"This is horrible," Ardee said.

"Bobby, you need to understand some things," Dr. Richie said. "Trauma—sexual trauma, being attacked—does attack your body. Bio-neuroscientists and my colleagues within the psychiatric community have learned within the area of Epigenetics that gene expression can be changed, and sometimes through trauma, it pushes people to do things, to harm themselves in many different ways. Almost like soldiers who have post-traumatic stress disorder, you're experiencing many of the symptoms of depression. Do you understand me?"

Robert stared into Dr. Richie's eyes and said flatly, "Yeah, I've thought about killing myself."

"I was afraid you might say that. It's not easy to admit that," Dr. Richie said. She exhaled through her lips. "That's why antidepressants can be dangerous. They sometimes have the opposite effect. But you've gotten this far, so let's get that out of your head. If you need to, you can call me. I have a 24-hour number for emergencies. This process can get tough, particularly when you get started."

"I'm not a quitter," Robert said.

Ardee clenched her jaw and fought back a tear for the loss of her childhood friend's innocence.

"I'm proud of you Bobby," Ardee whispered.

"For now, try not to talk about this outside this office. People don't just suddenly understand. They can't feel what you feel. It's about appropriateness—knowing when to share. It takes time, so trust me a bit to do my job. Okay?" Dr. Richie stared over at Ardee.

"I'm pissed off," Ardee said. She put her hands up in mock surrender. "But I understand. I promise I'll behave."

"Bobby, like I said, it takes time; that's my point. I can't snap my fingers and change what happened to you or how you see yourself, but I promise you, Bobby, in time, I can guide you to a sense of peace, love, and serenity. We need to build you a new emotional foundation. In the meantime, I'd like you to get a physical exam and draw some blood from you. I have some ideas for therapy that might just give you the boost you need to get back into your life. We can do this together, but I'll need your consent."

Chapter 16

Ardee drove her SUV down Richmond Road, heading due west from downtown. Robert stared forward through the windshield. At a stoplight, he glanced over his shoulder from the passenger side window, down at a brown-haired little boy with an innocent face. From the back seat of a four-door sedan, he waved up at Robert. Robert smirked and waved back.

"I'm sorry I got you mixed up in this." Robert hunched down in the seat.

Ardee pursed her thin lips and fiddled with the ends of her straight auburn hair. "Stop sayin' you're sorry. I can make my own decisions, and right now, I'm so ticked off." She shook her head in disgust.

"I don't know what to say," Robert said.

"Well, for one, don't say anything to anybody," Ardee said. "It's not the type of story people want to hear."

Robert snorted. "No kidding."

"Actually, I'm sorry. Sorry I said you're fragile," Ardee said. "I didn't understand…good God, this makes me even more determined."

"I'm glad you don't think so." Robert covered his face with his hands. "I can't cry anymore… Don't know how I'm going to handle work tomorrow. I'm a living, breathing buzz kill."

"Just buck up," Ardee said. "Stand tall. Fake smile, fight back smiling. Did I tell you I think I'm interested in being an FBI agent?"

"Really?" Robert said.

"Yeah, now I'm even more motivated. Maybe they'll let me focus on crimes against women and children; I don't know. They recruited me at school."

"That's cool," Robert said. "I could say, 'I know people in the FBI, so don't mess with me.'"

"Simmer. That's a long way away." Ardee drove across the apartment complex parking lot and up toward Robert's townhouse. Ernie and Steven were out front grilling burgers and drinking beer.

"There he is, the man…the myth," Steven said. He swigged his beer.

"Our man, Oob, ask your friend inside," Ernie said. "Want a beer?"

"Naw," Robert said. He turned to wave goodbye and noticed Ardee intently watched him walk toward the front door.

"Did your little fella spit?" Steven asked with a laugh. He and Ernie clinked their beer bottles.

"Come on; 'fess up, Bobby," Ernie said. He smirked.

"It's not like that," Robert said. As he reached the front door, he heard a car door slam and turned to see Ardee marching up the walk.

"Okay, get your stuff," Ardee said. She had her hands on her hips, and she stared over at Ernie and Steven. "I see you two knuckleheads haven't changed."

"Easy, sister," Ernie said. "It's late afternoon…"

"Whatever," Ardee said. "I've decided Bobby's going to hang out at my place for a few days. He's helping me with a project."

"I'll bet." Ernie chuckled.

"Why are you such a disgusting turd?" Ardee said.

"Bang; you're dead," Steven said to Ernie.

"Really?" Robert said. He shrugged. "I—I..."

"Shut up," Ardee said. "Let's go to your bedroom and get some clothes and whatnot... You're not staying here."

Steven and Ernie watched them leave as their burgers burned from medium to torched.

"I'll be damned," Steven said. "I think ol' Oobie's got a girl."

"And I think she could kick our butts." Ernie snorted and chuckled. "She's a feisty little thing."

"No kiddin'," Steven said. "I kinda dig it... might calm him down."

After a few minutes, a stunned Robert, clutching a suitcase and several shirts on hangers, dutifully followed Ardee out of the townhouse's front door.

"You all live like animals," Ardee said to Steven and Ernie.

"I don't live here," Ernie said.

"But you're still an animal." Ardee shook her head and grabbed Robert's hand. "Come on, Bobby. This will not do."

Ernie and Steven turned and gawked as a flabbergasted Robert got in the truck. He shrugged at them as Ardee backed out her SUV.

"You kidnapped me," Robert said.

"Shut up," Ardee said. "Don't get any ideas... Sorry, I doubt you're feeling frisky, and I don't need a man in my life right now. But I'm not going to just leave you there. They're bad influences right now."

"Oh, I didn't even think that," Robert said. "I'm not much on that sort of thing now... As you can image why."

"I'll get you a girlfriend. You're cute," Ardee said. "You used to be funny. Just need to get your sense of humor back, and then

I'll set you up. I've got pretty girls by the barrelful, and they're all looking for a nice guy with a sense of humor. We've had our fair share of boxes of hair that think they own us, but I don't think you've ever thought like that, so I'll give you a couple to pick from… But right now, your house is on fire, and Dr. Richie will help you put it out."

"But I'm nuts," Robert said.

"Don't say that again. You're not crazy," Ardee said. "Just some bad luck. It hasn't killed you yet, so you'll get past this. Besides, I've got skills setting people up."

Robert gulped, and he started to break out in a cold sweat. "Slow down."

"Bobby, I'm stopped at the light," Ardee said.

"No, your rapid-fire planning," Robert said. "I'm feeling dizzy."

"Sorry, I get on a roll."

"I do love to laugh," Robert said.

"I know," Ardee said. "That's why I thought you were cute. Girls like funny. Make us laugh—now there's the secret to a woman's heart."

*

Ardee awoke just past three in the morning. She yawned and decided she could get back to sleep if she drank some water and hydrated. She slipped on a baby blue cotton housecoat and slippers. With her hands in the housecoats pockets, she remembered she had a visitor in her guest bedroom as she went into the kitchen and filled a glass with spring water. As she tiptoed back toward her bedroom, she peeked through the gap in the guest bedroom doorway.

"I'm still alive," Robert whispered from within the darkness.

Ardee nudged the door open, slanted forward, and sat on the end of the double bed.

"Why are you awake?" Ardee asked. She sipped her glass of water.

"I don't know," Robert's voice resonated with thickened nighttime vocal chords.

"Bad dream?" Ardee asked.

"Yep, but it's funny... I don't remember them," Robert said. He chuckled.

"That's not funny."

"I know." Robert said. His shadow shifted his reality under Egyptian cotton, and he slinked his legs away from Ardee.

"I'm sorry," Ardee said. She only had one thought. She sensed a hole in Robert—a bottomless hole of childhood sorrows.

"Not your fault." Robert shrugged. "Just glad I didn't do anything stupid."

Ardee sipped the water and reached over to grab Robert's blanketed ankle.

"Why would you even think of doing harm to yourself?" Ardee said.

"It's hard to explain. It's like sometimes, when I went on a date, I would panic. I felt freakish, and I got tired of feeling stupid."

Ardee adjusted forward on the bed.

"I guess I really didn't know you," Ardee said.

"Yeah, well, at the time, I didn't want to hurt you," Robert said.

"I know," Ardee said. "It's okay now. I should have reached over kissed you and hugged you."

"I would have liked to be hugged." Robert grunted. "I would've felt safe for a while."

"I'm sorry," Ardee said.

"Stop. Now you're saying you're sorry."

"I know," Ardee whispered with a chuckle.

The bedroom quieted, and they were still for a few minutes within the shadows of their childhood remembrance.

"It just got worse the older I got," Robert said. He sat up and bent his knees toward his chest. "I would really try to come out of my shell, but…I don't know, like I thought through the future, and I'd talk myself out of asking a girl out. I know that's weird."

"I understand, now, why you would be distant," Ardee said. She sipped the glass of water and sighed. "You didn't have a chance. You tell someone what happened, and for the rest of your life they talk about you. Kids can be cruel."

"Yeah," Robert said. "Sort of like someone poured invisible acid over you. People can tell you not to feel dirty, but it gets really, really, lonely not being able to open up to someone. I had no one that wanted to listen, so I kept quiet. I tried to forget—ignore it."

"I won't lie; I'm angry," Ardee said. "I just don't understand. Why do people… Why do people pick on kids?"

"Easy target." Robert crossed his arms and gripped his hands. "I'm surprised I didn't kill myself. I used to think about it when I was in high school. I was tired… I couldn't sleep. Guess my brain was fried. Guess I'll be Dr. Richie's lab rat. I wonder what she'll find."

"I don't know, but just trust her. I'm going back to bed," Ardee said. She slinked up, stepped toward Robert, and kissed him on the forehead. "I'm your friend. If you need to talk, talk to me."

"Thank you," Robert said.

"For what?"

"I feel safe right now."

Chapter 17

"This might sting a bit," Dr. Richie said.

"Don't worry," Robert huffed. He had been jogging on a treadmill. Heart monitors taped to his chest. He was soaked with sweat. "I haven't run like this since high school. I can't feel my feet."

Dr. Richie tugged a rubber tourniquet above Robert's left elbow. Robert glanced over at the gold lettering from an academic fellowship with Dr. Richie's name emblazoned top center. His elbow felt as if a bumblebee had stung him.

"There. Just need some more blood, and then we're all done." She patted Robert on the shoulder like a good lab pet.

"What's this all about?" Robert asked. "Just to confirm I'm destined for the looney bin?"

Dr. Richie carefully labeled, with a dark pen, the tube of Robert's blood. Then she snuggled the sealed tube with ten previous tubes of Robert's blood.

"Well, I do thank you for letting me test you," Dr. Richie said as she buttoned her white lab coat. "The more I know, the more I can help you, build on the science, and help others. This Epigenetic science is opening up proof of theories that our bodies and minds react to environmental stimuli. It literally alters us, and if not dealt with, it can be tragically harmful. Or, we might be able to genetically heal as well... Exciting stuff."

"Do you really think there's something in my head?" Robert asked. He sucked in oxygen through his mouth, hoisted his chest up, and exhaled. He sat down on a metal chair in front of the treadmill. "Am I suicidal?"

"Scary idea?" Dr. Richie said. She shrugged. "Just saying the word suicide."

"Yeah," Robert said. His face flushed crimson. He stared up at Dr. Richie, his eyebrows furrowed.

"If you knew you had a cancerous tumor, would you want to get it zapped out of you?" Dr. Richie said. She leaned back against the lab table.

"For sure," Robert said.

"Well then, that's part of why you're here, but don't let me or the medical community fool you." Dr. Richie smirked. "We act like we know the answer, but most of the time, we are just hunting and pecking for answers."

He glanced up at Dr. Richie. "Just scares me."

"It takes time," Dr. Richie said. She clenched her jaw. "It's the mystery of the mind, that inner voice we all have. We think we can connect trauma with receptor genes in your brain. Just trying to dig inside you, without digging inside you." She leaned toward Robert and smirked.

"Trauma?" Robert said. He wiped his face with the towel and stared past Dr. Richie.

"Yes. Genes they've found from brain tissue, Epigenetic alterations of DNA," Dr. Richie said.

"I'm lost," Robert said.

"I can tell," Dr. Richie said as she chuckled. "Okay, you have DNA, essentially the protein instructions that make up our bodies."

"Okay," Robert said.

"Epi, which means above, and add that to genetics," Dr. Richie said. She shook her head. "I know, fancy doctor talk, but seriously, gene expression above your underlying DNA. So, how your life choices, things that happen to you, cause genes to either turn on, or off—different from your original DNA structure."

"So, you're saying, because of my childhood," Robert said, tying his tennis shoe laces, "I might have something inside me that might make me harm myself."

"Maybe is the answer. We're trying to devise DNA testing using blood," Dr. Richie said. She opened Robert's patient chart.

"Scares me," Robert said.

Dr. Richie stared down at Robert. She crinkled her mouth and tapped the pen against her lips.

"Let's stop dancing." Dr. Richie slid her glasses up her nose. "Tell me when you've thought about suicide?"

Robert smirked, fidgeting with the cotton towel as he dabbed sweat from his forehead. Dr. Richie examined his patient chart before gazing down at Robert.

"For a while, all the time." Robert flopped forward, his elbows on his knees. "I'm serious."

"I believe you," Dr. Richie said.

"When I told you I knew something was wrong with me after I took Ardee to a movie... I was a kid, but I didn't seem to think like the other kids. I wanted to be dead."

"I believe you," Dr. Richie said.

Robert glanced up and to the left of Dr. Richie at a clear bottle of hand sanitizer.

"My father had a nasty temper. He treated my mother like a dog," Robert said. He gulped and clenched his jaw, staring down at the square tile floor.

"Being beat down as a child," Dr. Richie said, "is not fair. There is nothing you could do—other than figure out how to survive. That was not your fight."

"I'd think about slitting my wrists, and then maybe they'd listen to me. I thought someone might care," Robert said. He stared forward at the beaker full of cotton balls and ear swabs. "I'd get a razor blade, but then I wouldn't do it for some reason. That's when I'd go jogging. As I got older, maybe I'd go rabbit hunting with Ernie. I'd have a shotgun in my hands, but I didn't want Ernie to find me—didn't think that would be fair to him. I don't like to hunt...don't like killing."

"And high school? College?" Dr. Richie asked.

"It was horrible in high school." Robert sighed and combed his moist hair with his fingers. "I never really tried. But I was poorly prepared, I'd panic around a girl I liked, you know, like Ardee. I'd try to hide. I'd act goofy. You know, make jokes."

Dr. Richie set his patient chart on the exam room desk.

"Tried what exactly," Dr. Richie said.

"Ah, dating, you know. I goofed a bit, but as I got older, I was very conscious of girls I cared about. Mostly, I didn't want to ruin their teenage years, didn't want them near me, didn't think it was fair. And to be honest, I didn't want them to ask questions."

"Ever think you could set some ground rules?" Dr. Richie asked. She shrugged and stared down at her colorful socks. "Tell her you just want to hang out, nothing serious. Maybe tell her to bring her friends, so that might take all the angst out of the evening, so you can just have fun and be friends. Nothing wrong with having friends from the opposite sex."

Robert sat back and with the towel over his shoulder. "Yeah, should've thought about that."

Dr. Richie scowled at Robert's patient chart. "And it seems like you've been drinking a lot." She sighed. "I suspect your samples will..."

"Yeah, but I'll be honest, being drunk doesn't work." He flipped the towel over his neck and smirked. "Sometimes if I ran across a girl I really liked, I'd get angry—say something nasty. Push 'em away, I guess."

"Angry? Why?" Dr. Richie asked.

"Because I felt robbed, I guess." Robert shook his head. He fiddled with the tip of the towel. "Like I should have been left alone. I should've learned sooner how to treat girls. I guess it's obvious I'm clueless."

"Bobby, you can't change the past," Dr. Richie said. She wiggled her foot in the air. "Like my socks?"

Robert stared at the kaleidoscope of woven color and grinned up at Dr. Richie.

"Yeah."

"I should get you a pair." Dr. Richie chuckled.

"I don't think so," Robert said.

"Slow down," Dr. Richie said. "Ask me why I wear them."

Robert leaned back in the chair. "Okay, why do you wear them?"

"They make me smile." She bent down and pulled her socks up and then grinned at Robert. "When I have a bad day, I inspect my socks. I have a secret. If I'm going to help you, I want you to understand me a bit, so you realize I'm not some cold, critical, clinical doctor who lacks understanding."

Robert glanced down at her colorful socks, then back up at Dr. Richie.

"All right," Robert said.

"Bobby, I like you. I like calling you Bobby. Seems boyish, but it's a happy name. I can see why Ardee likes you." She took off her glasses. "At least to me, it's a happy name."

"Just don't go calling me Robby. Creeps me out." Robert huffed. He sighed.

"Oh, I get that," Dr. Richie said. She took off her lab coat and sat down on a cushioned roller chair. "So Bobby, right now, I'm not a doctor; I'm just me, okay?"

Robert scooted forward and nodded. "All right."

"When I was a young girl, a teenager, I had an older boyfriend. As you might expect, one thing lead to another, and I gave in. He took my virginity," Dr. Richie said. She crossed her legs, sighed, and stared up at the tiled ceiling. "Stupid girl…"

Robert stared at her colorful sock and they both chuckled.

"At least you had a choice," Robert mumbled.

"Yeah, sort of," Dr. Richie said. She furrowed her eyebrows. "When you're young, the differences in age make a huge difference. Five years is a lifetime for your brain and body to develop."

"All right," Robert said.

"So, one night, he got what he thought he wanted," Dr. Richie said. She shrugged. "And then, he told his friends, and I was suddenly very popular—for all the wrong reasons. He came back for more, but then—after he had his fun, as you've already figured out—he dumped me."

"I'm sorry," Robert said.

"Oh, no need to say that," Dr. Richie said. She shook her head and crinkled her mouth. "It's life. You make mistakes, and besides, sex is not dirty, actually, between people who have an underlying friendship and love, it's a beautiful act. But here is why I tell you this tiny vignette of my own experiences. After he dumped me, the other boys—'cause dense boys do talk—asked me out a lot, and they just expected me to do the same thing. I had made myself the school plaything. I wanted to be popular, remember… Stupid girl."

"Oh, man, this is bad," Robert said.

"Yeah, well, I was at least smart enough to figure out what was going on behind my back. I had one friend who told me. We're still friends," Dr. Richie said. She tapped Robert on the knee. "But I was a teenager, and I felt used, as you might expect."

"Yeah." Robert shrugged. "I would imagine. I knew of a few girls like that. I could tell looking at them that they had disappointment in their eyes. I knew the look. I felt the same thing. Wish I didn't know that."

"But I was a lot older, and I willing participated. I was not assaulted… Big difference," Dr. Richie said. She turned on the cushioned chair to face Robert. "So, I got older, my body started to change, I wasn't the skinny cute girl anymore, and there were other new editions being rolled out." She chuckled.

"I get you," Robert said.

Dr. Richie unbuttoned her shirtsleeves and rolled the cuffs past her forearms.

"Take a look at my scars," Dr. Richie said. "You can touch them."

Robert stared down at the bubbled, angled slices dotting underneath Dr. Richie's wrists and forearms. He glided his forefinger tips along her bumpy skin.

"Damn," Robert said.

"Yeah, got that right," Dr. Richie said. "So, when I talk to you about suicide, in a sense, I'm reflecting over my own life—the work I had to put in to accept me, to love me. And remember, I just wanted to be popular. I never got pregnant, no abortion, and I'd had some say in the situation."

"Man, you tore yourself up," Robert said.

"Yes, I did, but I was lucky. My parents got involved," Dr. Richie said. She hunched down and patted Robert on the leg. "They were young parents and just didn't think through who I was with until I started carving my body."

"That's terrible," Robert said.

"Yes. It's a form of numbing, like drinking too much." Dr. Richie stared at Robert and smirked.

"I know," Robert said.

"Good news, they both took me for help straight away. They didn't hide from it. They likely saved my life. My parents were some of my best friends, and now that I'm a lot older, I miss them terribly."

Robert nodded and sniffled, staring straight ahead.

"So, the reason I wear these goofy socks..." Dr. Richie tapped Robert on the arm. "I wear the socks because they remind me not to take life so seriously—that life should be fun, and that I'm loved. Just that simple."

"Maybe I should get a pair," Robert said.

"Oh, leave that to me." Dr. Richie folded her sleeves down, put her lab coat back on, and adjusted the stethoscope around her neck.

"Okay, enough about me. I'm back to my doctoring ways," Dr. Richie said. "So when I hear a silent scream, I know what it sounds like. And it looks like…Bobby."

"Damn," Robert said.

"It feels good to talk?" Dr. Richie asked.

"Yeah, at least I know someone out there knows." Robert shrugged and coughed. "I just wouldn't want some kid to feel like I do."

"Well, me too, and good news." Dr. Richie clenched her jaw and narrowed her eyes. "I've got all the samples from you I need. Your lab rat days are over."

Robert wrinkled his nose and wiped the towel across his lips. He gazed up at Dr. Richie with the hint of tears.

"Why do people pick on kids?"

Chapter 18

Ardee tapped her fingernails along the steering wheel. The Sunday morning was washed in pure golden sunshine beams. It was a cool morning, winter approached. As the weeks had passed into months, Ardee was proud that Bobby was putting in the effort with Dr. Richie to face his childhood. As she strolled toward the red brick church, a mother bent down, her dress hemmed below the knee, and dabbed her fingers with her tongue to wipe resistant childhood grime off her little boy.

"Mom, yuck," he said, as he struggled for freedom.

"Stand still," she said. "I'm not going to kill you."

Ardee thought of Bobby. He had once been a little boy like this one, with thick brown hair, an unblemished face, and round puppy dog eyes. Years before, he had walked up this concrete path and into a living hell.

"Yes, dear? May I help you?" a middle-aged woman said. She sat behind a cherry reception desk in the church office, which smelled of disinfectant, age, and dankness. The fluorescent lights hummed with judgmental disapproval.

"Well…" Ardee said. She huffed and smiled. "Sorry, I'm nervous."

"Oh, no need to be nervous at the Lord's house. I'm Myrtle Dumbwoody. We've been members for three generations," she said, adjusting her reading glasses off the bridge of her nose. The black frames were attached to a fancy gold chain dangling around her skinny, wrinkled neck.

"Great. Well, you're clearly the person in the know," Ardee said.

"Oh, now, I'm just the eyes and ears for the church," Myrtle said. She tilted her head to the left and back.

"Okay, Mrs. Dumbwoody?" Ardee said.

"Oh, call me Myrtle."

"Okay, Myrtle," Ardee said. She adjusted the cuffed sleeves of her simple white blouse. "I'm hoping to find a church home—a place to maybe meet a good man and then someday, if we're blessed, you know, be a mother…have a family. I didn't grow up with a happy family, you know."

Myrtle beamed and examined the curvy, fit Ardee. "Oh, I've got several good men in mind already."

"Let me catch my breath," Ardee said, squeezing her hands on her hips. "But in the meantime, I'm hoping to volunteer, perhaps with a teenage class. Might be good mom training, I've always liked young boys. Maybe I'll have a few someday, if I'm blessed."

"Sugar, I know we need the help," Myrtle said, but as she engaged in mid-nudge-toward-her-nephew mode, from behind, through the opaque window with Assistant Pastor stenciled in block letters, the rumpled specter of Mr. Diabolus emerged.

Ardee held her breath and refused to back up. She ground her dress heels into the shiny, vanilla tile floor.

"I'm sorry for interrupting, but I overheard you," Mr. Diabolus said, fiddling with his silver belt buckle. His thin gray and black hair was slicked back by gel.

Ardee crossed her arms, and then made herself uncross them again. She forced a pleasant smile. *Act*, she thought. *Be patient.*

"I'm sorry, but I've not got real training," Ardee said. She slinked forward and glanced at Myrtle. "I guess I'm searching."

Myrtle waved her wrinkled hand at Ardee and pulled her light, cotton, baby blue sweater up over her nimble shoulders. "Oh, you seem trainable."

Mr. Diabolus's thick eyebrows furrowed. His ruddy cheeks creased with his grimace, as he scratched behind his ear.

"A pretty young thing working with the young boys, might not go over well," Mr. Diabolus said. He glanced over at an irritated Myrtle.

"What on earth?" Myrtle said. She gazed at Mr. Diabolus with a scowl.

"You know these days and all, with teachers getting caught—social sites and whatnot," Mr. Diabolus said. He nodded over at Ardee. "Not saying anything, but maybe on a trial basis, if Myrtle thinks it's okay with you being there. I can use the help. Youngsters can be a handful."

Ardee crossed her arms and put her fingers in front of her red lips. "I didn't even consider." She started to back out of the office. "This is embarrassing."

Mr. Diabolus slinked forward and patted Ardee on her shoulder.

"I'm sorry. Can never be too careful," Mr. Diabolus said. He smirked and played with the edge of his ill-fitting, Windsor-knotted, red club tie. "But, maybe you could come and sit in the back and shadow me for a while?"

Mrs. Dumbwoody puckered her lips and nodded approval.

Ardee thought it had been absurdly easy to waltz into the church and hook into a room full of defenseless children. She knew she had a reasonably pretty face and a healthy figure, so doors and assumptions favored her. The parents were deluded into believing their children were safe within the classrooms and halls of church. She knew she had showed up too late for Bobby, but her instincts nagged at her that there were other Roberts, Bobbys, and other names attached to tragic stares waiting for her. She had searched the social networking sites. She had noticed Mr. Diabolus had hidden and slithered within the virtual layers of idle chitchat and friends being friends, children connecting with children.

His page appeared innocent enough, with a welcome page to come to church. There was a review of his history—he was a reverend, and before that, an assistant school principal. Mysterious early retirement from the public school system was noted. The page had a hidden specter, pictures and pictures of children, and if she inspected carefully, it was in the eyes. Numerous faces screamed at her. If she was ever going to be FBI, this was a perfect window to walk through to test her commitment, and it was personal. It was for her childhood friend – her Bobby.

She had a plan. She would not go to the police, yet. She did not want Bobby to have to answer any questions, as he had already been humiliated enough. But she knew there were pictures of Bobby hidden some place, and she had to get the pictures back, while exposing a life-long predator who fed on the souls of innocent children. She had to descend into Mr. Diabolus's sick world. She had researched the profile. She would have to be patient and give him all the signs she was a predator too – that she lusted for young boys.

"That's a great idea," Ardee said. She grinned at Mr. Diabolus. "Clearly, you've been well trained. You're a man of God."

"Actually," Mr. Diabolus said. He stood up straight, his shoulders back, as if at attention. "I was called by God. It's my life-long calling to train children."

*

That one, Ardee thought. His suit jacket fit him uncomfortably. She had not pegged him because his parents had not purchased a properly fitting suit, but because the boy's face told another story.

148

His eyes screamed. *If he could only shed his skin and morph into another person*, she thought.

She had sat in the back of the church class for weeks listening to Mr. Diabolus drone on and on about the one true God, the evils of alcohol, drugs, premarital sex, predators who lurked at school and church, and to be extra careful who they talked with on social media sites. She wondered if the living God had been listening to this false prophet *blab, blab, and blab* on to the trapped children. He had the audacity to preach about child abuse in front of the church members. He hid right in front of them; he had been hiding in front of them for decades, and the parents had willingly exposed their children to evil—an evil just short of murder.

She had patiently observed the faces. There were at least two children under his control. Behind those faces, after listening to Bobby, she knew—she sensed—which ones cried out, who screamed at her in silence. Their names were Charlie, a slight eleven year old, with blond hair, and David, a normal-sized boy with dishwater blond hair, eyes blended between happy and sad. He was a kind soul, yearning for someone to hug him and tell him he was beautiful.

"Hi, I'm Ardee," she said. She held out her hand.

"I'm David," he said as he shook her warm, soft fingertips. "You're pretty, but you don't talk much, do you?"

"Oh, thank you," Ardee said. She grinned. "You look quite smart in your suit. Is that new?"

David shrugged and hooked his eleven-year-old finger between his neck and his snug shirt collar. "Yeah, my mom said I outgrew my other one. I can still wear the pants."

"She did good," Ardee said.

"She tries. Sometimes she…," David said. He stared down at his polished brown dress shoes, the laces tied at the top like waxed butterfly wings.

"Yeah," Ardee said, encouraging him to continue. She turned and stood parallel to David.

- "My dad can be really mean to her," David said. He opened and closed his Bible. "She has sad eyes."

"I'm sorry," Ardee said.

She glanced across the classroom at Mr. Diabolus reading scripture to a group of boys. They sat in a group across the rectangular classroom, where another helper aimlessly talked about himself, then read scripture, and then talked about himself again.

"I feel bad for her," David whispered.

"I'm sorry," Ardee said. *Just listen*, she thought. *Just sit here on this cold, metal chair and listen.*

"She can't protect me." David gripped underneath the metal chair after he glanced across the room at Mr. Diabolus. "But it's okay. She tries hard. I should try harder in school; it might make her happy."

"You like school?" Ardee retraced David's glance over at Mr. Diabolus and clenched her teeth.

"Sometimes," David said. He reached inside his coat pocket and slipped out a torn package of gum. "You like bubble gum? I like grape, but it makes my lips turn purple."

"Oh, yeah, then your mom knows you've been chewing bubble gum." Ardee chuckled and nudged David.

"Yeah, I guess, but I like it." He grinned.

"I do like bubble gum, but not all the time," Ardee said.

"Will you be my friend?" David glanced up at Ardee with intense, searching for trust—eyes.

"I'll be your friend," Ardee said. She winked at him.

"Okay." He swung his legs back and forth. "You're pretty."

"Don't you have other friends?" Ardee asked, gripping her fingers together.

"Sort of." He leaned in close to Ardee. "But I don't tell them much. Mom told me to be quiet and pray. And don't make stuff up. Do you like to pray? Sure you don't want any gum? Will you be here next week?"

Ardee checked her wristwatch. Sunday school was about to end and then there was the stiff-shirt formal church.

"No gum for me," Ardee said. She exhaled in anger. "David, you can talk to me if you want to, okay?"

David blushed and almost cried as he grimaced up at her.

"Okay... I..." David hunched down near Ardee. "Can I tell you a secret?"

Ardee leaned forward, her elbows on her knees, and whispered, "Yeah."

"I feel safe next to you," David said. "You wouldn't hurt me?"

"Never, but that's not a big secret," Ardee said.

And then, as if another person hid behind David's eyes, he blankly stared into Ardee's brown eyes.

"Yes, it is," David said. His unblemished face was like a blank piece of white copy paper, and then he shifted away as Mr. Diabolus stood up.

"Time for big church," Mr. Diabolus said.

David gulped and scooted toward the open doorway. A busy church hallway, with a human current, frothed toward the traditional Sunday service.

"Well, I think it's time for big church," Ardee said.

"See you later. Gotta go," David said. He scooted out of the class, into the Bible-thumping river of humanity, but he glanced back at her and waved as he disappeared through the doorway.

Ardee waved back and, without moving her head, glanced to find Mr. Diabolus. He had watched David skip out of the class.

"David's a good one," Mr. Diabolus said.

"He seems like a good boy." She picked up a three-ring binder left on a metal chair.

"So, I saw you talking with him," Mr. Diabolus said. "He's not much of a talker."

"Oh, he offered me some chewing gum," Ardee said. She watched Mr. Diabolus inspect the other helpers and wave to them as they left the room.

"You like that one—David?" Mr. Diabolus asked. The tone in his voice was a sick harbinger. "You've been watching him for weeks. Charlie, too. Charlie's not very smart. Sorry, sort of like his parents."

Ardee stopped walking toward the classroom coat rack and hugged the binder as she stared at over her jacket and purse. "Sorry?"

She decided to chum the predator water, puckering her lips and smirking sheepishly. "I do like young boys." Then she almost vomited and had to rapidly blink away tears.

"Oh, I see." Mr. Diabolus fidgeted with his silver belt buckle.

"Oh, yeah?" Ardee said. She licked her lips and played with the ends of her auburn hair.

"David's very obedient," Mr. Diabolus said. His tongue slithered between his chapped lips.

"I love obedient little boys," Ardee said. She blushed and clenched her jaw, flexing her calf muscle as she ground her shoe into the tile floor.

Mr. Diabolus stopped near the door and cupped her elbow to hold her back as the class emptied. After a few moments—eons of time to Ardee—Mr. Diabolus turned toward her. She could smell hints of his distinct, alcohol-laced cologne.

"I'm an artist," Mr. Diabolus said. "I go by Dandy on the net. I take retro photos. Do you like art?"

Ardee glanced away but tried to remain focused. A sick doorway had opened into the mind of a madman, and all she could see in her mind's eye was Bobby's tragic childhood.

"I love art," she said. "But some people don't appreciate the delicacy of it."

"I don't share with many, you know," Mr. Diabolus said. He rubbed his belly and reached over to rub along Ardee's forearm. She knew he was a testing her and resisted slapping or slugging him. It took all her effort to appear interested in his brand of…art.

"I don't think folks understand, not being enlightened and all," Ardee said.

Chum the dirty, filthy, perverted water, she thought. She stepped toward the coat rack, half concealed by the metal door.

"I've posed. It's not something I'm proud of, but you know, I was a little kid."

Mr. Diabolus slid between Ardee and the doorway, his pudgy hand slithering along her shoulder and down to her hands.

"Oh, yes, I see I've found someone who is a true art lover." He glanced around the empty classroom before turning to look out the doorway, and then whipped back around. "Would you like to come over and see some of my retro art?"

"Retro art?" Ardee asked. She placed the binder inside the closet and kept her arms down, her body open.

Mr. Diabolus ogled her from her thin legs, up each curve to her pretty face.

Kick the creep in the groin and beat him back to hell, she thought.

"Yeah, I call my photos retro, 'cause I use an instamatic camera. Some are in color, some black and white," Mr. Diabolus whispered. He grinned and fidgeted with his belt buckle. "I get sort of an instant gratification, so I can see my photos without having to wait."

"That's ingenious," Ardee said.

"Yeah, thought it up myself." Mr. Diabolus leaned in close to Ardee, his belly rubbing against her forearm, and glided his hand down her back. "Maybe you could model for me?"

"I'm not sure about that. It's been a long time," Ardee said. She slinked a few inches away—just enough to feign playing hard to get. She stared forward. "I guess you sensed my weakness…"

"Oh, yes – yes, I'm gifted." Mr. Diabolus snickered.

"I really should get going," Ardee said.

"Well, will you consider being a model for me?" He nudged in close to Ardee. "Can you keep a secret?"

"Don't tempt me; you know I'm weak. I thought I might get into church, you know...change my life." Ardee blushed, not from embarrassment or being shy, but from pure rage.

"Good, good. I'm a man of God; trust me." He gripped Ardee at the waist as he pulled her close to whisper in her ear. She could feel his hot breath along her cheek. "Maybe you can pose for me...maybe pose with a little boy, only from a pure artistic perspective?"

"Of course," Ardee said. "It wouldn't be art, would it?"

"I will give David to you. I own him." He smirked. "I can tell you like that. You're shivering."

"Not sure I understand," Ardee said. She crossed her arms and glanced away.

"Yes, you do. You're weak; you can barely control yourself." Mr. Diabolus grinned. "If you let me take the photos, you can play with David."

"Yeah?" Ardee said. She blinked her eyelids rapidly, her mouth as dry as pulverized concrete.

"One condition—it's mandatory that you be initiated, do you understand?" Mr. Diabolus said. He slid his hand down and patted her on the butt.

"Sorry, initiated?" Ardee asked. She wobbled a bit.

"My secret society. It's a small number I allow inside my artsy world," Mr. Diabolus said. He slid his pudgy hands up and hooked his fingers around her neck, squeezing gently. "I prefer children, but I sense you're a treat for me from God. Will you submit? Can I treat you like a boy?"

Ardee stared forward, almost in a trance, as Mr. Diabolus hugged her.

"Yeah," Ardee she finally whispered, her teeth chattering.

"I could tell the first time I saw you," He whispered. His thick arms slithered tighter around Ardee. "You like being a tramp, don't you?"

"Yeah," Ardee coughed out.

"Now, we understand each other. After I initiate you, you'll never talk, will you?"

"Never," she wheezed.

Mr. Diabolus kissed her forehead and licked her ear, smirking, before he squeezed her butt and patted her.

"You'll let the boys practice on you while I take my artistic photos?" He whispered, "That excites you?"

Ardee lost the ability to speak. She wanted to scream, but she kept Bobby's sad story, his sad eyes, in her mind. Now, she saw Charlie and David, as well. Her plan had worked well. *Too well*, she thought. She wanted to run.

"Hush, I've your answer. I can *feel* your answer." He ground close to Ardee. He whispered. "God will be watching. I look forward to your initiation and you modeling for me. We will become fast friends."

*

Ardee scampered from the church, her breathing erratic and her skin on fire. Within the relative safety of her SUV, she turned the air conditioning up to arctic blast. She sat inside and thought of little David and Charlie trapped inside the church sanctuary. They had not even gotten to be happy teenagers—just like Bobby. Both had been robbed of their innocence before they even knew what if felt like to innocently hold a little girl's hand and wonder what it might feel like to kiss her soft cheek.

As Ardee drove out of the packed church parking lot, she wondered if this was typical FBI undercover work. If so, she thought it might not be a good career path for her. She slipped out her cell phone and called Bobby.

"I'm coming over," Ardee said.

"Okay. I'm just sitting here, reading," Robert said.

After she knocked on the door, she barged inside the apartment and hugged Bobby as tightly as she could. "I'm sorry."

"Damn, Oobie." Steven glanced up from reading the newspaper. "I think someone likes you."

155

"Hush," Robert said. "I like hugs. You like my socks?"

Ardee backed up and scrunched her face, staring down at his feet.

"You are truly odd," she said. "But in a good way. Sorry, I was at a new church and started thinking about you. I just decided to come hug you… I hope you don't mind."

"I like hugs," Robert said. He smiled.

Chapter 19

"Well, I guess it's show and tell time," Dr. Richie said. She fumbled with her glasses.

"I like my socks," Robert said. "I guess fate spun me some colorful ones." He smiled over at Dr. Richie, but she had a serious, intent expression.

"Sorry, Bobby," Dr. Richie said.

"Sorry?" Robert asked.

"Where do I start?" Dr. Richie took in a deep, thoughtful breath. She exhaled through her puckered lips.

"Am I crazy?" Robert said.

"No. Okay, so I got all your test results back." She opened the folder. "You're physically in okay shape, though you need to lose some weight. Your liver enzymes are high, so you really, really need to cut back on your drinking, if not quite all together."

"I know. I expected you might say that," Robert said.

"I really like you, Bobby. You're a truly nice fellow. I have not had the opportunity to have meaningful talk therapy for quite some time. We don't have the time to just talk with our patients these days. It's about money and all. Clinically, I've gotten a great deal of insight from our visits. So thank you…"

"Most girls don't like 'nice'," Robert said.

"Until they get a bit older and date a few jerks," Dr. Richie said.

"I've been a jerk a few times."

"Stop. Let me get through this," Dr. Richie said.

Robert glanced over at Dr. Richie. She scowled and clenched her jaw.

"Not good," Robert said.

"No, not good." She shook her head.

"All right, stop pussyfootin' and get with it," Robert said.

"Sometimes science discovers new tests, and I really wonder if they are good, or if they open up a Pandora's Box, as it were." She slid her glasses back up her nose. "We did some DNA testing with your blood and tried out a new Epigenetic test that, unfortunately, came back positive. We did the test five times – same result."

Robert squirmed in the cushioned chair. "Positive for what?"

"If you think through it, I don't think you'll be shocked," Dr. Richie said. She blinked her eyes rapidly. "Within your DNA structure, within your stress response genes, we found what we think is a suicide gene. It has a much more scientific name, but for our conversations, that is ultimately what it causes."

Robert slumped back into the cushioned chair, his skin chilled with goose pimples. The lavender scent of the office did not calm him. Instead, he gulped and squeezed the end of the chair with his moist hands. "Damn."

"I don't have a magic drug. There are anti-depressants, but sometimes they have the opposite effect," Dr. Richie said. She scowled down at her shoes. "I'm sorry. I suspect the trauma from the attack did more than scar your brain. It triggered on the wrong gene. I don't view you as a lab rat. I view you as a human being— a person that I like. I'm not sure what to do…"

"I thought you all had all the answers," Robert said, combing his hair with his fingers. "Guess I'm cursed."

"You're not cursed, Bobby; listen to me." She leaned forward and patted Robert's knee. "Look at me."

Robert stared over at her.

"Good. Sometimes, just being aware of something makes all the difference," Dr. Richie said. She pulled a plastic bag from behind her.

"What's all this hot mess?" Robert said.

"I have a therapy idea." Dr. Richie fumbled into the bag. "I remember how you loved my colorful socks."

"Yeah, my roommate thinks I've gone off the deep end," Robert said with a shrug.

"Okay, I've come up with a strategy. Now hear me out."

"I'm scared," Robert said.

"And I'm scared for you," Dr. Richie said. "This whole Epigenetic gene expression science scares me, not to mention the ethical implications and how this science might be used against people."

"Yeah, I bet," Robert said.

"Here goes… I want you to do a couple of things between now and next week. You can call me anytime." She pulled out a pair of colorful, woven socks. "If you start to feel down, feel like drinking, I want you to do two things. First go exercise – get fit and release some positive endorphins, and I want you to keep these socks handy. Keep them where you can see them in your room, and if you think about harming yourself, I want you to put them on. Use them to think of a happy thought."

"You're serious?" Robert said.

"Yes. Until I can figure out how to turn off that nasty gene, I've got to get you smiling and thinking positive thoughts," Dr. Richie said. She rolled up her sleeves. "Remember these marks? They remind me where I *was*, not where I am today, so in a sense, if you put the socks on, they will remind you of the happy places you will

159

travel in your mind. The life you have yet to live – the now, the future."

"I'll try," Robert said. He started to cry, and a solitary tear glided down his blushing cheek. "I like…" He huffed, trying to regain his composure. "The socks…"

Chapter 20

"Now, you seem like a well-meaning young lady," Detective Sammons said. He was a tall, pro-football tight-end of a man, said. He twisted to readjust his holstered weapon. His blue jacket was purposefully large to cover the gun.

"Give me a moment," Ardee said.

"I gave you a moment a week ago. I don't have time for this cryptic dancing." Detective Sammons pointed up toward the building's fifth floor. "I told you then, I'll tell you now, we've got an entire department chasing after sexual predators. The Internet's full of them, but that's not part of my work. I chase *real* bad guys."

"What if I told you I know you used to go by Breck?" Ardee said. She crossed her arms and bit her lower lip, settling back in the cushioned desk chair.

"Well, I'd say nothing, I'm Detective Sammons, period." He scratched the top of his blond head. "So what? You got thirty more seconds."

Ardee glanced around the hectic, open floor plan police station. It smelled like three-day-old coffee.

"I know something about somebody." Ardee stared down at the tiled floor. "Someone you once knew, but I found out by accident."

"*Tick-tock, tick-tock*, sister. Be specific this time," Detective Sammons said.

"What if I found out inside a doctor's office?" Ardee said.

Detective Sammons squinted until his eyelids were almost shut and leaned forward. "You know, now I'm gettin' a bad feelin'." He tapped his lips with his thick forefinger. "Go on ..."

"Will I be in trouble if I tell you something terrible about a day you might remember, but I found out in a confidential situation...you know, the doctor-patient privacy?" She furrowed her thin eyebrows, staring intently at Detective Sammons.

"All right, I don't think so, but..." He glanced over at the elevator and nodded at Ardee. "Let's say I leave this badge in this desk, go downstairs, and just happen to be standin' in the parking lot, when you just happen to waltz by and tell me this or that, off the record."

Detective Sammons slipped off his gold badge, opened his top desk drawer, and locked it inside. Once he was outside, he balled up some chewing tobacco and shoved it inside his left cheek while waiting for Ardee to appear.

"See here now," he said when she arrived. "What you tell me is between us. This won't stand up in court." He spit at the trunk of the oak tree shading them from the mid-afternoon sun. "Understand?"

"Yes," Ardee said. She sucked in a full breath for courage. "All right, you remember Bobby Scott?"

Detective Sammons stood up straight on his lizard-skin boots and furrowed his brow. "Why, yeah." His cheek puffed out as he chewed at the ball of tobacco. "Damn, lost track of the boy."

"He's still here in town," Ardee said.

"All right, enough pussyfootin'," Detective Sammons said. "You sought me out and tracked me down for a reason. Now I know this involves Bobby, what's he done?"

"Nothing," Ardee said.

Detective Sammons wiped his nose with the back of his hairy hand. "Spit it out. I can take it."

"You chipped your teeth at summer camp," Ardee said.

Detective Sammons rolled his tongue behind his lips, remembering the day in question. "This ain't good."

"No," Ardee said. "And I'm mad as hell."

Detective Sammons stared past Ardee and up into the clear winter sky. He breathed out a long, thoughtful fog from his childhood memories.

"That SOB," Detective Sammons said. He shook his head.

"He was attacked, raped him," Ardee said. "By ..."

"Don't say another word," Detective Sammons said. He put his hand up. "It's a bit cold today, but not as cold as I feel right now. It's like all my blood just drained out of me. I knew somethin' happened to him that day, but I was kid so I just shrugged it off."

"You know who?" Ardee asked.

"Yeah, I know who," Detective Sammons said. "You know, kids are smart. I remember Bobby clammed up. He'd been flirtin' with a little girl, and then it was like we were all lepers."

"Kimmi," Ardee said.

"Yep. Cute little girl." Detective Sammons spat at the hibernating bluegrass and kicked the trunk of the oak tree with the toe of his boot. "So, what's Bobby doin' these days?"

Ardee crossed her arms and shrugged. "Not much. He's trying to finally graduate, but he's sort of stuck in neutral." She sighed. "I don't know. I guess I just like him. I came across him over near campus, puking his guts out with his friends. It was a total fluke."

"Too bad. He was smart as a whip. But more importantly, what've you been doin'?" Detective Sammons said. He stared into Ardee's eyes.

"Been going to church, volunteering in a Sunday school class," Ardee said. She gulped, she breathed out a slow breath. "Fifth grade boys..."

"Don't get yourself hooked," Detective Sammons said. He leaned his elbow against the oak tree.

"I'm going to get him." She furrowed her eyebrows and fiddled with the clasp of her purse.

"How?" Detective Sammons looked over at Ardee and smirked. "Wait." He spat and pulled out the ball of moist tobacco. "Go on."

"He invited me to his house. Asked me to be a model, model with a little boy. I wanted to kick him in the groin, but that's not going to protect these kids, and it's too late for Bobby."

Detective Sammons scowled. "See here, this is personal now. Model with a boy?" He scratched behind his ear. "Are you crazy? He's a big SOB, if memory serves."

"I'm worried about Bobby. I'm afraid he might kill himself," Ardee said. She exhaled, she clenched her jaw. "And I don't want him to know. I don't want him to be questioned. It might put him over the edge. And I know there are other boys in danger."

"Hey sister, just keep peckin' at me; no pressure." Detective Sammons shook his head. "Truth be told, my instincts told me to stay clear of that jerk-off. Sounds like Bobby didn't have a chance. Shame can be downright powerful motivator, according to the psychologists we work with. Damn it, I've had my fair share of suicide cases. Not too rare to figure out they had been molested or whatnot. I just don't understand it."

"He was always so sweet to me," Ardee said.

"Yeah, he was a nice guy," Detective Sammons said.

"I'm invited to 'Bible study' this Friday. The creep wants me to submit so he can take pictures of me. I'm sure he's got ideas. He thinks I'm like him."

"You're crazy," Detective Sammons said. "He could just as easily rape you and kill you, not to mention getting kids involved."

"That's why I'm here." She furrowed her eyebrows. "I didn't really think he would do this—didn't think it through, and now I'm in over my head. I need help."

"I'll say," Detective Sammons said, scratching his square chin. "But, you did the right thing comin' down here. Sorry I was grumpy earlier. I'll do what I can to keep Bobby outta this, but I can't make any promises."

"Thank you."

"Don't thank me now." He adjusted his gun holster. "I got half a mind to go find that monster and just put a bullet in his head, but that ain't goin' to help Bobby...or that little boy you mentioned. And I'm sure there are others."

"What should I do?" Ardee asked.

Detective Sammons stared across the busy parking lot. He was silent for several minutes, but then he winked over at Ardee.

"Tell ya what. I think you should go to Bible study this Friday," Detective Sammons said. He gave Ardee a once-over. "Go lookin' a bit butch, if you get my drift. You know what the sicko's plannin', don't ya?" ·

"I think I understand," Ardee said.

"With your face and figure, you might encourage him a bit, but whatever you do, we've got to protect those little boys. And, sorry, but I suspect they'll need to get some help. We're likely too late to the party."

"Bobby's all screwed up in the head. He's just confused ... I'm afraid for him," Ardee said. She leaned against a police cruiser and stared down at the blacktopped parking lot.

"Maybe I'll go pay the boy a visit," Detective Sammons said. "I've got your back. This is my world now, and I don't cotton to messin' with children."

"Don't do that. He'll know I squealed," Ardee said.

"Listen to me," Detective Sammons started.

"Don't. I don't want him to have to answer questions." She leaned in close to Detective Sammons. "He'll be humiliated."

"I've known him my whole life." He spit at the tree trunk again. "I've got a plan, and I won't be needin' to arrest anybody just yet. Just trust me. I won't fail Bobby twice."

"Are you sure?" Ardee whispered.

"I don't want to embarrass Bobby. Last thing I'd ever want to do," Detective Sammons said. He patted Ardee on the arm. "Besides, it's personal."

Chapter 21

"Hey there," Steven said after he opened the apartment door.

"Where's Bobby?" Ardee asked.

"Upstairs, asleep, I think," Steven answered with a yawn. "We were up late screwin' around. Cookout night. We cookout in rain, sleet or snow."

"What?" Ardee said, her eyes wide open. Her breathing was erratic.

"Why are you so nervous?"

"'Cause he didn't answer my calls." She barged inside and ran upstairs to Robert's bedroom.

"Hey, you're awful quick this mornin," Steven called after her. He almost dropped his half-full coffee cup.

Upstairs, at the end of a long corridor, Robert's bedroom door was shut. Ardee twisted the knob, but it was locked. Then she pounded on the door with her fists.

"Bobby," Ardee said. She pounded on the door. "Bobby, wake up."

No answer back from inside the bedroom. Ardee put her ear to the door, but it was just deathly quiet from inside the bedroom. She ran downstairs.

"What're you doin'?" Steven said.

"Give me a knife. Need to pop open his door." She yanked back the kitchen cabinet drawers. "It's locked."

"Calm down. He's just regroupin'." Steven sipped his coffee. He sniffled. "He probably thought I'd pull a Naked Man stunt on him, but I was too drunk to play Naked Man. Besides, Ernie called me a homo. I ain't a homo."

"Steven, I'm not kidding, you hear me?" Ardee said. She stared through Steven. "He's not right...he's fragile."

Steven hopped up and snagged a steak knife from a butcher block above the refrigerator.

"I'll knock it down if I have to," he said. He leaped up the stairs, skipping every other tread. Ardee scampered close behind.

"Hey, Oob?" Steven said. But there was no answer from inside. "Oobie? I'm comin' in ..." He gripped and twisted the knob, but it was still locked. He tugged at the door and stuck the tip end of the knife into the keyhole.

"Bobby," Ardee said. She pounded on the door while Steven worked.

"Screw this," Steve said, nudging Ardee behind him. He sized up the door, and then kicked his size-fifteen foot just above the doorknob, shattering the wooden door jam.

Inside the bedroom, the sole window cast a blue-grey haze across the end of Robert's double bed. One of his feet, covered with one of Dr. Richie's multi-colored socks, dangled outside the cotton bed sheets. Steven flicked on the bedroom lamp and shoved Robert's shoulder.

"Oobie, wake up," Steven said. Robert did not respond. "Oobie, wake up. Damn, Oob, you're all wet."

Ardee stood frozen at the end of the bed. After a few minutes, Robert stirred.

"Wha …" Robert looked up at them.

"What's on your hands?" Ardee asked, she sucked in a deep breath.

Robert's brown hair was matted with moisture along his forehead and down the sides of his face. He wobbled back up, stared over at Steven, and then up at Ardee.

"You wearin' mittens?" Steven said.

Robert tore the colorful socks from his hands.

"I'm all right," Robert said. He glanced up at Ardee. "I'm just hung over a bit."

"A bit?" Steven shook his head. "You don't remember?"

"I guess not." He stared groggily down at the cotton bed sheets.

"You were shakin' your head last night like you had a bumblebee inside your brain," Steven said. He smirked. "Ernie and me laughed our butts off watching you. Then you gave us the finger and disappeared. Like always…"

"Bobby, why?" Ardee whispered. "Just stop drinking."

"'Cause Dr. Richie told me to," Robert said.

"What on earth?" Steven said. He shook his head and folded his arms across his chest. He shoved Robert. "That's double gay."

"Shut up," Ardee said.

"I ain't a homo," Robert said, scowling over at Steven. "Dr. Richie told me to, if I was feeling bad. Wear these socks... I don't know why I put them on my hands. I don't remember."

"You scared me," Ardee said. "Just answer your phone next time. You can hang up, but I just wanted to make sure you were all right. That's all."

Steven sat back and smirked. "Oobie, I think she digs your chili." He hopped up and strolled toward the door. He smirked over at Ardee. "Hang in there. I'll give you two some space."

"You just can't help yourself, can you?" Ardee said.

"Naw, I'm just joshin' with ya. I'm harmless," Steven said. He turned at the doorway. "Guess I'll need to fix this mess. Maybe I should be a fireman."

"It's my fault. I won't lock the door anymore," Robert said. He rolled up onto his left elbow.

"Okay, then. And I'll promise not to go all Naked Man on ya," Steven said as he flicked wood splinters from the door jam. He winked at Robert and then bounced back down stairs.

Ardee pulled out Robert's desk chair and sat near the bedroom window. "Talk to me."

"I'm sorry," Robert said.

"Stop apologizing. Just talk; tell me…tell me everything."

Robert sighed and pulled his knees to his chest.

"I swear, I was minding my own business," Robert said. He shook his head. "Then, from nowhere, I got these images popping up in my mind from when I was a boy, when I took you to a movie, and…and other stuff. My heart started pounding. I don't know, I just started sweating, like I ran a mile or two. It's embarrassing…humiliating. What am I supposed to do? And now, Dr. Richie tells me I have this gene in my brain, telling me to kill myself."

"I don't know," Ardee whispered. "I don't know what to say."

"I'm sorry," Robert said. He blew a harsh breath through his lips. "Sorry, you came across the likes of me."

"Shut up," Ardee said.

"Don't tell me to shut up," Robert said, his expression growing hard. He squinted at Ardee until his eyes were almost shut. "I've been an adult most of my life, it's true, and you deserve a better friend. The best thing you can do is forget I even existed… Just leave and forget about me. It's not your fault; it's not your fight."

"I do what I want," Ardee said.

"I know, I know you want to be tough and go all FBI agent, but you came back into my life by accident," Robert said. "I'm not looking for sympathy. I'm screwed up, and it's going to take me time to get my life in order. Thank you for trying… Thank you for helping me."

"Why do you push people away?" Ardee said.

"It's not fair to them—not fair to you." Robert gazed at Ardee. "I think you're the prettiest girl I ever saw; I've not changed my opinion. But you need to live your life, go be an FBI agent, go find a good man with a normal childhood, who loves you more than life itself and have a bunch of pretty kids, and... Just do me this favor? You go live a happy life. I'll be all right."

"No, you won't." She shook her forefinger at Robert. "You dumbass, I like you. I care about you, and I know there's another side to you—a kind, funny, thoughtful man."

"What're you sayin'?" Robert asked. He shrugged.

"I don't care about your screwed up family." She leaned forward, her elbows on her knees. "I don't know; my instincts tell me to hang tough with you. I'm not a quitter, and I don't think you are either."

"Are you crazy? What could you possibly see in me?"

Ardee slipped off her coat and shut the broken door.

"Move over; you need a hug," Ardee said. She kicked off her tennis shoes.

"You're crazy," Robert said, but he did as she asked.

"Hush," Ardee said. She snuggled in behind Robert. "Now, try to rest. I'm right here, and I'm not going anywhere."

Ardee kissed Robert's forehead and hugged him close.

"I don't know what to say," Robert whispered. "Feel like a little boy."

"Shh... I do dig your chili," Ardee whispered.

Chapter 22

Thursday evening came with a crisp, clean, dark blue sky, as desolate darkness approached.

"Yes, sir?" Steven said after answering a knock at the door.

"Bobby, or rather, Robert Scott live here?" Detective Sammons stood at the door, wearing a dark blue jacket. He stepped back, turning until his shoulders perpendicular to the door.

"Yeah, I'll go get 'im," Steven said.

After a minute, Robert peeked out the doorway, wearing a t-shirt and blue jeans.

"Yes?" Robert asked. He stared at Detective Sammons.

"Remember my face?" Detective Sammons asked. He grinned, his gaze certain from practice—dagger like.

Robert studied his face and shook his head. "No, I'm sorry." He noticed Detective Sammons's holstered weapon. "Something happen? Ardee all right?"

"Yeah... Something happened a long time ago," Detective Sammons said. "It was the day I chipped my front teeth."

Robert pursed his mouth and furrowed his eyebrows. He glanced up into the naked, leafless oak tree searching for the answer.

"Breck?" Robert asked. He chuckled and opened the front door all the way. "I'll be."

"Yep. Been a long time," Detective Sammons said with a smile. "I'm a police detective now, believe it or not. I'm the youngest detective on the force."

"Wow, that's great." Robert reached out and rapidly shook Detective Sammons muscled hand. "You're big as a house. Wow, look at you... Hey, come on in. Sorry."

Detective Sammons strode inside the modest apartment and glanced around at the college boys' byzantine existence.

"Bet ya'll got some beer," Detective Sammons said with a chuckle.

"Heck, yeah. Can I get you one?" Steven said.

"Ah, another time. I'm sorry, this isn't a social call," Detective Sammons said. He twisted his shoulders and rubbed his neck before looking Robert in the eye. "Bobby, I think you should have a seat."

Robert sat down at the kitchen table and the wooden chair creaked at the glued joints. "What's this about?"

"I met...ah...your friend, Ardee. Pretty girl," Detective Sammons said. He glanced over at Steven, who was staring down at Robert, and nodded. "This might get real personal real quick. You mind him hearin' this?"

Robert clenched his jaw and sucked in as much oxygen as his lungs would hold. "Naw, I guess he's bound to eventually find out," Robert said. He stared down at his bare feet.

"What's this about?" Steven asked, leaning back against the kitchen counter.

Robert held up his hand to Detective Sammons. "Wait, give me a second." He glided his moist palms across the cold, slick kitchen tabletop, gathering his thoughts. "What do you want to know?"

Detective Sammons grunted to clear his throat. "When we were at summer camp, after Kimmi nailed me with a rock," Detective Sammons said. He grimaced and pointed at his teeth. "What'd that SOB do to you?"

"What the…" Steven said. He stared down at Robert. A wrinkle emerged from his between his eyebrows and jagged across his forehead.

Robert stared down at the kitchen floor. "Well, guess, I'm might as well." He shrugged. "First time, he got me and locked me in a closet. I guess that's why I'm still claustrophobic."

"Bobby, just say it. I'm not here to judge you," Detective Sammons said. He scowled.

"What do you mean by locked you in closet?" Steven asked.

"I wasn't even ten, but I was flirting with Kimmi. She threw a rock and hit Breck, better known at Detective Sammons," Robert said. He blushed and scratched the top of his head. "I got in trouble, and…uh, I got attacked."

Steven sprang forward. "Hey, who?"

"Ah, breathe," Detective Sammons said to Steven. He stared down at Robert. "Bobby, just breathe and tell me. I have a very important reason. I need to know whatever you can remember, because a little boy's life is on the line."

"Damn," Robert said.

"No kiddin'?" Steven asked. He stared up at the ceiling. "This why Ardee's been after you?"

"Yeah," Robert said.

"No kiddin'," Detective Sammons said over at Steven.

"Flipping monster's still at it?" Robert asked.

"Yep," Detective Sammons said.

"Diabolus, he's a preacher, or at least he acts like one," Robert said. His face went blank, his eyes unemotional. "Sorry…sorry you have to hear this."

"I've likely heard worse, but it's usually not quite this personal," Detective Sammons said. "If memory serves, he was our elementary school principal."

"Yeah, and junior high, but I'll get to that. Well, after you left with Mr. Gibson, he took me inside the cabin, locked me in a closet, and chased all the other kids to dinner. He came back about an hour later, pulled my pants down, and spanked me," Robert said. His ears burned with embarrassment, and he concentrated on just breathing.

"Oobie, what the hell?" Steven asked.

"Well, he pinned me up against one of the wooden posts that supported those bunk beds, ground into me and, ah, made me...you know," Robert said. He puffed out causing his cheeks to balloon. "First time I ever, well...you know. This is humiliating."

Silence descended within the three men, each sensed the specter of childhood death. Detective Sammons opened the sliding glass door and a whoosh of cold air attacked the tension.

"Need to get some air," he said, turning back to Robert and Steven.

"Damn, Oob," Steven whispered.

"Well, I'm not done," Robert said. He shrugged.

"What else?" Detective Sammons said. He supported his back against the sliding door jamb, half of him inside.

"Got me again at school. That's when he snapped a bunch pictures of me and this other kid, Willis." Robert looked at Detective Sammons. "You remember Willis?"

Detective Sammons scratched his square chin.

"Yeah, fat kid. You know 'bout him don't ya?" Detective Sammons asked, his voice a low growl.

"Sorry, I lost track of him," Robert said, shaking his head slowly.

"Didn't you tell on him?" Steven asked.

"Yeah, but my parents didn't believe me." Robert gave a hopeless shrug. "They acted like I was the bad guy. He was a preacher at church—you know, mind the adults, they know best. I just kept quiet. I didn't tell my sister or anybody."

"I'm sorry Bobby, but I had a case about a year ago," Detective Sammons said. "It was Willis."

"He into drugs or something?" Robert asked.

"Nope. I'm sorry to tell you this, but Willis committed suicide," Detective Sammons said. "His mother found him out in their pasture. She said he loved being near the horses. He ambled out from the barn he worked at and shot himself one early morning as the sun came up."

"Why?" Steven said.

"Left his mom a note. Told her he couldn't live with the shame, the memories," Detective Sammons said. He shrugged. "I didn't push for answers from his mom—saw no point in it, but now it all makes sense."

Robert sprang up and slid between Detective Sammons and the sliding glass door to the patio, where he collapsed and vomited. His whole body moved with each breath he took.

"Bobby, don't say another word," Detective Sammons said. Dropping down on one knee, he patted Robert on the back.

"Sorry, Oob," Steven said.

Robert screamed for his childhood. He spit at the lawn. He dry heaved all the remorse inside his lungs. "All I want is to be normal, I'm tired of this. This sucks."

"All right, let me get this over," Detective Sammons said.

Steven handed Robert a cotton towel and then set a kitchen chair next to him. Robert sat back on his legs, twisted, and stared up at Detective Sammons.

"What's Ardee done?" Robert asked, gulping for air.

"She's trying to defend you," Detective Sammons said.

"That feisty little thing sure digs Oob," Steven said with a grin.

"Now, I think she's the one who's going to need defending, and to be honest, this has gotten real personal with me," Detective

Sammons said. He shrugged and adjusted his gun holster. "And those kids, someone needs to help them."

Chapter 23

Ardee felt her stomach acid bite at her throat. She thought she might vomit as her boots crushed the thin layer of frost blanketing the concrete sidewalk. A few random cars passed nearby, their yellow headlamps slightly blinding, revealing the sparkling moisture sliding down the storm drain.

She strolled near Mr. Diabolus's street corner. The street was lined by a collection of silent, swaying oak trees, naked of their leaves. It was a normal, quiet, ho-hum, everyday middle America street where all the homes appeared to match the other. They all had white aluminum siding, each with a single story and a single car garage at the end of a short driveway. But then there was a house, at Mr. Diabolus's address, where most thought nothing significant ever happened.

Down at the far end of the dark street, Detective Sammons sat inside his unmarked four-door sedan. As was the plan, he flicked his headlamps twice.

Ardee nodded and breathed in a long drag of cold air, chilled by the winter breeze and fear. She released a vaporous fog. But then, in her mind's eye, she saw Bobby's face. She saw his sad eyes and the same sad eyes of the church boys, David and Charlie. She clenched her jaw, curled her hands into fists, and marched toward the front door. Her gloved hand shook as she knocked.

"What did you do to your hair?" Mr. Diabolus asked. He stood within the doorway, wearing a simple long-sleeved cotton dress shirt and dark slacks. He pushed back the creaky metal storm door. Behind him, from within the modest home, were the sounds of young boys teasing each other.

"Oh, I thought it might do better?" Ardee said. "You know.. Pictures…" She combed back her hair, now short and brown, and unbuttoned her coat.

"Yes, you're a lovely flower. You'll be a great model," Mr. Diabolus said. He ogled Ardee, from her brown leather-riding boots, past her Glen plaid skirt cut above her knees, and up to her striking face.

"Oh, yeah." Ardee's vision blurred as she walked inside on wobbly legs. The house became quiet and still, and two boys turned to stare at her. The tall one stood like a hungry, battle-tested soldier. The home smelled of body odor, dank age, and anticipation.

"I can tell you're excited. You're shaking," Mr. Diabolus said, gliding his puffy hands along her neck and shoulders as he helped her slip off her winter coat.

"Hi, Ardee," David said. He flinched away from Mr. Diabolus. "You can take me home now, but my mom's at work. We can play video games."

"Ardee doesn't want to take you home," Mr. Diabolus said and nudged David aside. "I'll have to talk with your mother. You've been bad, and you *will* pay a penalty."

"Sorry," David whispered. He hunched down but grappled onto Ardee's leg.

"You'll be okay," Ardee whispered. She reached down and squeezed his soft hand.

In the front living room, there was a semi-circle of three dining table chairs, and on the other side sat the master dining chair. Atop the coffee table laid a Bible and a nylon dog leash. Now she understood what Bobby said about his skin feeling as though acid had been dumped over his head. She glanced away from the ritualized setting as stomach acid stabbed up her throat. Her lungs demanded more oxygen.

The boys wore simple brown monks' robes, and they were barefoot. From the kitchen, she saw one more boy with blond hair come out of the bathroom, barefoot and in same monk's robe. She knew the face—Charlie, but she did not recognize the taller child, who was perhaps almost six feet tall and athletically built.

"Why the robes?" Ardee asked.

"Oh, it's my secret society," Mr. Diabolus said. He rubbed his chubby hand up toward her neck as he chuckled. "Reminds them they're here to serve me and God, like Old World monks living lives of service. Makes the photos seem more artsy, I think."

But the children's expressions told another story—a painful story, and even though they appeared like young boys, they were all adult-like behind their eyes. Ardee looked down and saw that David had sad eyes—eyes like Bobby's.

David carefully watched Mr. Diabolus. The other boys fidgeted as if they expected something to happen. The tallest boy, who had jet-black hair, smirked at her with greedy expectation, and his eyes glazed over, as if he were high on a drug. No, he seemed drunk—uninhibited.

The boys kept rubbing at their groins as if a snake had bitten them. They all leaned forward, bent at the knees. Charlie crinkled his face and breathed hard gusts of air.

"Won't we get caught?" Ardee asked.

She squeezed David's hand and clenched her jaw, staring at each pre-teenager, and wondering what the monster had done to them, how he had humiliated them, and how he had likely manipulated their parents.

"I'm a man of God," Mr. Diabolus whispered. He caressed Ardee's neck with his moist fingertips.

"So? I just want to be careful," Ardee said with a gulp. "You know, no one will expect me to...well, you know."

"Oh, I love little boys, too," Mr. Diabolus said. He hooked his clammy hand further around her neck, and squeezed, ogling her yet again. "I love little boys, and they love me, but tonight, I'm going to enjoy taking pictures of your initiation. You'll make my art so much better. I'll red marker them as extra special."

"I don't understand," Ardee said. She almost screamed. She tried to back up, but Mr. Diabolus clasped her neck a bit harder and nudged her forward, deeper into the house.

"Societies have initiation rites; you know that," Mr. Diabolus said. He sighed. "You've changed your mind?"

"No. Ah...no, of course not," Ardee said. She twisted her shoulders.

"Good, I have a surprise for you," Mr. Diabolus said with a chuckle. From behind her, with his left hand still grasping her neck, he slithered his right arm around her waist. Into her right ear, he whispered, "The tallest boy, he's rather...shall I say, gifted. Not too bright, you know. A boy in a man's body."

Ardee felt a rush of blind rage and squeezed David's hand.

"Oh." He yanked his hand away.

"Sorry, sorry." Ardee winked at him.

Mr. Diabolus squeezed her neck and pulled her close to his fat belly.

"Yes, I understand," Ardee said.

"No more names," Mr. Diabolus said. "I own them."

He released his grip, waltzed away to shut the front door. He flicked the front deadbolt shut.

"All right, what's next?" Ardee whispered. She looked hesitantly down at David.

*

After he saw, the house blinds pulled down, Detective Sammons growled and tapped at the steering wheel. "I don't like this."

"Why?" Robert said. In the front bench seat, he sat next to Detective Sammons. Ernie and Steven were in the back of the cruiser.

"Instinct," Detective Sammons said. "This might go downhill real fast, so just give me a head start, and then come in behind me. Just let me do my job."

*

"But you're sure?" Ardee said.

A tiny wireless surveillance earpiece, similar to a hearing aid, exposed their conversation to Detective Sammons.

She rubbed her neck and slightly backed away from the master dining chair, staring down at the coffee table, where the Bible and a dog collar still laid. The dog collar was an immediate concern. The fact that a Bible was in the room made her want to scream. She glanced at the tall man-child, thinking he had probably been sexually abused to the extreme, because he stared at her as if he had been stallion-teased and prepared to breed, the way they did at the local horse farms.

"Their parents think we're just into a Bible study," Mr. Diabolus said, fidgeting with his silver belt buckle. He shifted behind her, grasped her neck again, and whispered in her ear. "I separated them from the rest, identified the ones with naïve parents. I picked that big one for you off my Internet site—he's only twelve—big for his age. His mom thinks I'm trying to help him get off booze— mentor him, you know."

"He *is* a big boy," Ardee said. She twisted her shoulders to create some space from the overheated Mr. Diabolus and averted her gaze from the aroused man-child by closing her eyes and taking a deep breath.

"Yeah, sorry. I had to have him first," Mr. Diabolus grunted. "He's a very aggressive boy. I just gave him a few pops of bourbon, and then did whatever I wanted. I think his old man got him before me, so I'm not sure I own his soul. But he'll model— do anything you want as long as you supply him with booze."

Ardee felt her stomach clench. She wanted to scream. She wanted to kick the predator in the groin. But, she knew she needed to be patient. She had to get evidence. She knew the cavalry was not far away.

"Yeah?" Ardee asked. She held her breath.

"I promise I'll try to make him slow down as I take the photos, or they might be blurred." His breathing was erratic. "Not sure you'll be able to walk after, but that's what you want, right?"

Ardee felt frozen in space, her feet cold.

"Yeah, yeah, but what about Charlie...and David?" Ardee glanced at the man-child. He needed serious help. He was not even thirteen, and yet he was drinking and was already sexually traumatized.

"I got them into trouble. The parents only listen to me now since, of course, I'm a man of God. None of them will ever talk." Mr. Diabolus paused and hummed a church song. "After you go through initiation, I'll teach you how to manipulate them. It's easy."

Ardee closed her eyes. She scowled. She tried to remain calm and resolute. *Focus on the result*, she thought.

"Okay, sounds...great," Ardee said. She gapped open her mouth to breathe.

"You're still shaking. Maybe you could use a pop of bourbon? It'll calm your nerves," Mr. Diabolus asked. He kept his grip around her neck, as if she was a life-sized Barbie doll. "Might help you get in the mood. Then, before you know it, you'll be naked— modeling for me and having fun before God."

All she had to do was flick a light from inside the house— a signal for Detective Sammons. But the blinds had been drawn down, though, and they appeared thicker than normal, so very little light could be seen coming from the house. Just in case, Ardee wiggled her leg to make certain her handgun remained strapped to her calf.

A good backup plan, she thought. An old gun her father had given her for protection, a gun he had taught her how to clean and use.

She thought the sight of this insanity would almost do the trick—give them enough evidence to arrest the child predator and stop the madness. Detective Sammons had told her he would listen —told her to be patient and let the old fart talk, and not to eat or drink anything.

"I'm good," Ardee said.

"Little boys, this woman will be joining our secret group tonight," Mr. Diabolus said. He arrogantly waltzed Ardee toward the top of the circle of chairs. "Sit in your assigned seat."

"I thought you were different," David whispered.

Ardee gazed down at David. "I am."

She wanted to pull her handgun out and put a bullet into Mr. Diabolus's head.

Just breathe, she thought, *Focus*.

She needed to let him talk, to let Detective Sammons collect the evidence. Either she signaled, or he would bust down the door. She knew he was listening, but she had one last goal. She wanted to figure out where the monster hid the pictures of Bobby. Once she had the photos, Bobby would no longer exist within Mr. Diabolus's madness. Bobby would never have to answer questions.

"But..." David whispered.

"Little boy, do not disobey," Mr. Diabolus said. He nudged Ardee to the center. "Woman, you will kneel before me. You will no longer have a name. You will only talk when ask if you want to join us. Do you understand?"

"Yeah," Ardee whispered. She wondered how long to play out this insanity. Detective Sammons had assured her he was down the street. She had seen him blink his car headlights. She knew if she got into trouble, he would bust in the door. She steeled herself to keep up the act. Mr. Diabolus had taken all the bait. He was showing off for her, showing her how in control he was.

*

Detective Sammons sat inside the cruiser shaking his head. He double-checked the recording device and made sure his weapon loaded. "Frickin' monster... Just don't kill 'em, all right?"

"I don't know, Oob. I'd kick me some serious ass," Steven said.

"Yeah, that girl loves you," Ernie said. He shifted in the back seat.

"I know. Tell us when," Robert said. He clenched his jaw.

"Gettin' there fast. This guy has this all planned out," Detective Sammons said. "Just do me a favor and beat the hell out of him before I arrest him. I don't care if I get in trouble for it."

*

"You will do as told if you are to become part of my secret society." Mr. Diabolus said, pointing his forefinger at Ardee. "Do you understand? I want you to drink from this cup – my initiation cup."

"Yes," Ardee said. She glanced behind her at each of the three hooded boys. The man-child and Charlie were to her left, while David sat to her right. David and Charlie were still, as if not wanting to be noticed, but the man-child stared at her. He kept wetting his lips with his tongue, gulping, and fidgeting.

She took a microscopic sip.

Mr. Diabolus took the drink back and inspected the cup and smirked at Ardee. "I said take a drink, not a sip. You in, or not?"

"Yeah, yeah," Ardee said. Now she had no choice. She prayed Detective Sammons was on the way. She shut her eyes.

"Sorry, my bedrooms are not fit for modeling work— not big enough. My art needs space." Mr. Diabolus fidgeted with his silver belt buckle again. "Will you submit to me as your master? While you're here, I'm in charge."

"Yeah," Ardee said.

She gulped the juice down. It tasted like grape juice, but her throat stung, so she knew it was spiked with alcohol or something stronger. The clock started ticking in her mind. She thought it was time to stop and flick the light switch. But she didn't, curious what else he would say, even though the light switch was within easy reach. Her handgun was a few inches from her right fingertips. Before she could decide or act, she had to blink her eyes to focus. She shook her head as if to recapture a clear thought and realized that whatever was in the drink was working.

"I am now God's emissary for you. I will take your soul, and I will own it. As I take each photograph, your essence will be trapped inside. You will have to please me to get them back. Do you understand?"

"Yeah," Ardee whispered, her mouth dry. She thought about the light switch—maybe flip it before things got weirder.

My soul, essence trapped inside the photo? The man is insane.

But she had to keep blinking. Her eyes were unfocused like foggy binoculars, and her skin tingled.

"No, don't," David said. He gripped the bottom of the wooden chair. "Run ..."

"I'm okay." Ardee shook her head. "I think…"

Her face blushed crimson. Her breathing became even more rapid, and she gulped, glancing over at the light switch. She looked back at the man-child, who seemed prepared to pounce on her like an African lion hunting prey.

"Little boy, quiet," Mr. Diabolus said. He pointed at Ardee. "Woman, you were not authorized to speak. You should feel warm. Giddy?"

"Yeah," Ardee said. She shook her head, knowing the drink had been laced with something powerful. She knew she was in trouble, exposed, but she couldn't move, as if she was a blow-up plastic plaything doll.

"Good. You, boy, get my camera," Mr. Diabolus said.

A few moments later, Charlie brought back a sealed instamatic camera. He appeared terrified, confused. Mr. Diabolus tore open the packaging and pointed the instamatic camera at Ardee. He clicked the trigger and the flash sparked like a lightning bolt in her face. Then there was the whirr of the motor, the smell of chemicals, and an instamatic photo slid from the mouth of the camera.

Ardee snapped back, a memory of the flash floating within her blurred eyesight. She sensed what Bobby felt, as if a part of her essence, her humanity, had been stolen.

Mr. Diabolus got up and untucked her blouse. She didn't resist. Her hands dangled at her sides, and she wobbled. He dropped to one knee, between her and the light switch, and there was another instamatic flash as he took a photo of her from the side. Like a practiced cowboy, he looped the dog collar over her neck.

"I own you?" Mr. Diabolus said.

Ardee hesitated. She wondered if she should just shoot him, but she had lost her ability to grip. Her fingers were almost limp, and they trembled as she wobbled. She shook her head once more in an attempt to focus.

"I own you?" Mr. Diabolus asked. He grunted.

He nudged her with his knee before gliding his hand down her back, where he unclipped her skirt button and revealed the zipper.

"Ah, yeah," Ardee said. With her fingertips, she tried to grapple at the nylon dog collar.

"Boy, you stand next to the woman," Mr. Diabolus said. He strolled to the other side of Ardee, acting like a professional photographer.

"I don't want to," David said. He started to cry. "It hurts, I don't want to, it hurts. It won't go down. It won't stop." He glared at Ardee. "I thought you were different."

"It'll be … all right," Ardee said. She gently reached out for the little boy. She grasped at empty air.

Mr. Diabolus sprang over. Ardee glanced up just as he smacked her. She collapsed. He tackled her and dragged her by the hair as David screamed. The boy scampered to hide behind the master dining chair.

Ardee tried to fight the large man off, but he was well more than six feet tall and in excess of three hundred pounds. She knew a narcotic was also in her system. Before she could do anything, the man-child hugged her by the ankles. She tried to wiggle away, but they dragged her back, hog-tied her hands behind her, and cinched the dog leash harder. Mr. Diabolus ground his knee into the center of her back as he yanked her head back.

"Now, boy, like I showed you," Mr. Diabolus said.

The man-child yanked off her leather boots and began to rope her ankles together. The handgun dislodged. Charlie snatched it with his tiny hands and gazed at the barrel like it was a thick piece of chocolate cake and he was a starving child.

"You brought a gun," Charlie whispered. He slid his forefinger near the trigger.

"I own you," Mr. Diabolus said. He grabbled with her neck and held her face close to his. "Do you understand? You only speak when asked. And guns are bad."

The man-child snagged the handgun from Charlie and handed it to Mr. Diabolus. He checked the chamber and unloaded it before setting it on the coffee table with a thud.

"That was not wise," Mr. Diabolus said. He grunted. "You will now have to pay a penalty. I will have to treat you like a boy and not just as a model. Sorry, you disobeyed me. I own you, and it's penalty time."

Ardee stared over at the light switch. *Please hurry, Detective Sammons*, she thought.

"Leave her alone," David said. He ran at Mr. Diabolus like a football cornerback but bounced off, but he clawed at him. Mr. Diabolus backhanded the boy across his face.

· Charlie sat staring at the floor, shaking. The man-child rubbed his moist palms on Ardee's legs and glided his fingers up toward her knees. He had a crazed, rabid-dog stare in his eyes.

Mr. Diabolus flipped her face down like a freshly caught Maiden of the Sea. She wiggled and tried to scream, but Mr. Diabolus cinched the dog collar a bit tighter, making her cough and spit out mucous. Mr. Diabolus slithered on top of her and ground into her.

"Woman, I own you," Mr. Diabolus said. He breathed hard as he stuck his tongue into her ear. "Remember, you submitted to me – I own you now. If you don't please me, I'll turn you in to the police. I'm a reverend – a man of God. Who will they believe?"

The young boys sat shaking. David sobbed and hid his stinging, red face with his trembling hands.

"Leave her alone," David whimpered.

"See, woman, their parents think we're in a Bible study," Mr. Diabolus said, chuckling. "I'm training them to please me and God. I own them, too."

Ardee wiggled and huffed. Mucous dripped from her lips, and her eyes were glazed with a viscous fluid.

"Let…go," Ardee whispered. *Please come, Detective Sammons*, she thought.

"Silence woman. Guns are bad," Mr. Diabolus said. "You submitted to me, and now I own you. Never bring a gun to the meetings again. Now, if you calm down, I'll loosen the strap. You have modeling to do. You will allow the boys to disrobe you, and then you will lay here silently."

Ardee closed her eyes and tried to remain calm. She was certain Detective Sammons was coming.

In fact, he was, with his weapon drawn as he approached the house. Robert, Steven and Ernie stood in the street; their heavy breaths choo-choo puffed from their mouths—the steam of revenge vaporized from their bodies.

"Good, good. There now." Mr. Diabolus slithered his pudgy fingers through Ardee's hair as he got up off her. "Boy, prepare her like I showed you."

Ardee lay still, frozen in place, begging Detective Sammons to bust through the front door. She stared over at the light switch, but she couldn't move her hands. The gun her father had given her for protection was out of reach, the barrel watching her from the coffee table. She had not expected Mr. Diabolus, at his age, would be so swift to attack her. Then she realized he had carefully planned the attack, beginning with the drink laced with a powerful drug. This was not his first time; this was a practiced, orchestrated sexual attack and humiliation.

"Will you do as told?" Mr. Diabolus said as he pulled her onto her knees. She swayed, but he cupped her neck to steady her.

"Yeah," Ardee coughed out. She knew she was powerless.

Detective Sammons will be here soon, she thought.

She could sense her skirt zipper being twisted, tugged. Her feet were naked and cold, lashed together. She felt Mr. Diabolus pants unbuckle, and the polyester slithered past her waist and onto the floor.

Please, Detective Sammons, please. She closed her eyes.

"No." David said. He whimpered.

"See boys, women are here for your use; humiliate them." Mr. Diabolus grappled Ardee's shoulders. "I was humiliated as a boy, but they'll not get me twice. I was called to do this... to teach you, train you...mentor you."

Mr. Diabolus slipped Ardee onto her back and sat back in the master dining chair like a fool king. His rubber-soled shoes pushed against her shoulders as he held a tight grip to the dog leash wrapped around her neck.

She opened her eyes and foggily gazed up at the milky ceiling. She gulped for moisture, her mouth dry. She twisted her head but still could not see the front door. Her neck stung, and her head throbbed. Her legs were lashed together at the ankles.

"You, boy, I've got the woman prepared and under my control," Mr. Diabolus said. He lightly tugged at the leash.

"Woman you will be silent. Boy, hand me that camera I dropped. It's over there under the chair."

"No, leave her alone," David said. He crawled near Ardee and brushed back her hair, whimpering. "Leave her alone."

"You will do as told," Mr. Diabolus said.

The man-child handed over the instamatic camera.

Mr. Diabolus triggered the camera—*flash*. Ardee blinked involuntarily and felt how Bobby must have felt—isolated, humiliated, and half-naked.

"You, read the Bible verse." Mr. Diabolus pointed at Charlie. "I want good pictures of this one. I'm going to pray over her as I take her soul. Boy, prepare yourself. I want you to unbutton her shirt after this next photo."

"Yes, sir," Charlie whispered. He sniffled as he retrieved the Bible from next to Mr. Diabolus.

"Now, I will teach you how to submit," Mr. Diabolus said. He sucked in a deep breath, turned, and pulled at Ardee. "Remember, you asked to be initiated. I demand you be a good model. My art is too important, too valuable for God. You will do whatever I demand, because I own you."

"Leave her alone," David said. His tiny hands balled into fists.

He crawled over and grappled onto Ardee's waist.

"It's not your turn," Mr. Diabolus said. "He's first." He nodded over at the man-child. Ardee noticed the man-child had a hint of tears in his eyes. As he clenched his jaw, his lips smashed together.. Behind his eyes hid confusion, betrayal, and pain, but he stood up like a good soldier.

At that moment, Detective Sammons thunderously kicked the front door open. He pointed his handgun directly at Mr. Diabolus, who involuntarily dropped the dog leash and the camera.

Ardee huffed out a relieved thank you as David climbed on top of her, hugging over her head. Charlie screamed as he hunkered down beneath the dining chair.

"You sick SOB. Hands up!" Detective Sammons said. He kept the gun pointed at Mr. Diabolus. "Ardee?"

"I'm... not right," Ardee said. She turned her head to the side, she coughed and spat. "I think..."

"Leave her alone," David whimpered, sliding protectively between Ardee and Detective Sammons.

"Boys, stand over there in a nice single file line. Turn around to face the wall," Detective Sammons said. He slinked forward, keeping the gun pointed at Mr. Diabolus' fat head as he untied Ardee. "You, too, little man. I'm not goin' to hurt her."

"Promise me," David cried, tightly hugging Ardee. "Don't hurt her; I don't want her to hurt, too."

"Damn, you may be old, but you're quick," Detective Sammons said, glancing at the ritualized setting. He shook his head. He clenched his jaw. "Move along, little man. I know you're being brave. I'll not hurt her."

Ardee sprang up and wobbled to her feet, pulling her skirt up. With energy she didn't know she had, she screamed and scissor-kicked Mr. Diabolus square in the groin.

He moaned out all his breath as he flopped down to his knees. Ardee shifted back, took a deep breath, steadied herself, and then kicked him in the head. His nose splattered with blood.

"Slow down, honey," Detective Sammons said. He grabbed her hand and held her back. His weapon pointed down.

"I had to do that." She turned to Mr. Diabolus and spat, "You stinkin' rapist."

She adjusted her skirt, sat down, and tried to compose herself. After a few moments, as Detective Sammons inspected the house, she slipped her boots back on and hand combed her hair.

"I can't think straight, he drugged me, think I'm goin' to throw up."

David snuck over near Ardee and his fingertips touched her forearm. "I'm sorry."

"Thank you, David. You're a brave boy," Ardee said as she hugged him. "You're safe now."

Mr. Diabolus rolled up off the floor and he shook his head. He held his bloody face in his fat hands.

"I've got rights," Mr. Diabolus said. He nodded at Ardee. "She tricked me. She submitted to me for training."

Ardee sprang over and kicked Mr. Diabolus in the gut. He fell forward, moaning on the carpeted floor.

"Creep!" Her chest bellowed. Her forehead glistened with angry sweat.

"I said slow down," Detective Sammons said. He put his thick hand up and pulled Ardee back. He glanced at David and over at the other boys.

"Boys, Ardee's goin' to take you all to get your clothes back on," Detective Sammons said as Mr. Diabolus. He shoved the gun into Mr. Diabolus's vast gut. "Shut up... Just give me a reason."

Ardee straightened her blouse and then flicked the back of Mr. Diabolus's greasy head.

David hugged her around her waist, followed by Charlie. It was as if they had all snapped out of a trance. The man-child appeared stricken, he crawled into a dark corner of the kitchen.

"I knew you would save me," David said.

"Damn..." Detective Sammons looked at the man-child hidden within a dark shadow.

Ardee moved toward the older boy and gently touched his foot.

"I'm not going to hurt you."

In the kitchen corner, he yanked his feet back. He hugged his knees, pushing his shoulders into the wall. He stared down at the cold linoleum floor

"I'm going to die," he whispered, moaning for his childhood.

"No, you're safe now." Ardee blinked back her tears.

"I'm going to die... Are you going to kill me?" He twisted and covered his face with his hands. "I've been bad... I get beaten when I'm bad."

David and Charlie poked and prodded at the man-child, pulling him out of the darkness, and into the light.

"It's okay; hold my hand." Ardee's hand was steady, certain, confident. "Hold my hand. You're safe with me...and David and Charlie. We're not going to hit you."

"I'm scared," he said. His shaking hand reached out for Ardee. "I'm scared... I would have hurt you."

"Come on; let's get you back to your parents," Ardee said. She carefully, gently guided them out of the kitchen and down a narrow hallway. As she expected, the first bedroom had their clothes strewn about. She stared down at David who tightly held her hand. "Did he take pictures of you too?"

"He took pictures of all of us," the man-child whispered. "He made me drink stuff... He did things to me."

"Said he would show everybody if we misbehaved," Charlie said. He shook his head and shrugged. "No one would listen."

"He hides them in his bedroom," David said. He pointed toward the next-door bedroom. "Can I go home?"

"Yes," Ardee said. She backed out of the room. "I'll be out here while you change clothes. You're safe with me." Ardee rubbed her neck and glanced down the narrow, dark hallway at the master bedroom door.

*

"I guess I'm about your size. I really hope you resist," Detective Sammons said, eyeing Mr. Diabolus before holstering his weapon.

"Son, I'm a reverend. Release me. I was doing the Lord's work. I'm called to save souls," Mr. Diabolus said. His face and lips bled, and his left eye was swollen.

"Sure you are." Detective Sammons yanked Mr. Diabolus up by the shirt collar and navigated him onto the master kitchen chair, where he handcuffed both his arms to the chair's arm rests.

"That woman is a whore," Mr. Diabolus said. He spat. "She intended to shoot us. Guns are forbidden. I think she was going to rob me."

"Careful. Don't go shootin' your mouth off," Detective Sammons said. He shook his head and waved his forefinger back and forth.

"I'm a man of God, and I have rights," Mr. Diabolus said. He grunted.

"Yeah, most of the time that's true." Detective Sammons unclipped his badge. "See here? I may lose this tonight. I worked hard to earn this, but right now, I'm not a detective. I'm goin' to walk out that door... I'm goin' to take those kids out of here, and I'll be gone for about an hour or so...just depends. Goin' to talk with them, and then I'll call for backup. I'm not sure if you'll be living or dead by that point, but it's not goin' to be up to me."

"Or what?" Mr. Diabolus spat at Detective Sammons.

"Man, oh man, you are not smart." Detective Sammons leaned back and almost tripped over a dining chair. He wiped the frothy saliva from his jacket. "And you are a seriously sick person."

Mr. Diabolus grunted. "Whore needs training; she was asking for it. And I was *mentoring* the boys. I own them."

"You don't own crap." Detective Sammons rubbed his forehead and smoothed his blond flat top. He looked around at the modest home's sparse furnishings and stared down at Ardee's handgun resting on the nearby coffee table before smirking. "Been at this awhile? Had this all planned out."

"I'm a man of God. I've been called to minister, to train children," Mr. Diabolus said. He leaned his head back, he sniffled.

"So, let my small brain understand. Molesting little boys, and if I figure right, humiliating a tied up woman... That's ministering?" Detective Sammons asked. He gripped the handle of his weapon.

"She submitted to me. I asked first, because she was being initiated," Mr. Diabolus said. He snarled. "I was going to teach the boys how to treat a whore. The pictures are just visual aids; that's all."

"I see," Detective Sammons said. He grunted, as Ardee guided the boys out toward the front door. She had a deadly stare locked onto Mr. Diabolus. "Okay, I'll be back. I'll not touch you or anything, like that handgun. Don't want to mess with evidence and all." He turned to leave. He smirked certain Ardee's gun a useless antique. "Oh, and by the way, I brought with me an old friend of yours."

Ardee stepped back from the front door. "Bobby?" she whispered. A solitary tear sparkled in her eye like a translucent white diamond. She shook her head and stared at the carpet. "I didn't... I don't want to be an FBI agent."

"He could've killed you," Robert said, hugging her.

"I had to get him. He hurt you," Ardee said. A few stubborn tears dripped down her bruised cheeks.

"I love you," Robert said, as he held her tight.

"I love you, too," Ardee whispered.

"You're safe now," he murmured.

"I know where he hides the pictures," Ardee whispered after a moment.

"I told her," David said, grinning from below.

"All right, we'll go find 'me' together," Robert said. He looked over at Detective Sammons. "But I have something else to do first."

Then Steven and Ernie entered the house. They hugged Ardee and stood next to her.

"Oob, that the *sumbitch*?" Steven asked.

Ernie just scowled over at Mr. Diabolus.

"Yep." He glanced back at them.

"Well, I see the gang's all here." Detective Sammons said. He addressed Mr. Diabolus and pointed at Robert. "Remember him?"

"No," Mr. Diabolus said, smirking. "Well…yeah. Clearly he has come to save me, since I own him."

"You're a kook, and yes, this is a grown up Bobby Scott," Detective Sammons said. He marched toward the front door. "And he brought with him a few friends, just to show them what a maggot looks like. You remember, right? He's the boy you raped at summer camp, and then you got him again at school. Figured you got away with it, didn't ya?"

"I'm called." Mr. Diabolus smirked. "Oob, let's beat the hell out of him," Ernie said.

"Yeah," Steven said. He punched his fist into his other palm.

Robert kissed Ardee on the cheek and glanced down at David.

"This is my friend, David," Ardee said. The little boy hugged Ardee as he hid behind her.

"Hi, David," Robert said.

"Hi," David said, hiding his face in Ardee's side. He whispered. "Ardee's my friend."

"She's my friend, too," Robert said.

"Oob, want us to hold him down?" Ernie asked. He slipped off his jacket. He dropped it on the floor.

"Yeah, just say the word," Steven said.

"All right, but don't kill 'em," Detective Sammons said, turning toward the door. "I can stall for maybe an hour, but then I have to let justice take its course. I might get into trouble for that, but I don't care right now."

Robert glanced toward Mr. Diabolus and then turned to gaze back over to his friends.

"Well, just do me this one favor. Get out of here," Robert said. He clenched his fists and glared over at Mr. Diabolus. "Just give me some space. This is my fight."

Chapter 24

"Look me in eye," Robert said, staring through Mr. Diabolus.

"Say you're sorry, and I'll not beat you like a dog."

Mr. Diabolus gazed up at Robert with a blank, unemotional expression, suffused with the fragrance of depravity, of innocence stolen, and hints of self-satisfaction.

"Remember my face?" Robert asked. He pointed at his face with his forefinger.

Mr. Diabolus grunted. "I own you." He leaned back into the dining table chair and scowled down, twisting his cuffed wrists.

"Why? Why did you molest me? Just tell me you're sorry; that's all you have to do," Robert asked.

"You're weak. Look at yourself. I own you, and I always will."

"You don't own me," Robert said.

"I enjoyed you. I remember vividly. The day I took you, I got in a rush, forgot to control myself. I could have used you for so much longer... I remember watching you cry in the shower – little Robby." He wet his lips.

"You're not ashamed? I was little boy." Robert's eyes glazed with painful moisture memories.

"You're so weak...so pathetic." Mr. Diabolus grinned and gazed up at the textured ceiling. "Cry, cry, cry, wimpy boy... I bet you're gay."

"Why are you so happy?" Robert asked.

"I own you. I still have the pictures, so I have your soul. You were so photogenic, I should have gone after just you and not that fatty, but I was just young, horny, inexperienced."

"You son of bitch," Robert said. He shook his head.

"Hey, I'm a reverend. Watch the language, boy," Mr. Diabolus said.

"And you were going to abuse my friend tonight," Robert said.

"She's a whore."

Robert screamed as he punched Mr. Diabolus square in the face. He snarled like an enraged Bobcat, and then he noticed the handgun. He picked it up and pointed it between Mr. Diabolus's crusty, grey eyebrows.

"I don't care if they arrest me," Robert whispered. His grip was tight, inexperienced, and the gun wavered in his hand as if it were a drunk barrel—unfocused on a target. "You're *sick*, have you no shame?"

"Shame? I'm called to train, to mentor," Mr. Diabolus said. He grunted. He glanced down at Robert's shoes. "You're shaking. You'll not shoot me. And you're wearing girly socks? You must be gay."

"I have to do this. I have to kill you. You have to be stopped," Robert said. He sucked in and out for oxygen.

"Oh now, thou shalt not kill," Mr. Diabolus said. He smirked. "Turn the other cheek, and I'll be able to save you...even though you're old now."

"You almost ruined my life," Robert said. He shook his head. He wiped his hand across his forehead.

Mr. Diabolus sensed that he needed to choose just the right tone, the exact words, with the practiced precision from a charismatic master manipulator. "Now child, you've been to Bible study. I'm proud of you. Don't you remember reading, 'Vengeance is mine sayeth the Lord'?"

Robert shrugged. "I know vengeance is the Lord's, but…you have to be stopped. You have been right under everyone's nose for decades."

Mr. Diabolus wiggled in the chair. "I'm not afraid. I'm old," he said, and then hummed a church song. "God loves me … God loves all the little children. I'm simply a child of God."

"One moment… Hold that thought," Robert said. He stepped over and dragged back a chair to sit in front of Mr. Diabolus before spinning the gun's chamber. Mr. Diabolus intently watched the chamber spin like a circus wheel and noticed it had one bullet. It looked like the sloped top of a nuclear warhead in a silo in a Nebraska cornfield.

"God loves you, and so do I," Mr. Diabolus said.

"Okay, tell me about this God. I want to enjoy this—how your perverted brain thinks God loves you?"

Mr. Diabolus sniffed at Robert like a French pig searching for truffles in a lush forest. "I'm a reverend, you see. I've studied the Bible, Robby."

"Really? So taking pornographic pictures of children whose parents trusted them to your care seems normal?" Robert asked. "Sexualizing innocent children before their bodies are ready, that seems normal? What God would want?"

Mr. Diabolus grunted. "I'm capturing their essence. I was told to; it came to me in a dream. I've been called, I'm telling you." He closed his eyelids and wet his lips. "My mission in life is to capture your essence for safe keeping… I simply baptized you, Robby."

Robert pointed the gun barrel up. "To the unaware, you might seem quirky, a bit weird, but sane." He scrunched his lips. "But you are criminally insane. You sexually abused me and others, and each of us was scarred for the rest of our life. And you think God has sent you out as the crusading happy-horseshit missionary, snapping photos of kids and then abusing them for your own sick pleasure. *That* seems okay to you?"

"You simply cannot know the mind of God," Mr. Diabolus said. "I'm a reverend, cleansed in the spirit. I've been *called* by God."

"Thank you," Robert said. He clenched his jaw, his eyes a deathlike stare.

"Oh, you're most welcome," Mr. Diabolus said. "Untie me, and I can mentor you back to God."

"No, you don't understand." Robert shrugged. "You've given me, with your own words, all the motivation I need to kill you...tonight. This is for Willis."

Mr. Diabolus stuttered. "Now, that would be a mistake, Robby. Thou shalt not kill, especially not a man of God."

"Don't you *dare* call me Robby," Robert said. He flipped open the gun chamber and grappled for another bullet within his fingertips, then he held the barrel close to Mr. Diabolus' face.

"Say you're sorry. You almost killed me," Robert said.

"I've killed no one," Mr. Diabolus said. He smirked. "I just captured your essence. God loves me. I'm a mentor."

"Molesting a child is one step from murder, but you might as well have pulled the trigger. Humiliation. I can't cry about it... I'm numb right now," Robert said. He shifted forward. "But, I owe it to you to see, up close, the bullet that I'm going to put back in this chamber. I do not care when the gun goes *bang*. I'm numb to it. I wonder how it will feel for you, to be surprised when the gun goes off and the bullet smashes into your brain. Will you know you're dead? Will you be shocked for a nanosecond? Will you hang on for a moment, twitching and flailing in front of me? I wish you could tell me, but sorry, you will be dead... *Bang!* Just like that. And you'll never touch another child. You'll never ruin another life."

Mr. Diabolus snarled at Robert. "I'm not afraid."

"Yes, you are. I can see in your face. You're an old, insane, pathetic subhuman. But you don't want to die. You think you'll never die. And I am taking great pleasure having the power over you—the power to kill you," Robert said.

He slid the bullet into the gun, spun the chamber with his fingers, and snapped it into place. He shoved the cold barrel between Mr. Diabolus' eyes. "*I* own *you*... Goodbye."

Robert calmly pulled the hammer back with his thumb and squeezed the trigger. *Snap!*

Mr. Diabolus screamed and shook, his eyes wide, expecting an instamatic flash of death. He twisted at his cuffed wrists.

"Oh, I thought you weren't afraid? Guess it might be in the next chamber. Hmm, darn it. I have just one in there, or are there two? But that's not being fair to you. It should be a surprise," Robert spun the chamber again, and it snapped into place. "Goodbye."

He calmly pulled the hammer back with his thumb and squeezed the trigger. *Snap!*

"Please, please, don't kill me! I'll do whatever you want," Mr. Diabolus said. He whimpered. He jerked at the handcuffs, pushing away from Robert. The chair teetered backwards, and Mr. Diabolus hit the carpet with a massive thud, cracking the wooden chairs back support.

Robert spun the chamber and sprang forward, standing over Mr. Diabolus. He scraped his tennis shoe across Mr. Diabolus's sweating face and pointed the gun barrel down, in between Mr. Diabolus's eyes.

"I don't want anything. Now, I just want you to die," Robert said. He calmly pulled the hammer back and squeezed the trigger. *Snap!*

Mr. Diabolus screamed. He trembled. He started to cry, tears streaming down his face. His face contorted, making him look like a terrified, humiliated, injured little boy.

Robert dropped the gun onto the coffee table, but he changed his mind and picked it back up. He glanced over at the modest kitchen.

"Don't go moving around," he said. "It only will get worse for you." He opened the front door and found the boy, David. "Show me. Take me to the hiding place."

David gazed up at Ardee as he held her hand.

"You sure?" Ardee said.

"Yeah."

"I don't know... It might bring back bad memories," Ardee said.

"I need to make a point. He doesn't seem to care," Robert said.

Detective Sammons turned his back, a halo of streetlight over him as he walked toward the wet street.

Robert looked at Ernie and Steven. "I need you two to pull his carcass upright and scare him while I go find the pictures of me and Willis. I know what I have to do now."

"Anything, Oob," Steven said. Ernie just snarled and grunted.

Chapter 25

As she stepped inside the master bedroom, Ardee glanced at Bobby. She could see his sad eyes and sensed why he thought he'd had an out-of-body experience. The sensation of a Black Death evil permeated the vanilla-painted bedroom walls, and she reached out to hold his hand.

Each wall had religious paintings—such as an old-fashioned print of a tanned, European Jesus with a wooden cross—nailed to the wall underneath. The soffit of recessed lighting created a halo effect over the Son of God's unlikely likeness.

A double bed centered the room—made in the military style, and Ardee imagined she could have bounced a quarter off the baby blue cotton blanket. The pillows were fluffed in a fancy hotel style.

"Show me…" Robert said.

"Up there." David pointed at the bedroom closet. He scampered forward and shoved open the wooden accordion-folded doors. "Up, there …"

Ardee yanked the light bulb chain, and a dull yellowish wash of light filled the tiny space. The galley of shirts, pants, and polyester suits hung on plastic hangers exactly a quarter of an inch apart. On the shelf above them were rows and rows of shoeboxes.

"Oh, God," Ardee whispered. She leaned up on her tiptoes to retrieve the nearest box. Inside was a long row of square instamatic photos. She pulled one out and cringed. It was ghastly.

"Bobby, don't look." Ardee pushed and shoved Robert and David toward the doorway and out into the narrow hallway. "Let me try to figure this out. Besides, it's cramped, and you...you... Just don't look. This might take some time."

She composed herself, wiped her eyes, and pulled out another picture. Across the white top, it had, written in a black ink pen, the exact date, time, location, and name. The name belonged to a real person—a person who might have still been alive, though she did not recognize the name.

She clenched her teeth and studied the photo. She did not recognize the young boy. Judging by his appearance and clothes, the photo was from a long time ago. It was dated August 6th, but there was no year noted. She put it back and slid the box back into the drawer.

"My God, he's been at this for generations," Ardee gasped. She had her hands on her hips as she gazed over at Robert. "Bobby, let me do the searching. I think it best that you... You should not look at much of this. It's gross, and I think it would be bad for you. Just trust me."

"What's gross,?" David asked.

"He took pictures of me, too," Robert said. He nudged David out of the bedroom and further into the hallway.

"When you were a boy?" David asked.

"Yeah. I'm just like you," Robert said.

David stared inside the bedroom at Ardee and then looked up at Robert.

"Will you be my friend?" David asked.

"I'll always be your friend," Robert said. He patted David on his maturing shoulder. "You can call me Bobby."

"Hi, Bobby." David smiled and grasped Robert's hand. "I like calling you Bobby. It's a happy name."

Inside the bedroom closet, Ardee studied the front of the shoeboxes. On the front of the boxes, within the metal label slip pasted to each shoebox, were beginning and ending dates and block letters. The letters, Ardee guessed, were related to the location. Mr. Diabolus would not use a code; that was too complicated. He was meticulous. He was simple. She did notice that a few had red-inked stars above the dates.

What year was I a student at Briar Hill? she wondered.

It only took her a second. Her skin tingled, and she felt separated from her body, as if she were a ghost floating closer toward her Bobby's pictures. She understood what he meant as she sensed the purity of her heart whisking into nothingness. She searched for the correct shoebox within a lineup of childhood sorrows.

She knew what Bobby meant; as if a part of her—a gene within her DNA—had been altered. She understood why Bobby never told anyone why he felt like a freak. Why his skin felt like someone threw a bucket of acid over his head.

Ardee felt tears of rage form as she thought of the photos of innocent boys and innocent girls, all sexually assaulted. Disoriented, she realized she was going back in time, toward her own childhood, to when she was pure, pristine—innocent. She shook off her childhood thoughts, she breathed in and out, she puffed.

"This has to be it," Ardee whispered. The date on the box was before he was thirteen.

Bobby would have been ten, eleven? No, he would have been a little older, Ardee thought. She realized Mr. Diabolus had hunted and terrorized Bobby at school. Ardee tried to guess, as she pulled out a shoebox, which year she thought might be close to the assault date. As she studied another photo, she realized she knew the face. He had sat next to her in seventh grade social studies. He had

207

become a prominent lawyer, but was known for being a thoughtless playboy. He had children scattered up and down Interstate 75.

She slid the photo back in place and stepped back. Somewhere hidden within the closet, Bobby's stolen likeness resided, but she realized it also contained stolen pictures of many of her childhood friends. She fought back the instinct to scream, to cry. Stepping back, she noticed one of the drawers had a red star above the date in block letters: B.H.

Ardee slid the box all the way out and turned to set it on the nightstand, though she didn't really know why. Her instincts told her to, as if Bobby had whispered in her ear, "That's the one."

Within the box, there were pictures of grade school children, several of whom she remembered. One was now a prostitute, addicted to methamphetamines. She studied another photo. He was a recovering alcoholic, but he had gotten his life back in order and was now in medical school. Another was an old high school friend, who'd committed suicide in college for some unknown reason.

Then she noticed a section with red magic marker marked across the top, toward the back of the shoebox. With her forefinger and thumb, she pulled the entire section up and out. She dropped them on the bed, her fingers feeling as though they'd been dipped in corrosive acid.

"What is it?" Robert asked.

"Don't come over," Ardee said. Her breathing erratic, her chest heaved.

She backed away and fell into the closet, crashing through Mr. Diabolus's clothes. She covered her mouth, wanting to vomit and scream at the same time. She understood how a silent scream felt...looked.

She crawled back toward the bed to glance through the photos, fidgeting with her torn skirt and breathing in deep breaths. Her pulse was pounding inside her mind, causing her bruised face, neck, and head to throb.

"Damn him," Ardee said. She shrieked.

"She okay?" David asked.

"Yeah, she just found me," Robert said, staring up at the ceiling. Ardee tore Mr. Diabolus's shirts and pants off the wire hangers and stomped on them. All of Bobby's descriptions made sense to her now—why he felt the way he did, why he never told anyone. The photos said it all. It was his life's balance sheet—snapshots in time, at the exact moment of the death of his childhood, the moment of total and complete desolation.

"Bobby, I don't have words." She sniffled.

"Why's she crying?" David asked.

"She loves me," Robert said. He squeezed David's hand.

"Why?" David asked.

"I don't know."

Ardee collapsed to her knees and prayed. She begged for wisdom, for courage, for guidance. It was the only thing she could think to do. After a few precious minutes, she wiped the tears from her eyes with the back of her hands. Then she got up and made herself study the photos—photos she would never be able to forget.

Red stars for Mr. Diabolus' favorites, Ardee realized. That was the reason he had remembered Bobby. He had been a pretty boy. He'd had unblemished, perfect skin, without a hint of one pimple. He'd had full, pink lips and hypnotic hazel eyes. Even as a boy, he'd had a solid, maturing athletic build. He was genetically lucky. And he was the polar opposite to Willis.

It was in the eyes, she thought. At first, Bobby and Willis both appeared terrified. The color photos screamed with their harvest-peach cheeks dotted with tears. It was the instance of violent trauma and expectant death captured in each photo. As their t-shirts disappeared, in each photo as they were repositioned in front of the bathroom stall, it was in their eyes. After each instamatic auto flash, their red eyes traveled from terror, to hopelessness, to shame, to numb, to death. In the last photo, naked, stripped of his dignity, a humiliated Bobby's eyes were dead—a blank, stone expression. An expression a poker player spends a lifetime trying to perfect. He had been taught how not give anyone the power to know his thoughts; he had been taught how to hide in plain sight. Bobby had earned his poker face PhD the old fashioned way...the hard way. His childhood innocence was gone forever before he was a teenager.

Ardee realized why he had never tried to kiss her in a half-empty movie theater—why he thought he needed to protect her that day. Oddly, she understood why he had felt safe just holding her hand. He just wanted to connect with her—to be friends. He connected a pleasurable childhood discovery—an innocent kiss— with pain.

Ardee had walked in Bobby's socks back into his childhood. The socks did not fit her—they were big, but she could take the socks off. Forever within Bobby's mind, the socks woven with tragic DNA memories.

"Ardee?" Robert asked.

"Wait," Ardee said. "Just wait... Give me some more time." She sat down for several minutes to find some composure, to get her mind right. She collected the photos of Bobby and Willis, she now understood Bobby. She was numb, as if trapped inside a milky cloud.

As she wobbled to her feet, it occurred to her that, above her, within each shoebox of tragedy, there were countless other Bobbys. Not her Bobby, but Robert, Bob, Robby— the list of names was endless—they were all up there. They all had their own unique story, like the uniqueness of the irises of their eyes as the photo flashed during the exact moment they'd had their innocence stolen. The younger the boys were, the more their brains were scarred—their DNA chemically altered, and the more difficult it was for their minds to mature. Hidden within their subconscious was the shame, driving some to act perfect—to attempt obsessive perfection. It was the polar opposite for other victims, as they had developed drug and alcohol addictions, turned to prostitution, and did anything to numb the senses. For some, the final solution to stop the silent screams inside their minds, the common link, the memory of abuse drove them toward suicide.

The pictures were of the living and the dead. They had lived their lives as college professors, prostitutes, judges, hardened criminals, doctors, lawyers, drunks, drug addicts, ministers, politicians, real estate agents, hair artists, insurance brokers, famous entertainers, mothers and fathers, brothers and sisters. Every child had come from every lifestyle. Mr. Diabolus had made no distinction between rich or poor, upper or lower or middle class. The common life thread, as if the sisters of fate had spun an ancient prophecy, was that he had manipulated them...and their parents trusted him. He'd had power and control over them. The pictures were snapshots of frozen moments of tragedy, capturing the exact moment of the loss of their childhoods.

"Let's go into the kitchen," Ardee said. She hugged Robert tight and they strolled toward the kitchen with him and David. She turned on the lights and held the pictures like a deck of cards. "You sure?"

Robert nodded his head and glanced down at David. "Turn away. Go stand on the other side of Ardee."

She handed him the stack of photos. She blushed with her palm along his forearm, then she and David backed away. She stared out the kitchen door into the backyard as angelic skiffs of snow began to kiss the dormant bluegrass. She bent forward, like a loving, protective mother, and wrapped her arms around David. A solitary translucent teardrop for lost childhood traveled down her cheek.

Robert spread the photos across the white Formica countertop and crossed his arms. "Damn," he huffed. He glanced over at David. "Sorry, excuse my language."

"It's okay, Bobby," David said. He gripped Ardee's shaking forearm.

Robert gathered up the photos, staring forward. "Enough, Ardee. Take David out the back, right now."

He marched into the living room and found Steven and Ernie sneering at the seated Mr. Diabolus. Pulling up the handgun, he pointed it between Mr. Diabolus's eyes.

"Oob, careful. That ain't no toy," Ernie said.

"Yeah, beatin's one thang," Steven said. He shifted near Robert and whispered into his ear. "Shootin', that's permanent like."

"Like being raped?" Robert said. He pulled back the hammer and squeezed the trigger as he stared at Steven. *Snap*.

Mr. Diabolus yelled and he squirmed for his life, like an ancient fish caught at the banks of the mighty river of life.

"Sorry, I'll eventually find that bullet for you," Robert said with a shrug. "I'll keep flipping the chambers. It should be a surprise… Yeah, don't want to cheat death."

"Come on, Oob." Ernie nudged Robert. "Put the gun down… Let's just hit 'em."

"No," Robert said. He dragged the dining chair in front of the whimpering Mr. Diabolus and held one the photos in front of the man's face. He handed it to Steven and another to Ernie, before holding the third photo up to Mr. Diabolus's sweaty face.

"Damn, Oobie," Steven said.

"So, look at me and Willis. See the terror in our eyes. Is that our essence?" Robert asked.

"What? That's my art," Mr. Diabolus screamed. "You stole my art."

"Art? What tha?" Ernie said, as he and Steven examined the photos.

"Guess you'd like me to put the gun to my head?" Robert said. He pointed the loaded weapon at his head. "Right?"

"I don't care," Mr. Diabolus said. He smirked. "Might do you some good…"

"You're one sick bastard," Steven said.

"Damn, Oob," Ernie shook his head. "Don't know what to say. Just shoot the sumbitch."

"Good idea," Robert said. He stepped back and pointed the gun at Mr. Diabolus. *Pow*!

Chapter 26

The bullet whizzed past Mr. Diabolus's fat face, missing by a microscopic amount. It clipped the tip of his ear and plunged into the carpeted floor. "Now you know what it feels like to be terrorized." Robert screamed for his childhood. He pressed the hot gun barrel to the trembling Mr. Diabolus's temple. "You're not worth wasting the bullet, but you can wonder for yourself what happens to old pedophiles in prison. And if you don't get convicted, best o' luck out here, 'cause everybody's going to know everything. No more secrets."

"Damn, Oob," Steven said. His hands gripped his knees, and he shook his head. "Thought you shot 'em."

Detective Sammons peeked into the house, his gun drawn and pointing down. Mr. Diabolus was shaking as if he had seen the Devil incarnate. Detective Sammons smirked.

"Bobby, just hand the gun over. I don't think you need that anymore." Detective Sammons swiftly moved toward Robert.

"Guess not," Robert said. He coughed and then spit on Mr. Diabolus. "That's for my friend. Don't you even look her at wrong."

Ernie slapped Robert on the back. "Nice shootin'." He hugged Robert.

Then Steven hugged him. "Proud o' ya, Oob."

"Sorry, I didn't think that antique would even fire, glad you're bad shot." Detective Sammons said. He scratched his square chin.

"Thanks," Robert said. He grabbed back the photos he had given to Ernie and Steven and handed them to Detective Sammons. He wiped his face. "Now you go back to work and take these. I'll stand in court; I'll point him out."

Detective Sammons flinched and sauntered backwards.

"But Ardee…" Detective Sammons said. He held up his open hand. He stuffed the photos inside his coat pocket and scratched behind his ear. "That's not a fun time. We won't even make it to court for a while, but real soon, the whole town will likely find out. This is goin' to get nasty. Lots and lots of questions."

"I know," Robert said. He noticed Ardee and David standing near the open front door crying waterfalls. "Someone has to stand up for these children. No one ever said they were sorry to me, so this will be my way of letting the others, those kids, know someone cares."

Chapter 27

Ardee drove her SUV up in front of Robert's townhouse. He sat out front on the top concrete step, cooling off after a mid-afternoon jog. In the wintertime air, his body released a foggy steam, as if a childhood fire had been extinguished within his skin. His face was less chubby, and his eyes were clear, as if he were molting into who he should be.

"This is a pleasant surprise," Robert said. His arms dangled over his knees, his fingers dripping sweat drops as his angst riverbed dried up.

"Want to get some dinner later tonight?" Ardee asked. "Maybe come out and we'll go riding. I've sort of got a surprise for you— someone I want you to talk with. I think it's important."

"Riding? I've no idea how to ride a horse." Robert grinned.

"Trust me; I'll teach you," Ardee said. She shrugged.

"Well, I do trust you. Got nothing to hide from you. Let me get cleaned up," he said. He took off his multi-colored fleece cap, unzipped his warm-up jacket, and wiped sweat from his face. "Don't come close. I'm rather ripe."

"Yeah, I picked up your scent." Ardee chuckled. "That cap's like your funny socks."

They strolled inside the townhome. Steven was stretched out over a blue fabric Strata lounger.

"Yeah, Dr. Richie strikes again," Robert said.

"Hey, girl," Steven said.

"Chop, chop. Daylights burning… Let's get going." Ardee said, with a wave in Steven's direction.

"Simmer, don't tease me."

"I don't tease," Ardee said. "Giddy up…" She sat down.

"Hey, there. Want a beer?" Steven asked.

"Thanks, but I'm not in a mood for beer. I'm driving," Ardee said. "Maybe next time."

"What've you been up to?" Steven asked.

"Went searching for someone special," Ardee said. She smirked. She winked at Steven. "Bobby's lookin' cute."

"Yeah, skinnier he gets, you know, he's more like his old self." Steven flipped open a sports magazine. He glanced at Ardee above the glossy pages. "A couple cute girls were hittin' on him the other night. I guess they read the newspaper. They were treatin' like he was an abused puppy dog."

"I see." Ardee ran her fingers through her hair, which had been colored back to its natural auburn shade, before fidgeting with her handbag's zipper.

Steven hid a smirk.

They listened to the apartments plumbing turn on and turn off. After an uncomfortable twenty minutes, Robert emerged from upstairs, wearing his classic uniform—a baby blue button down, khaki pants, and brown shoes. His tan barn jacket was folded over his forearm.

"It's not fair," Ardee said.

"What?"

"Boys can get ready so fast, but your hair's still wet," Ardee said.

"Oh, I'll be all right," Robert said. He shrugged.

"At least you have hair," Steven said.

"No, go dry your hair," Ardee said. "I don't want you getting sick."

"Okay, okay," Robert said. He trudged back upstairs and returned ten minutes later. "This work?"

Ardee stepped over and ran her fingers through his thick, brown hair. "Well, I'll let it pass this time."

"Don't worry about me," Steven said. "I'll just be here, lonely, maybe reading a book."

"Simmer," Robert said, as walked out the front door behind Ardee.

"Hope your little fella gets to spit," Steven mumbled.

"Dude, it's not like that," Robert whispered back. He pointed at Steven through the side window.

"Oobie, you might be surprised," Steven said, after he sprang up to watch them drive away.

*

"Ever been out here?" Ardee asked. She didn't wait for an answer. "You know Keene Farms has been here for decades. All the horsemen know about it."

The gray, bulbous clouds had floated north to allow the sparkle of golden, late afternoon sunlight. The thick Kentucky bluegrass was emerging from dormancy, and the terrain was light brown—pale, with only a few clumps and patches of new green growth. The oak and ash trees towered along the fence lines that stretched over the terrain, marking farm from farm and pasture from pasture.

"Never been past the gate," Robert said. He glanced around at the rolling landscape. A cluster of horses grazed in the far pasture as she drove toward a white horse barn with a red metal roof topped by a hexagonal shaped crow's nest. The weather vane rooster pointed true north.

"Driven past here a thousand times. It's been years since I've been out here. I think Briar Hill's just over that hill."

"Yeah, I remember," Ardee said. She reached over and squeezed Robert's hand. "I have a surprise for you. I hope you'll forgive me."

"You're already forgiven," Robert said. He glanced at Ardee. "Glad you colored your hair back to auburn."

"You like it?" She fidgeted with her hairline.

"I'm not hitting on you, but I think you'd be pretty bald, with long hair, short hair, whatever hair." Robert grinned at her.

"Thanks." She blushed and drove toward the open barn doors, near what locals might have called a 'horse palace'.

Robert hopped out and followed behind Ardee with his hands stuffed in his barn jacket pockets. The distinct scent of horse manure, bales of hay, and worn leather permeated the cool, dry air. As they entered the barn, a few horses scratched at their stall floors with their hooves, nibbled at their feed, and snorted vibrato puffs of air.

"I love horses," Robert said, patting one along its nose. "They're so huge, so powerful, and yet so gentle, so fragile."

"Just don't get caught doodling behind one if they're having a bad day," Ardee said. She patted along the hairy mane of the same chestnut horse. "They'll send you to the hospital."

"I'll bet," Robert said. He stared quizzically at Ardee. "But you don't just ride these horses? These are thoroughbreds; only the little people get on them."

"Little people?" Ardee tried not to laugh.

"Yeah, brave little Oompa-Loompas in bright and shiny silks." He laughed. "You've got to be seriously brave to ride these horses going at those speeds around a dirt track."

"Yeah, you're right. You just don't ride these horses." She smirked. "You have a way with words Bobby."

Robert noticed she was acting nervous, fidgeting with her short hair. They got halfway inside the barn when Ardee wheeled around on her boots to stand in front of Robert. She embraced his face and kissed him. She kissed him hard.

"I hope you'll forgive me," Ardee said.

"Well, ah… I, ah, guess I finally got my kiss, so I'm not sure I need to forgive you." He blushed and tasted her lipstick, whispering. "You can kiss me again if you want."

But there was something behind Ardee's happy, brown eyes. Robert could tell something was wrong, he sensed it, from how her warm hands embraced his face. He thought the kiss was good, but he wondered if there was something else as they entered the barn office.

"I want to acquaint you with someone," Ardee said. She had the hint of tears glistening in her eyes.

"Hello, Robert?" The voice was unfamiliar, raspy. It came out breathless, like a slow tire leak.

A large African American woman, hidden by the shadows of the late afternoon sunlight, was partially concealed by a square wooden post. A filtered cigarette wafted concentric rings of smoke toward the tile ceiling from within a forest green Depression glass ashtray. It was huddled with an extinguished crowd of its other carcinogen brethren. From within the shadows, the woman hobbled forward into the office lamplight.

Robert's feet froze to the pine-wood office floor. He glanced over at Ardee and saw tears streaming down her face.

"We've never met, but I think we've a tragic bond."

"How so?" Robert said. His neck hair gathered with a field of goose pimples.

"I'm Willis's mother. My friends call me Sparky," she said. "I know. It comes from my happy face after a few drinks. I should know betta."

"Bobby's friends call you Oob?" Ardee asked with a sniffle.

"Oobie," Robert said. "That's drunk speak for Bobby at three in the morning. I used to get ticked at my roommate. They'd be up late drinking when I had to be at work the next morning, so I used to storm downstairs and yell at them to keep it down. They'd say, 'Aw come on Oobie.' So now the name's stuck."

"Well, Oobie or Bobby or Robert," Sparky said. She hobbled over and hugged Robert. "Even though he's gone, thank you for defending Willis' honor. I think he's smiling at you from a happier place."

"It's really Ardee you should thank," Robert said. He gazed at Ardee as he continued to hug Sparky.

"How so?" Sparky asked.

"Ardee lured him out. He could've killed her," Robert said. He patted Sparky on her lumpy back. "Thanks to Detective Sammons, she's not going to have to answer any questions. I've just been the one talking, answering questions. I'm not embarrassed anymore. Those pictures are just pictures now. But, Ardee defended me, so the least I can do is protect her."

Sparky wiped a tear from her pudgy face. She moved over and gently hugged Ardee.

"Oh, my lands, you brave little flower." She kissed Ardee on the hands. "Thank you."

"Just want to give credit where credit's due," Robert said. He smiled over at Ardee.

"Will you all walk with me?" Sparky asked. She wiped her cheek, slipped on her winter coat, and picked up a paper sack off her desk.

They left the office and moved through the far side of the barn and out into a nearby pasture. Within the pasture, encircled by a white fence, was a simple monument. Carved across the top was the name *Willis*.

"This breaks my heart. It's a gift from the farm owners. They're extraordinarily kind people," Sparky said.

Robert stared down at the monument.

"Willis loved horses," Sparky said. She wiped away the brown dirt and grass clumps from the monument. From within the paper bag, she pulled out a simple tubular candle, then she set it near Willis' name.

"Why here?" Ardee asked.

"This is the spot where Willis took his life one morning," Sparky said. She nodded toward the east, to a nearby line of towering oak and ash trees. "It was December 28th, he watched the sun come up, just over there, one more time. He sat here with a few favorite horses, and well…"

Ardee sat down, tucking her legs underneath her, and covered her mouth as she cried.

"He liked this spot?" Robert crossed his arms, staring across the grassy pasture. He leaned back against the fence post. A horse with a reddish-chestnut coat loped over and nudged its nose near the fence, grunting and scratching at the turf. It sniffed and snorted near Robert, so he reached back and patted the horse along its nose.

"His favorite spot. Early in the mornings, he'd come out here with the horses and watch the sun come up." Sparky smiled through her tears. "Made him feel happy. The horses were his friends."

"It's pretty here—peaceful," Ardee said. "Hardly a sound. I can hear myself breathing."

"Yeah, I placed his ashes underneath," Sparky said. She lovingly glided her hand across the cold monument. "I think he would have wanted to be buried with the horses, but they don't let you do that."

"He's safe now." Robert choked and coughed, holding back tears.

"I failed him" Sparky whispered. She stared into the distance of merciless time and huffed out a mother's regret. "A mother should protect her child."

Ardee turned to stare up at Robert.

"It's not your fault. We didn't tell anybody," Robert said. He kneeled down next to Sparky.

"A child should be able to tell his mother everythin'," Sparky said.

"To be honest, I tried, but people just assume…whatever. I felt humiliated, ashamed," Robert said. He shrugged. "I think it's hard for people to know how you feel. They don't realize what trauma does to a child's brain. You just don't shake it off. I didn't understand, but I guess I got lucky."

"That what happened to my boy?" Sparky asked. She patted Robert's left hand.

"I'm no doctor, but I think so," Robert said. He glanced over at Ardee. "Ardee hooked me up with a doctor, and she explained how a suicide gene gets turned on. You don't even know it. Has to do with stress genes and whatnot."

"Go on," Ardee said. She nodded over at Robert.

"To be honest, I probably would've shot myself, too, or done something to make the memories go away," Robert said. "Guess I got lucky. She saved my life."

"Hush," Ardee whispered.

"You two, just stop with the dancin'," Sparky said. She observed Ardee and Robert with a pleased expression. "Trust an old woman to know love when she sees it. You best not let her wiggle away."

Robert stared down and yanked up blades of grass. He glanced at Ardee and then over at Sparky.

"I'll not let her get away," Robert whispered.

Ardee shifted close to Robert and grabbed his hand.

"There, good," Sparky said. She breathed in a deep breath. "I can't do anythin' for my boy. He's gone, but I was hopin' you two might…well, light this candle from time to time to remember Willis."

Ardee held the candle close.

"We will, every year that I'm alive, on December 28th," Robert said, squeezing Ardee's hand. "We'll come out here…" Robert finally began to cry, tears dripping down his face.

"Just let it out, honey," Sparky said.

"We'll come out just like Willis did," Ardee said. She kissed Robert on the cheek and hugged him. "I love you, Bobby."

And as the years and decades passed, Robert and Ardee abided by their promise.

Chapter 28

"Grandpa, why do you wear funny socks?" Charlie asked. His head bobbled just above the kitchen table like a hairy balloon tethered to an overworked string. His happy reflection showed in the smooth cherry finish.

"You're like a little bumblebee." Robert chuckled and sipped his coffee. He smirked over at Ardee. The kitchen was temporarily quiet, but the upstairs floorboards squeaked with family activity.

"I'm not sure how the boy is so awake." Ardee blinked and yawned. Her tall, white mug steamed like a miniature nuclear reactor cooling tower.

"The boy has worn me out, and the sun's not even up," Laina said. She snuggled back in the wooden chair and tightened her housecoat. She blinked her green eyes and yawned. "Dear brother, who is keeper of the candle this year?"

"Me. My number came up," Robert said. He spied Charlie zipping near the edge of his chair and reached out to snag the six-year old. "Got you, little huckleberry."

"Grandpa," Charlie said. He giggled and twisted to hug his grandfather. "I like your funny socks. Are you a circus clown?"

"Charles," Ardee said. She stared a hole through her grandchild. "Respect your grandfather."

"Yes, Grandma," Charlie whispered, backing away.

"I simply sit here, wondering what he will say next," Laina said. She covered her mouth as she glanced over at Ardee and winked at her brother. "Ah, to be an innocent child..."

"Indeed, sister." Robert winked at her. "Like holding a little girl's hand, and wondering what it would be like to kiss her cheek."

"Yes, it's true. Our children have that piss and vinegar gene," Ardee said. She batted her eyelashes. "I blame myself." She crossed her legs and brushed off dirt from the soles of her knee-high brown leather boots.

"Can I borrow some of your funny socks, Grandpa?" Laina asked with a laugh. "They make my walking boots fit better."

"Oh, of course," Robert said. "You know where to find them by now."

Ardee chuckled.

"What?" Robert asked. He had negotiated Charlie onto his lap.

"I stole – borrowed – a pair for the same reason," Ardee said.

"Well, I am a world-wide woven sock magnet," Robert said. He sheepishly grinned.

"I shall return." Laina said. She stood and the chair groaned with age. "I hear the herd forming upstairs. I better get with the plan."

"We'll wait." He hugged Charlie and kissed his forehead.

"Can I have some funny socks?" Charlie asked.

Robert brushed back his thick brown hair and glanced over at Ardee.

"Someday, but not quite yet," he said.

"But why?" Charlie asked.

"Just tell 'em. We don't keep secrets round here," Ardee said.

"See, Grandma said I can have pair." Charlie grinned at his Grandma.

"No, my lovely bride said I can tell you why," Robert said, pulling Charlie close. "Remember to listen to what someone says, not what you want them to say. If I tell, I trust you will never keep secrets from your parents or from us. Deal?"

"Deal," Charlie said, hugging his grandfather's neck.

"Okay, deal it is," Robert said. He stared over at the six-burner cooktop, the stainless steel double oven, and inspected the massive kitchen's granite countertop. He sighed and turned Charlie to face him.

Ardee got up and shifted her kitchen chair closer to them, sliding the hot coffee mug forward with her palm. "I get to be the witness."

"Grandma…" Charlie giggled.

"Listen; this is serious," Robert said. He stared into Charlie's eyes.

"Okay, Grandpa," Charlie whispered. He hunched down.

"When I was a boy, not much older than you are, some bad things happened to me," Robert said. He puffed his breath, slow, methodical. He held Charlie's puffy cheeks steady with his fingertips and gazed into the boy's innocent blue eyes. "Things that I pray you will only read about and never fully understand."

Charlie hunched down further, his doe eyes quiet, curious, as he stared at his grandfather and then over at his grandmother.

"What kind of bad things?" Charlie whispered.

"An evil man did bad things to me," Robert said. He tapped his wrinkled fingers on the tabletop like he was playing a piano. "Let's just say, he stole from me, stole something precious, more valuable than gold or diamonds. Does that make sense?"

"That's not nice," Charlie said. "Mom says stealing is bad."

"Not nice, indeed," Ardee said. She uncrossed her legs and sipped her coffee, twisting atop the antique wooden chair, she set

·her elbows on the kitchen table, and she gazed out the great bay window into the darkness. She whispered, "Good boy…"

"Well, what he stole you cannot see. What he stole you only have once in your entire life, and once it's gone, it's gone," Robert said. A slight memory tear sparkled in the corner of his eyes. He sniffled and sighed.

"I'm sorry, Grandpa," Charlie said. He frowned and crawled up to hug his grandfather. "But why?"

"You're a good boy," Ardee said as her lips quivered.

Robert kissed Charlie on his blameless forehead. "I don't know why. God doesn't give all the answers. And no one ever said they were sorry."

"I love you, Grandpa," Charlie said. "I'm sorry."

Ardee's eyes glistened with moisture.

"So, a friend gave me some funny socks so I would remember to smile, to think happy thoughts. I wear these socks even today, to remind me to smile and seek happiness. They're woven, sort of like how your body was interwoven to create you." He straightened his legs to reveal his socked feet. "That's why this particular morning, I always slip my boots on last, before we all go out in the front pasture to light that candle."

"Is that why we light candles?" Charlie asked.

"Sort of." Ardee said. She wiped her eyes with the back of her hand. "I think you've learned enough. Let's go upstairs and investigate Grandpa's sock drawer. I'll let you model for Aunt Laina."

Ardee held her hand out for Charlie.

"I get socks too?" Charlie said. "Yeah?"

"Remember our deal," Robert said. "No secrets. Secrets are bad, okay? You're approved for funny socks detail."

"Yes, Grandpa, no secrets," Charlie said, as he skipped toward the back staircase with Ardee. She turned and winked back at Robert.

Robert sat alone within the custom kitchen enjoying the sounds of family. He dangled his legs out in front of the chair and inspected his colorful woven socks. He thought of Dr. Richie; he thought of holding Ardee's hand in an empty movie theater. And the he smiled and sipped his coffee. After a while, he got up and slipped on his boots as his family gathered to go outside and walk into the front pasture to remember Willis.

"Bundle up. It's cold, but clear," Robert said to his tribe. "And I love each of you the same. I love you more than life itself."

Robert stood next to the front door, and one-by-one his family hugged him as they walked out. He happily gazed at each face, winked at Laina, and kissed Ardee. They held hands and let Charlie carry the candle. And Robert realized he had all he ever wanted. He was blessed to be old. He was blessed to have lived a lifetime of unconditional love.

EPILOGUE

On December 28th of every year, we gather as a family. Early in our marriage, our children had wondered why we lit an old candle out in the middle of a horse pasture and stood, shivering, next to a granite monument. They knew something terrible had happened. People talk, children tease, and nothing disappears from the Internet. It is the human condition to try to understand or shield our minds from reality, but we wanted to wait, let them mature a bit, before we explained. We had learned to be patient parents.

Each year, we would get up early in the morning before the sun awoke. Sometimes the sky was clear, the stars sparkled, and under the protection of the silvery moon, our grumpy tribe trudged out toward the monument. It was typically cold and damp. A skiff of icy frost hugged the thick Kentucky bluegrass, which was dormant at about mid-boot. We released the horses early – just as Willis had. Our flashlights attracted them like giant wintertime fireflies. They snorted out fogs of childhood death, and we dodged their deep steaming pies of degradation as we patted them along their hairy manes. They scratched their hooves near the fence posts as we recited the Lord's Prayer. I usually had nothing much to say, as I stoically waited for dawn to emerge above the tree line. I did not want my children to see me cry. I thought I would appear weak. In fact, I was just being a fool. It's okay to cry for my childhood. I decided not to make it habit, I let the sadness go.

Ardee would hug our children. "Be brave, have courage and audacity, and I don't care what others think, blaze your own trail. Hear me?"

Our children would respond in whispered stereo. "Yes Mother." She was determined our children would grow up within her protective cocoon to take risks, she allowed them to make mistakes, to skin their knees without leaving a permanent scar, but then she taught them how to clean up their wounds, pick themselves up, and move forward. She never again talked of being.

an FBI agent. She realized it was not her destiny. Instead, she had a much more valuable career – she was an active, attentive mother. I couldn't think of a higher compliment for her.

And Ardee devised numerous family golden nuggets. She demanded we be together to share a meal at least once a day—it did not matter the meal. We just had to all be together at least once during the day. If I was traveling for business, I had to call in. It was her only rule – "Just let hear your voice, one time a day". It was her way of keeping an eye out, to protect me, and to know what our children planned to do, or what we had been doing. In truth, she was in conspiracy with all the other attentive mothers to watch for potential predators lurking in and out of our lives. She had faced down a real predator, and she knew what to look for. Sadly, they were usually right in front of us.

*

As we walked toward the pasture, the snow crunched under our boots, and I glanced over at my lovely bride. Ardee was wonderful, smart, and humble—my best friend. I didn't deserve her. And happily, that morning, her intense stare told me she loved me. That was the only look I needed.

Charlie proudly carried the candle in his arms, but I had to keep him moving forward since he couldn't help but study his brand new pair of colorful socks.

"He's weavin' like a tiny drunk man," Laina said as she chuckled.

"Charlie, your socks aren't goin' anywhere," Ardee said. She frowned down at Charlie.

"Yes, they are," Charlie said. "They are taking me out to the pasture."

"Hush," I said. I shook my head and smirked at my sister.

*

Ardee was careful about telling anyone about my childhood— because she did not want me to have to answer any questions. I think that was how I knew she loved me. We protect the people we love. We think of them first, before we think of ourselves. But, I wanted to protect her too, so I stepped forward. I talked, and I let the shame go. I wanted those young boys left alone. I wanted to give them the space to work through their pain, to figure out on their own terms who they wanted to be.

Even so, I recognize, even today, I have a distance to me. I'm easy to talk to, but difficult to know. I guess I will always be hesitant, careful, always on high alert. It's not easy to just stop worrying, wondering, but my anxiety has cooled, my thoughts from youth that were a tempest storm, are now the nectar of a pure mountain stream.

I do not want another person to feel like I did. And I did not want my children to fear life; I wanted them to be special, to take life by the reins, to charge forward and be who they should be.

I gazed up into the clear sky. I could almost see heaven beckoning just past the stars. It was a cold morning, with the smell of trampled hay and crisp air. I could see our family's blue-gray shadows and the fog from their loving breaths. The monochromatic moon smiled down at us, as we abided by our promise to Willis's mother. It had become our moment to reflect what we had done in the past year and what we were planning for the next.

I was determined to be successful. I felt like I owed it to Willis. We built up a good savings, and we bought the horse farm and all the surrounding land. We even bought what was left of Briar Hill. Then we had a Weeping Willow tree planted just north of Willis's monument site. Ardee thought it a fitting symbol to remember him by. With the constant changing of seasons, as the leaves turned, each time we noticed the willow, we remembered Willis.

But one day, Ardee and I stopped making up excuses. Our children were in their early teens, so one late summer afternoon, we sat them down near the monument and had a family picnic. Then, we told them everything, every single detail we could remember about my childhood and the night Ardee had defended me. We did not filter. We told them about summer camp, school, the trial, the photos of Willis and me, why Willis committed suicide, and why his mother asked us to remember Willis with a simple lit candle on December 28th—the day Willis had taken his life as dawn had emerged just above the line of oak and ash trees. I guess Willis, in his own way, wanted to feel the warmth of the sun splash his face one more time. I cried for Willis. He was my childhood friend and life was not fair to him, but I know, we don't get to choose our family, and then life happens.

At first, it jolted our children. Suicide gene or not, the idea of taking their own lives because of shame and humiliation, thankfully to them, was unthinkable. The thought of their father sexually abused and their mother attacked seemed a horribly bad dream, but it was reality. They learned reality was a tough monster, but it was better to face life than hide from truth. We thought it important not to have secrets, even secrets about suicide and sexual abuse. I thought Willis's mother would have approved.

"Talk about it and put it out there. Don't fear it," I told them.

They were upset, angry, wanting to exact some sort of revenge. Then, through their tears, they realized their mother had already defended her Bobby. And her Bobby had defended their mother. We bonded, and from then on, we understood each other.

I guess that is why we got so many hugs from them. And we happily hugged them in return. They knew, no matter what, they could call us and we'd have their backs. We were a family. They knew the most severe punishment was my and Ardee's disappointment. And I'm proud they never felt the fear of coming home, being screamed at and whipped like a rabid dog with a looped leather belt. It's not fair to pick on someone who can't defend themselves.

Regardless, I love hugs. I think unconditional love is accepting someone's imperfections. It is the seed born from not having any secrets. It is being able to look another in the eye and tell them "I love you" without saying a word.

I think if we all took the time to slip on another person's socks, to view the world as they view the world, we might take a pause, and perhaps not worry about minor differences.

So there was nothing more to say. The business of living was left to each of us. And in time, the ceremony had blossomed into a family ritual. It was our family's post-Christmas gift—the gift of life, the gift of renewal.

We were determined our children would grow up in a home full of happiness and laughter, and not full of paranoid secrets. And neither of us would expose them to the twisting of faith for advantage. After we told them everything, from then on, each time they did something special, I would give them a pair of my funny, colorful, woven socks. They would wear them with pride. At first, their friends thought it odd, but then, one by one, our children were empowered to explain why. I had nothing more to hide. Occasionally, I had a quiet conversation with one of my children's friends, and we would anonymously pay a professional—someone like Dr. Richie—to talk with them, and I think we helped save lives too. I will leave the saving of souls to others.

I continually had to order a new sock supply, because I had started to include my children's friends in our colorful sock campaign. We ordered so many that I gave in, found some investors, and we bought the company. We manufacture Bobby's Socks across the planet. It seems the market is vast, in the multiple of millions, unending, a worldwide epidemic. We continually need to manufacture a massive, brand new inventory. We typically sell out and our storage facilities stay empty. We have given up trying to keep pace with demand or make faulty sales projections. Even our most ambitious growth forecasts have been well under real worldwide demand.

I truly wish we would go bankrupt, but we won't. The Bobby's Socks Company—thrives. Each year, we make a huge profit, and then I cry for unseen children's faces.

We have been successful beyond imagination—so much so that Ardee encouraged us to create a trust. It's a massive trust, in the billions and billions, set up for the sole purpose to fund safe places for abused children. I do not care about their skin pigmentation, who they have affection for, or chosen religion. To me, we are all the same—I understand them and they understand me.

The kaleidoscope of colorful woven socks at first became a fashion statement. Then, the socks became a warning sign – we are all watching, paying attention. Because every child is special, every child is unique. Children should know there are others who will defend them, protect them from the harm of sexual abuse, and fight back against predators. All they need is a non-judgmental ear to listen and a place to feel safe. But not all homes are safe places. Sometimes it takes courage just to survive. Safety and trust are everything for an abused child, even for most adult survivors. Memories don't just magically disappear.

For us, we made certain our children knew God loved them, God accepted them, and that life is not set in stone. Life is meant for living, and evil lurks, at church, school, anywhere. They need to recognize it when they see, and don't run from it. Face it head on. Take action.

*

A thick crowd had formed around the monument site. Another year had quietly passed. Charlie studied the people's faces.

"Are these people your friends? They have funny socks on like me," Charlie asked. He looked up at me.

"Some are," I said. I patted Charlie on the back. "They're invited to share with us. Some of them had some bad things happen to them, like me, and some know someone like me."

"Oh," Charlie said. "Does God love them, too?"

"God loves everyone," I said. "Just love God in return."

*

We cannot know the mind of God, or understand why life can be ugly, why people abuse children, or why we have extraordinary

238

happy times, too. God does not exist in the fantasy of our own manmade boxes, and I don't think God's testing us. I don't think we are a bunch of lab rats with God as the eternal scientist. Our challenge is straightforward life choices. And I think God *is*. Just that simple. I think the Devil exists, too, the reason it takes courage to seek happiness. We can't let the Devil lure us into the evil of being complacent. Doing nothing is a choice, not an excuse. Fighting back against evil, even evil in our own hearts—I think that is when God smiles. I think that's where the bright light of wisdom hides. We have to seek it, but it comes with a price. That's the reason I think character is revealed after a tragedy, not before. As said many times by others—talk is cheap, and everyone has to pay the toll.

For me, wisdom came with a brutally high price, but if I had to trade my own life to protect just one child from my fate, I would die with a happy smile.

Shine a bright light on truth and hate will wilt, dry up, and blow away. But, unfortunately, the vast majority of the universe is made up of Dark Matter, trying to choke out the sparkle of timeless light. It takes courage to shoot your rocket ship into the dark void of space, to realize you cannot change the past, and expect bright candlelight to guide you back toward safety.

*

As we gathered near the monument, beneath the protective branches of Willis's Willow, a cold breeze washed us, cleansed us, and I thought about my life. There are still moments that flash in my mind – terrible moments. Sometimes, I feel like all the blood in my body has drained out, down through my feet—as if I stand naked to the harsh sting of an ice storm. But I steady my thoughts; I take in a deep, reflective breath, and I pray a thankful prayer to God for grace. I remember that I am blessed, that I have lived a long life, and that I have a happy marriage and a beautiful family. I think it was because I decided to seek happiness and molted from the depravity of shame that made me different—that made me unique.

I had a lifetime of pain before I was even a teenager, but I faced the reality. Then I let it go; it no longer has any power over me. And every night, I pray no children ever feel like I did.

I guess Dr. Richie's sock therapy worked. She saved my life.

*

Charlie carefully placed the candle on the monument next to Willis's name. We stood at the center of the dense crowd, and candlelight surrounded us. Over the years, I had told our children we'd leave the pasture gate open. Everyone was welcome. This was not an invitation-only gathering. The news spread, and friends of friends seemed to appear. And then strangers appeared with their own candles on that date, just before dawn.

I moved the modest candle a bit to reveal Willis's name, and I thought of his chubby, sad face. I bent down on one knee, cupped my grandson Charlie's tiny hands with mine, and snapped the fireplace lighter so we could light it together.

"Do you like my socks, Grandpa?" Charlie whispered. He nudged at me and grinned.

"I do," I said. "I love you. When you wear those socks, remember you're wearing a piece of my heart. Remember, no secrets?"

"I love you," Charlie whispered. "No secrets."

I gazed up at Ardee, and she smiled at me through her tears. Even though she was well into her seventies, I thought she was as beautiful as the first time I ever saw her on a school bus ride to Briar Hill. In truth, she was even more beautiful. Her beauty shone from the molten fire behind her brown eyes.

As I gazed down at the flame swaying back and forth, kissed by the cold breeze, I was surrounded by our family, friends, and others who had joined in our cause. Charlie hugged me, and I thought from the black wick tip, a blue-hot flame had blended into a forever-golden teardrop—teardrop for the loss of a child's innocence, a teardrop burned from a stained heart. My heart, and the hearts of those like me.

We held hands and recited the Lord's Prayer. We faced east, and waited for the dawn to emerge above the jagged tree line. I glanced at my family, and the other faces that were bathed with the twinkles of tears.

Then it occurred to me, the candle had become a beacon in the early morning. We were together for the millions of hidden faces joined in our broken circle, to pray within the communion of open hearts for the sexually abused child, for the victims with silent screams behind sad eyes.

ABOUT THE AUTHOR

Nathaniel Sewell lives in the Midwest with his wife, RD and their King Charles Cavaliers – Maggie May and Pink Petunia.